OUT
OF THE
NEST

This is the first book of
The Deep Woods Adventure

The continuation of the search is contained in
book two, entitled
INTO THE HIGH BRANCHES

The treacherous journey home is contained
in book three, entitled
TO FIND A WAY HOME

Book one of the Deep Woods Adventure

OUT OF THE NEST

by P.M. Malone

Illustrated by Terry Lewison

*Raspberry Hill, Ltd.

This is a work of fiction. All characters and events portrayed in this book are fictitious. Any resemblance to real individuals, places, or events is coincidental.

A Raspberry Hill, Ltd. publication
P.O. Box 791
Willmar, MN 56201

ISBN: 0-9631957-0-0

1st printing: September, 1991
2nd printing: January, 1992
3rd printing: December, 1994
Printed in the United States of America

TO MY WIFE, WANDA, AND MY DAUGHTER, MELISSA,
WHOSE LOVE OF ALL THINGS LIVING,
AND TENDERNESS TOWARD THEM,
INSPIRED THIS STORY

AND TO MY SONS,
DAN, MIKE, CHRISTOPHER, AND JUSTIN,
WHO LISTENED TO MY TALE...AND
MADE ME WANT TO TELL MORE

OUT OF THE NEST

LIST OF CHAPTERS

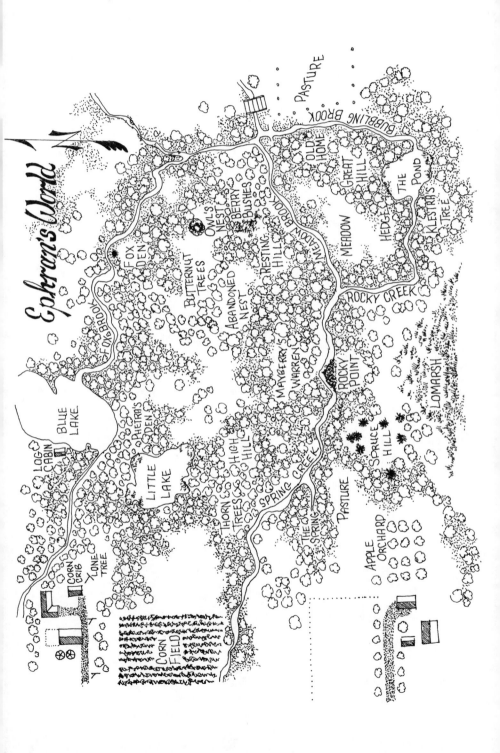

INTRODUCTION TO OUT OF THE NEST

What? an English sparrow sing?
Insignificant brown thing,
So common and so bold, 'twould surely bring
Tears of laughter to the eyes
Of the superficial wise
To suggest that the small immigrant could sing.

(From "Did You Ever Hear an English Sparrow Sing?"
by Bertha Johnson)

Most of us, I think, whether we live in a large metropolitan area or call the countryside home, have no idea (or indeed, even an interest) in the notion that animals might be real individuals and that they have their very own definite and distinctive personalities and character. I refer especially to the creatures that inhabit the green forest, the wide blue sky, and the hidden pond. And I include some of those that live with us by accident of birth but who, given the chance, might survive and perhaps even flourish in the unforgiving, yet wonderfully free and untamed woodland.

I suppose that this lack of appreciation for individual worth shouldn't surprise me. We do it within our own species; spurning those who are unlike us. Can they think and perceive? Can they feel anger, and excitement, and love? We say we cannot tell one from the other -- and we weary at the attempt.

I have always delighted in the woods; from the time timid Spring flowers struggle through still-frosted leaves of last Summer, to steamy days of butterflies and thunderstorms, to the intense burst of color as the forest directs life's nectar into the deep earth, to those consecrated snowy days of cathedral silence beneath towering oak and ash. I admit, however, that it took me a very long time to appreciate the fact that the inhabitants of that wondrous realm, far removed in many ways from our own, were so unique and fascinating. Especially squirrels, who, I can say with authority born of love, are intriguing and erudite beyond imagination, and who have an amazing sense of affection and humor.

As you stroll along the banks of gurgling streams, roam through meadows of waving grass, and pick your way among tangled oak and lofty cottonwood, I suspect that you too will perceive that a great deal more happens beyond the Hedge of brambles and along the shores of The Pond than you would have dreamed. I hope you might discern that those who live and love and learn there have something to tell us - - even if it is not always imparted in sounds or sights we readily comprehend.

Before we set out on our journey along Bubbling Brook and Rocky Creek, I ask that you lay aside anything that might slow you down, catch on the thorn bushes, or crush the wildflowers. Preconceived ideas and prejudices are particularly heavy and cumbersome. Wear a brightly colored jacket and soft boots which make a bit of noise (squeaky leather will do just fine) -- we don't want to surprise or frighten our hosts and hostesses. You may want to pick up that crooked elm branch laying there, to use as a sort of walking stick. Don't worry about lunch, we'll be back before long. By all means watch the forest around you, there will be many fascinating things to see. But don't keep your eyes on the earth all the time. Look up now and then -- and behold the high branches.

THOSE FOUND IN THE DEEP WOODS;
IN THE EARTH, TREES OR SKY

Ephran (Ee - fran): A young, curious gray squirrel who lives with his family in the north woods.

Mianta (Mee - an - tah): Ephran's "first" sister; a female littermate.

Phetra (Fet - rah): Ephran's "first" brother; a male littermate.

Odalee (Oh - dah - lee): Ephran's mother.

Jafthuh (Jaff - the): Ephran's father.

Fetzgar (Fets - gur): A muskrat who lives in The Pond.

Winthrop: A large white owl.

Maltrick (Mall - trick): A wily red fox.

Mayberry: A male cottontail rabbit.

Truestar: A female cottontail. Mate to Mayberry.

Blackie: A female black and white farm cat.

Rennigan (Ren - a - gun): A bachelor buck fox squirrel.

Cloudchaser: A large drake mallard duck.

Marshflower: A female mallard. Mate to Cloudchaser.

Klestra (Cless - trah): An excitable red squirrel. Ephran's closest friend.

Smagtu (Smag - too): A shy skunk.

Kaahli (Kay - lee): A beautiful female gray squirrel.

Laslum (Lahs - lum): Kaahli's first brother.

Aden (Aye - den): Kaahli's and Laslum's father.

Roselimb: A female gray squirrel. Mate to Phetra.

Fred: A yellow hound dog.

Frafan (Fray - fan): Ephran's "second" brother. From Odalee's next litter.

Janna, Tinga and Ilta: Ephran's second sisters.

All is a search, is it not?
            One within another...
And yet another.

Song of Syntenaar,
Canticle III

CHAPTER I

ACROSS GREAT HILL

But mother," Mianta whined, in a voice that was not Ephran's favorite, "if it lasts as long as you say it does, I'll never be able to sleep through the cold season!"

"Very probably not," mother answered. "I have not known a gray squirrel who could sleep so long, and I very much doubt that you will be the first. You will want to get up and stretch, to nibble on a seed or a nut. You may even want to leave the nest to sun yourself. But, I warn you, stay near our tree. Do not wander far from your den.

"The air will be bitter then," mother continued, "and the trees and the bushes will fall asleep..."

She hesitated and scowled.

"May I ask what you are giggling at, Phetra?" Her lips did not smile, but her eyes sparkled, and Phetra could tell that she wasn't really angry.

"The trees and bushes have no eyes, mother!" he laughed. "How could they fall asleep?"

"Small one," she replied, "Does the wind need a mouth to sing? Does the snake need paws to run? Do the clouds need wings to fly?"

Phetra's smile shriveled. Mianta observed him from a higher branch, a smirk on her pudgy little face. Ephran knew what she was thinking: She was glad she hadn't said it!

It seemed strange to Ephran to be speaking of cold air. The day was so warm and still he didn't even feel like running and playing. It was a far better day for talking and learning. So the entire squirrel family; mother, father, and their three little ones lay comfortably on thick boughs, high among the cool green leaves of their tree.

"They will sleep," mother went on, "to save their strength for the time warmth returns to the sun and drops of water come from the clouds."

"Many forest animals besides us will be asleep too, but not all of them," interjected father, who was sprawled on a nearby branch. "Foxes and owls don't seem to need to close their eyes much. And a lot of those who do sleep will do so under a heavy blanket of snow..."

"'Snow'?"

Three little faces turned toward their father.

"Well yes...snow," he repeated, surprised at himself for being caught without his usual nimble reply. "Bits of white water. Light as milkweed down. Gets very thick on the forest floor. It's...ummm...sort of like feathers. White feathers from the sky, I suppose you could say. Yes, that's it! Feathers. Ah...but very cold, you know, not warm at all..."

He looked pleadingly at mother and she came to his rescue.

1

"Snow is difficult to describe," she said soothingly. "When you see it, and when you feel it with your paws, then you will know what snow is."

"Are foxes able to run in snow?" Ephran asked.

"You bet they can," said father. "Never try to race with a fox, snow or no snow."

"Why don't foxes eat acorns and butternuts and other things that grow on bushes and trees?" asked Phetra.

"That's a stupid question!" said Mianta. "Everybody knows that they don't eat nuts or fresh buds and that's that. Who cares why or why not?"

"Mianta!" Mother had a stern look on her face. "Your first lesson should have been that there are no stupid questions, except perhaps from those who think there are. Phetra, all I can tell you is that foxes and other hunters have little taste for the good things that grow from the earth. I don't know why."

"Maybe because there's no excitement in chasing a bouncing acorn," mused father.

At the end of the warm season Ephran waited impatiently to see these bits of white water that father had tried so hard to describe. Though he waited and waited, they had not come. Finally, bright eyes grew blurry and little eyelids heavy and he had fallen asleep as the last of the red and yellow leaves tumbled from the trees. When he finally woke up, really woke up, he didn't know how long he'd slept, but it must have been a very long time.

Ephran, first borne of those borne last warm season in the nest of Jafthuh and Odalee, his father and mother, lay as quietly as he could. His belly made a sad little growling sound and squirmed around inside. He spied no seeds or nuts in the faint light. He knew he'd eaten some and evidently everyone else had too. Food might still be there, hidden beneath the sticks and dry leaves that made up the floor of the nest, but digging around would likely wake someone else.

Mianta, his sister, and Phetra, his brother, lay on either side and the only way he could tell they were breathing at all was the tiny timid movements of their chests every time air moved in and out.

He'd entertained himself for a time, watching bits of dust dip and hover and chase each other in the ray of cheerful sunlight that had poured through the smooth hole in the big oak tree. He had puffed softly in their direction and smiled as they scurried and darted out of sight in the dark recesses of the den. The light had dimmed and faded now. Clouds must be thickening over the forest.

He simply couldn't lay still any longer. He had to get up and stretch his legs. He'd just slip outside for a moment or two. That should be all right. Surely there would be something to eat nearby. There always was. Maybe a fresh bud or a forgotten acorn near the roots of the oak.

And as long as he was out there anyway, he'd take a peek around the neighborhood -- see who and what was up and about. Then, he promised himself, he'd come right back and curl up in the nest next to mother.

Squeezing carefully between Phetra and Mianta, Ephran crept toward the pale shaft of unsteady light that shimmered from the hole. He glanced at father and mother with every other step and tried to avoid treading on any particularly dry leaves or twigs. He stopped in his tracks when father rolled up unto his side and snorted in his sleep. The outside air brushed his whiskers. It was still cold, but not nearly as bitter as it had been. The other times he'd awakened during the cold season the air had been so frigid that he'd taken a few nibbles from a stale acorn, cuddled close to another warm squirrel body, and went right back to sleep.

With a final look at his sleeping family, Ephran scrambled through the hole and unto the thick branch beneath it. The world had changed! The trees on Great Hill were totally bare. They seemed to be standing too far apart. No leaves could be seen. They had to be buried beneath a layer of white that was everywhere. Bubbling Brook was silent and, under a darkening sky, the skittish air stirred up a whorl of tiny crystals. Ephran's warm green woods, full of happy sounds and sweet smells, was gone. This new woods was fascinating. It certainly deserved a very close look.

"Scree! Screee!" A piercing cry broke the silence.

Now there was a voice he recognized! Mr. Bluejay was up on Great Hill, scolding something or someone. It wouldn't take long to see what was giving the old bird cause for a tantrum.

By the time he made his way to the crest of the Hill, the noisy bird had flown away and there was no sign of what might have unsettled the blue jay, on the ground or in the sky. He knew he should get back to the nest but another sound distracted him. This time it was the grinding squeal of breaking wood. How could that be? The air was barely moving. One should really try to find out about these things, he told himself, and so he set out through the treetops once more, crossed over the top of Great Hill and, heedless of beloved branches, out of sight of the oak.

Once again no exciting event, no new or amazing discovery, awaited him. All he saw was that a large and crooked limb had indeed surrendered its rotting grip on a maple tree. But there had been no need for swift-moving air to make it fall; the juices in the branch were long gone.

Ephran's stomach grumbled again, just as a fluffy flake drifted in front of his nose. It was not a feather. It had to be snow, snow the way it looked before it covered the earth and became one big white mantle. He glanced up to the solid gray sky above and saw that it was as devoid of feathered ones as was the forest below. Then, as though a hole

3

opened in the thick overcast, the air was full of flakes, floating slowly and gracefully to the earth. He watched and smiled as snowflakes drifted down on the peaceful woods; so still, so beautiful that he was mesmerized. It was a long while before he realized he was looking through the bare branches, at The Pond.

He remembered last warm season when he, mother, and Phetra had crossed Great Hill and explored this wonderful spot. He knew they had been in one of many whitebarked aspen trees along the far bank. The trees all looked alike and he couldn't tell which one had been their resting place .

On that sunfilled, breath-deep-and-smile day The Pond had been a little world of its own. A whole line of frogs had perched on lily pads, puffing up their spotted necks and making deep croaking sounds. There he saw, squatting in the snow, the ramshackle den of sticks and reeds where an old muskrat had reclined, contemplating his domain over an uplifted nose.

"Hello there!" Ephran had called out.

Phetra had "shushed" him, telling him not to talk to dangerous animals, but mother only smiled. She assured her sons that this water creature was no hunter.

He'd ignored the treeclimbers at first but Ephran begged mother to learn his name so she had introduced herself saying, "Mr. Muskrat, I am called Odalee. These are my sons, Ephran and Phetra."

"Fetzgar's mine," he said shyly.

"A fine name," she said, "a name with character." And she'd charmed the old fellow into a halting conversation about water, and trees, and hunters, and 'young 'uns'. About how long the days were getting and how soon the time of walnut ripening and of scattering of cattail fur would be upon the forest.

A waterlogged branch, no longer visible under the snow, had barely floated in the still water and a group of mudturtles found it an ideal place to enjoy the hearty sunshine. They were nervous types however and splashed into the water like stones the moment Fetzgar made a move in their direction.

Ephran could almost hear the yellowheaded blackbirds' loud discordant serenade, sung from thick brown and green bullrushes that surrounded The Pond. And how he'd laughed to see agile waterbugs with long skinny legs trace zigzag paths on the surface of the smooth water!

He wanted to return after that first visit but something always seemed to interfere. What with lessons from mother and father preparing him for his 'time alone', trips up Bubbling Brook, and excursions to The Meadow, he hadn't gotten around to coming back.

Now, like the rest of the forest, The Pond had changed. It lay silent, white, and cold. No birds or animals were to be seen. The cattails and bullrushes were withered, bent and broken. Fetzgar's dens were covered with undisturbed snow. Although the woods possessed a certain splendor, it was a frigid and indifferent beauty. There was no one to talk to, no one to play with and, apparently, nothing to eat. Everything seemed to be asleep.

That's what he should be, of course: Asleep. He'd better get back to the nest. It seemed that would be the only place to find a few dried seeds or a leftover nut after all. If he woke someone up, well then he woke someone up, that's all there was to it. He could always disturb Phetra. His brother would fall right back to sleep anyhow.

Just as Ephran made up his mind to backtrack over Great Hill he noticed the male rabbit.

"At last," he thought, "someone to talk to! Someone who might know where to find something to eat."

He was about to shout a greeting when another movement in the brown reeds, not far from the rabbit, caught his eye. Ephran knew at once what it was: At the edge of the hardened water a red fox stalked the cottontail.

The shorttail was crouched near a clump of bare sumac bushes and had been nibbling at something or other in a patch of shallow snow. He wouldn't be able to see the fox from where he was and the air was nearly still. So no warning, no musty fox smell, would be carried to his twitching nose. Despite that, he must sense danger, for his large round eyes seemed even more alert than usual and his long ears were held stiff and straight. Well, nearly straight. One of the ears would never be straight. A notch marked the place where the left ear had healed crooked. The deformity might be a souvenir of a family disagreement. It might as well be the outcome of a close call with a hunter.

Ephran didn't know this rabbit. Not that it made any real difference. Rabbits and squirrels didn't have much to do with each other anyway, except to answer an occasional question, usually involving directions to this or that warren or this or that walnut grove. For some reason though, at this time, in this quiet and hostile forest, Ephran felt he ought to do something to warn the cottontail. After all, was the fox not one of "them", a hunter? And was it not seeking one of "us", the hunted? He knew, deep down inside, that if the situation were reversed he'd appreciate some kind of warning. But what kind?

"If you're the first to sense danger," father told them, "let your family in on it. You all have quick feet and loud voices. Use them."

He could, of course, run rapidly along the thick bough he lay on. It had collected a layer of large white flakes, and clumps of it, falling from the tree, might distract the fox and give the rabbit time to understand its predicament. The branches were slippery and cold though, and even older and more experienced squirrels would have trouble maintaining their balance under these conditions. Especially

5

"AT THE EDGE OF THE HARDENED WATER
A RED FOX STALKED THE COTTONTAIL"

with a fox below, watching every move! What if he should slip and fall?

Maybe he should scold and chatter in his shrillest voice. That would certainly signal the rabbit that something was amiss! But, if he gave away his position the fox might follow him home. Then the hunter would know where the squirrel family nested. It could watch from a hidden place. It could wait for a mistake to be made.

Oh dear, what should he do?

Well, he could lay very still on the branch, as though he was part of the frozen tree. And, in a way, he was frozen.

Just as the fox crouched to spring at his victim, a pair of whitetailed deer sailed gracefully over a low bramble hedge and landed nearly atop the rabbit. Their arrival, though not noisy, was so sudden and unexpected that it sent the already uneasy shorttail bolting along the fringe of The Pond. Distracted for but a moment, the fox looked back toward where the rabbit had been, to discover he was too late. Lunch disappeared behind a clump of wilted bullrushes.

A tiny plume of steam, unnoticed by the foiled hunter, arose from a high branch as Ephran exhaled a long sigh of relief.

CHAPTER II

THE MANY COLORED ONES

The deer picked up where the rabbit left off, poking soft noses into crisp drifts, searching for tender shoots. They ignored the hunter with the thick red tail. He was no threat to them. Ephran kept very still as Mr. Fox cast a disgusted glance at the intruders, then slipped off through the Hedge, a redbrown shadow against white snow.

Father had been right; at least one hunter was out and about, looking for a warm meal. There were probably others. A gust of damp air sent a sudden shiver through Ephran and he got to his paws. He crept along the branch, freeing wisps of snow which, like little puffy clouds, drifted away from every step he took. The branch was smooth. He gripped it firmly, and used his long bushy tail like a balance stick to keep from falling.

It was past time to go home and he wished he hadn't meandered so far away in the first place. The search for nibblies had been a failure and he had nearly witnessed a cottontail's last breath. He didn't care to think about it. And he wouldn't dare consider going further in this direction, around The Pond, even if he knew something to eat lay that way. After all, somewhere nearby was Lomarsh, spawning ground for most of the terrible things that afflicted the animals of the forest. Or so everyone said.

The old oak wasn't far away but it would take time to retrace his path. Snow still lay soft and deep in the low places and his short legs would never get him through it. As always, he wished he could fly. But he was a squirrel, and the route through the trees was the only way. It was always the safest way.

Again, as though she stood next to him, he heard mother's words: "Keep to the high branches," she had told her young. "That is where you are secure; far above the earthhunters. From there you can see the edge of the world. You can see where the sun blossoms in the morning and where it hides at night. You will be able to see farther than any other animal in the forest."

At this moment his visibility was limited by the crest of Great Hill and, before he reached the summit, his ears detected peculiar sounds ahead. He stopped and listened. The noises he heard didn't seem to belong in the snowy woods but he wasn't frightened. What he heard now he'd heard before and his mind went back to that day with Jafthuh...

Early last warm season, when the leaves were new and when he was still very young, father had taken him along the banks of Bubbling Brook, past the rabbit warren, on one of many 'learning trips'. That special day Jafthuh spotted some of the most unusual creatures that Ephran thought he'd ever lay eyes on. From the topmost limbs of a tall ash they had watched two very large animals, animals that actually walked on their hind legs! They were in a grassy place across the water and they set up a terrible clanging and clattering with heavy sticks, wielded by delicate front legs. The sticks had thick shiny tips and were swung with great force, striking thinner and longer sticks that had already been poked into the soft earth. When many of these sticks had been set in straight lines, like tiny saplings without branches, the creatures strung a long vine between them.

"Father, what are they doing?" Ephran had whispered.

"Don't know, son. Sure act like the forest belongs to them though, don't they?"

"Can we go closer, father?"

"No. Not until they've gone. They're unpredictable. And dangerous."

Ephran peered at the animals on the far side of the brook. "Dangerous"? They certainly didn't look dangerous. Those bodies were not built for speed...and there were no wings or claws. If either possessed long, sharp teeth it wasn't obvious from here. Actually, despite their size, they looked sort of topheavy and clumsy. Phetra might shiver at the sight of them and Mianta's teeth would chatter if they looked her way, but these funny visitors in his woods didn't bother him. No sir, they were curious things. That's all they were.

"What are they called, father?"

"Many Colored Ones," replied Jafthuh.

And of course they were. Many colored, that is. Ephran realized the only common color of those in the pasture was their paws.

"They're usually very noisy," father continued in a low voice, "remarkably careless and apparently unafraid. You can almost always hear them coming through the fallen leaves and twigs on the forest floor. I've stayed hidden and watched plenty of them stumble around. Can't count how many different colored pelts I've seen."

Afterward, when they had left, he and father carefully inspected what these creatures had built. They marveled at the shiny and rigid vine, studded with sharp thorns, strung tightly between the smooth, stone-hard branches they had fixed in the earth. Only later did Jafthuh and Ephran understand that this place would be a cage of sorts - for those gigantic gentle pets of The Many Colored Ones called 'cows'. The vine would keep them from wandering off into the woods.

Back in the nest Ephran told his brother and sister of the encounter. They were fascinated and wanted to see for themselves these most unusual visitors. Disappointed faces greeted father's words when he told them that he and Ephran had watched as the strangers left the clearing at the edge of the forest.

"They are not actually creatures of the woods at all," mother had said. "They tend to nest together in flocks, like blackbirds just before the cold season. A few of them, outcasts perhaps, dwell near the woods and seem to be provided for from the goodness of the land as we are. Only they grow their food in massive plots of black dirt and build large dens of square stones or slices of trees..."

"Oh, mother!" Mianta breathed, "have you been near their dens?"

"Close enough," said Odalee, as she picked up a plump walnut and inspected it for worms.

"It would be great fun to watch them as father and Ephran did," said Phetra.

"At a distance...," said mother between bites, "at a good distance. Some do not grow food, or perhaps it is not enough for them. In any case, those creatures are hunters."

"Hunters?" gasped the young ones.

"Yes, hunters," said father. "They have sticks that make a horribly loud noise. Thundersticks, they're called, and they roar so loudly that a bird or animal near that sound might fall and lay still. The Many Colored Ones have lots of strange and wicked things like that. All of them seem to make more noise than the bluejay and smell worse than the skunk."

"Oh, I'm glad I didn't even see them," said Phetra in a wavering voice. "They must come from Lomarsh."

"You trembling fieldmouse," said Mianta to her brother, tilting her nose in the air and flicking her tail in his face, "Those old Many Colored Ones don't scare me any."

But her big eyes had betrayed her.

The sounds Ephran heard now were the same as he'd heard that day -- the garbled sound of their chatter. As before, there were two of them. At that moment Ephran wished that Jafthuh was awake and right here, next to his son on the bough. However, father was sound asleep in the den.

Ephran was more curious than anything. The tiny showers of snow he caused to tumble from the branches seemed to go unnoticed, and he soon found himself almost directly above the Many Colored Ones. Each of them carried, in their front paw, a bright red thing with a long, shiny snout -- a snout with teeth on both sides! They ambled slowly along, funny looking beasts, tripping now and again on fallen branches beneath the snow, stopping under one tree and then another, gazing up to study the branches, babbling to one another the whole while. Ephran had no idea what they were doing but he giggled once in a while when one or the other of them nearly fell in the snow. He wondered if they might be outcasts, the kind mother had mentioned, looking for a place to build a den. Fascinating though they might be, Ephran wasn't sure he was really excited at the prospect of having them for neighbors.

11

He certainly didn't care for it one bit when they stopped at the base of the huge oak that he called home. They peered into its massive limbs for a time, then one of them (mostly brown and blue) bent over the toothy object it carried. With a quick motion of its front leg The Many Colored One made the nasty, noisy thing come awake with an ear-splitting roar and a cloud of dense smoke. Almost gently, it lay the growling and fuming thing near the base of the oak. Splinters of bark and dark red wood sprayed out unto the virgin snow. The long snout with its shiny silver teeth sunk into the tree as though it was soft as mud.

Ephran's fascination turned to cold dread. Now he understood: These creatures were not just amusing visitors. They meant to harm his tree! That wasn't the worst part -- his family must still be inside! At that moment a sleepy face appeared at the same hole Ephran had climbed out of a short while ago.

"Mianta!" Ephran cried.

His shout was smothered by the monster's awful roar as it sank its teeth into the oak. His sister disappeared and he was sure that she hadn't seen or heard him. She must be going to rouse the family, if they hadn't already been stirred awake.

As he gazed intently at the hole, waiting for his kin to scramble through it, he realized that the great oak was trembling. At first he thought it odd, for the air was really very quiet and even in the warm season's most ferocious storm the sturdy old tree barely quivered. Then the oak seemed to moan as if in pain and it leaned toward the tree in which he hid.

There was no time for a second look. Everything had become confused and terrifying. He turned on the branch so quickly that he nearly lost his balance. The massive tree groaned again -- a long, deep, and sad sound. Ephran ran higher up the trunk and onto a limb opposite the giant oak. His jump to a small poplar was not graceful -- the limb was tiny -- but he didn't fall. Then to a larger box elder, a cluster of basswood, and finally to a stately, slender ash where he turned and looked back just in time to see the oak collapse heavily into the tree in which he'd been hiding a moment earlier. It twisted slowly, with immense dignity, and under its ponderous weight the other tree buckled and gave way. With mighty thunder both trees crashed to the snow-covered earth.

Ephran's panic was now complete. Inconceivable though it was, his home, that monumental work of countless warm seasons, was destroyed. And it had taken only a few moments. How could those shiny objects do this? What unbelievable evil power had The Many Colored Ones concocted? Father had spoken of the noise and the smell, but he hadn't mentioned the phenomenal strength.

His family was still in the downed tree. Could they have survived that great crash? If they had, would they find a way out? And if they found a way out, could they escape The Many Colored Ones with their loud noises and senseless destruction?

It was no longer possible to think. Fear and instinct became overpowering -- and Ephran ran. He ran through the treetops as far and as fast as he could. He ran without looking back. He ran until he was exhausted and lay panting and shivering in the uppermost branches of a thick-trunked elm. Away from those terrible shiny teeth that, without remorse, were carving his home into small pieces.

CHAPTER III

LOST FAMILY AND EARLY OWL

It took a long while for Ephran's heart to stop pounding against his ribs and before he could reflect on where he'd run to. All he knew for sure was that he'd crossed Meadow Brook. That slow flowing and peaceful ribbon of water, now frozen and hard, had been the boundary of his world. Its meeting and merging with Fox Brook had been as far in this direction that father or mother had taken him. Ephran found himself among trees he'd never seen.

A nearly overwhelming sense of loss and loneliness engulfed him and, for a moment, it seemed he could scarcely breathe. Should he go back and try to find his family? Could he find his way back? Did he really want to go back? Those terrible monsters with the silver teeth might still be there. Even if he could find his way back, his family would certainly have run from The Many Colored Ones -- if they were able to run. Assuming they could run, which direction would they go? This was all his fault. If he had only stayed where he was told to stay...

Ephran lay curled, nose tucked under a front leg. He shivered now and then as fewer and fewer flakes from the sky floated by. Finally they stopped entirely, and he wiped the tears from his eyes with damp little paws. He tried to be brave. And he tried hard to think. He must think!

He had observed that, on clear days, the sun unfailingly arrived over Bubbling Brook, twinkling and smiling, and that it always disappeared in a blaze of wonderment over the edge of The Meadow. That must mean something. And he had noticed that, more often than not, air moving from where the sun rose meant that clouds would soon come from the opposite direction. He had felt that the air sliding down to the big oak over Great Hill was generally warm air whereas air that came from the place where Bubbling Brook and Meadow Brook joined was much cooler. Somehow he should be able to use these and other things, like a damp or dry feeling on his whiskers, to foretell what the sky might do and to help direct him to other places in the woods. It was all quite complicated and confusing though, and very hard to keep one's mind on.

If he weren't so hungry perhaps it would be easier to think. When he'd first left the den his stomach had been making noise... and he still hadn't put so much as a stale thistle seed into it. For a moment he wished he could rummage around in the nest but the nest, of course, was gone. Any leftover seeds or nuts were spilled carelessly in the snow.

While he lay on his branch the clouds split open and the sun, low in the sky, shot streams of orange light through feathery gray plumes at the edge of the overcast. Longlimbed shadows of his resting tree stretched down a steep slope and into an undisturbed snowfilled hollow. Crisp tufts of baneberry and shriveled cocklebur poked up through the whiteness. To either side of the clearing were clumps of scrawny bushes. From their otherwise bare branches dangled small clusters of brownish berries. Food! Relics of the warm season that had somehow escaped the bright eye of the nuthatch and the chickadee!

Fear or no fear, loneliness or no loneliness, a young treeclimber had to eat -- and those berries were as tasty-looking as anything Ephran had seen in a long while. The problem now was; how to get to them? It was hard to keep his paws still while he looked, but eventually he spotted a bridge to dinner. An aspen had toppled from the woods into the clearing and its trunk lay nearly atop the bushes. It had been difficult to see, white bark against white snow, but it would allow him to reach the lovely fruit.

He tried to be careful as he ran, keeping the bushes in sight the whole time. When he finally reached the aspen, and scampered down its long trunk, he was impatient. He snatched a berry, bit down too hard, and squealed. This was a rock, not a berry! He hesitated for a moment before spitting it out and that was long enough for the berry to soften and fill his mouth with a tart and wonderful taste. He took another berry in his paws and held it in his mouth until it became soft. Then he swallowed it with relish. They weren't as satisfying as an acorn and they certainly didn't make the meal a big butternut would. They held a hint of sweetness, however, and were filling. He knew, if he ate enough of them, he'd be able to sleep without the misery of a grumbling stomach.

He finished his meal, seated comfortably on the broken aspen, facing the dusky sky. This time of day, during the warm season, the air would be filled with wonderful evening songs of the mourning dove and the redbreasted robin. Those songs made Ephran both happy and sad. He would very much have liked to hear their music now. However, it seemed that the robin and the dove had not returned from wherever they went to escape the cold season.

Ephran, lost in memories of a warmer and friendlier time, was unaware of yellow eyes that watched him from the edge of the forest. The eyes belonged to a large white owl named Winthrop.

It was too early in the day for Winthrop to begin hunting and he hadn't really gotten down to business yet. He'd been dozing in his nest when he heard the squeal of a squirrel. The very least he could do, he decided, was investigate. He could enjoy the sunset if nothing else came of it. There would be plenty of time to spend in the dark.

The appearance of the little gray treeclimber was a trifle surprising -- not many of them chattering and jumping about in the trees at the end of the cold season. At first Winthrop watched with a sense of drowsy detachment, much as he might gaze at billowy clouds float across the moon. It was only after he'd watched Ephran eating for a while that he realized that he was very probably as hungry as the squirrel.

Without a sound, the big white owl spread his wings and slid away from his perch. Ephran picked that moment to decide that he'd better find shelter for the night. As he turned on the aspen, the dark shape in the air caught his eye.

He grinned with delight. If there was one thing he would really like to be able to do, one wish he could have fulfilled, it would be to fly. To think of being able to spread beautiful and powerful wings and to soar...soar high over hills and valleys, up into great white clouds, through the trees above Bubbling Brook! It made him smile to think of it. Could this be a pigeon? Perhaps a dove. No, the bird was too big. Slow, deliberate wingbeats...not a crow either. What could it be then? And what was a bird doing, fluttering around so late in the day, when the sun was almost gone? What kind of bird came out to fly when the sun was going down? ...Then he remembered what sort of silent wings cast night shadows in the moon-filled woods. Then he recognized what was swooping through the chilly air toward him.

Much to his credit, Ephran did not panic. He had every right to, but he didn't. He knew, without thinking, that he had few if any choices. Though he avoided deep snow earlier, it might prove a friend right now. Just as the owl reached the fallen tree, Ephran leaped and sank out of sight.

With a flap of heavy wings Winthrop came to rest on the aspen. What happened to dinner? Had it jumped? Or had it swooned into the deep snow in sheer fright at his awesome presence? Either way, if he was really hungry he'd better shake those old tailfeathers. He flopped down into the snow and began to scatter it in all directions with his wings and feet.

Odalee had once said, "Watch -- and remember everything you see, even if it seems not worth remembering at the time. You never know when a new path will lead you home."

"Yes, mother," her young had nodded in unison, with no real understanding of what she meant.

Well, Ephran thought now he maybe knew part of what she was getting at. While he had been thawing berries in his mouth he'd noticed last warm season's grass, still visible beneath the aspen. The tree had obviously fallen before the snow came, and the broad trunk had shielded the earth and kept the flakes from accumulating beneath it. That observation, unimportant as it seemed at the time, proved to be his deliverance. Ephran used the clear path to scurry back to the safety of thick trees.

So, as things turned out, Winthrop was the one who ended up facing the wrong direction. Even if he'd been facing the woods he may

17

" THEN HE RECOGNIZED
WHAT WAS SWOOPING
THROUGH THE CHILLY
AIR TOWARD HIM...''

not have noticed a flash of gray disappearing into the bushes and trees. Though his sight was dim until the light faded, other eyes were alert. Someone watched, as someone always did in the big woods. Nothing went unseen.

Ephran clung to the side of a shaggy-barked tree, opposite the owl. He hadn't had time to be frightened -- not until now. Though he hadn't run far, his pulse raced madly and air came and went in short gasps. He waited until his breathing slowed, listening the whole time for the whisper of wings overhead. After what seemed an eternity he found the nerve to peek around the tree. In the gloaming he scrutinized every branch for an unnatural looking bump or a peculiar stubby limb, one fatter than the one it grew from. At last he was satisfied -- the owl was gone.

The sun had nearly buried itself below the brow of a hill crowned with spruce and yellow birch. A pair of chickadees chirped happily as they flew to their resting place in the thick evergreens. A pheasant crowed in the distance. Ephran shuddered. He had never spent the dark hours by himself. He always thought that the first would be arranged by father.

"Early next warm season," Jafthuh had said to him, "I'll show you a new part of the forest. You'll be expected to stay there for a while..."

"Will it be a fun place? Will Phetra and Mianta come too?" Ephran had asked, smiling and thinking he sensed a family adventure in the offing.

"No," said father, looking away from his son's eyes, "we'll expect you to stay alone."

"'Alone'...?"

Ephran had been so shocked that for a moment he thought his ears might be deceiving him. Could father really mean that they would leave him, all by himself, in a strange part of the forest?

"Why would you do that, father?" he'd asked, trying to keep his voice steady and the tears from spilling.

"So that your mother and I feel confident that you know how to find food and how to escape hunters. You must understand that when your mother delivers her young there won't be enough room in the nest for everyone. You simply can't stay with us forever."

What a dreadful thought! Dismay showed clearly in Ephran's eyes, shining though the tears.

"Don't be upset, Ephran," Jafthuh had said gently. "We wouldn't do this if there was no need." He gazed off into the faraway sky. "Your mother and I have tasted sadness, you know. Those who would be your first brothers and sisters were swept from the nest one day by a strong wind, before they knew how to care for themselves. It seems a long while ago." He looked back at Ephran, the usual good humor gone from his face. "A fox was waiting for them, you see. You must be prepared."

Right now Ephran wished he was more like Phetra and able to just listen and do as he was told. But there was a voice inside that insisted that he find things out for himself, that he go out and learn as much as he could, that he get to know and understand who and what he was going to have to deal with if he planned to survive in the big forest. It was basically a good voice, and it really wasn't the cause of his problems. He'd been warned about straying from the family tree before he was ready. Father and mother understood he wasn't ready. Now he understood too.

Well, no good fretting. He'd have to do the best he could, ready or not. Before anything else he'd better find a place to spend the night. A fork in a high tree would do but would provide no protection from the cold -- or from a possible return visit by the owl. A spruce would offer cover and some warmth, but the branches were too small and prickly to allow a decent night's sleep.

It was nearly dark when the last rays of light outlined a cluster of leaves near the top of tall tree far back in the woods. It looked lonely and out of place in the leafless forest but it was a welcome sight. Although not like his family's cozy den, he knew what he was looking at. It was a squirrel's nest.

When he arrived he found the nest abandoned, and his spirits drooped. He'd hoped, foolishly he knew, to find one of his own kind snuggled in the leaves. Unfortunately, from its appearance, Ephran could tell that the nest had had no occupant this cold season. Many of the sticks and leaves used by the original builder had long since fallen to the forest floor. And there were holes in the bottom almost large enough for him to slip through. If he wanted a reasonably safe and warm place to sleep, some repair work was going to be needed.

There were no fresh leaves, of course, but there was enough left of the crumbling nest to provide adequate cover. With a bit of rearranging he managed to curtain the holes and, when he did lay down with his tail curled around him, he found it wasn't too uncomfortable. His comfort was incomplete, however, even though his stomach no longer complained and his paws were not cold. His distress was in his mind, for he had no idea where he was and he couldn't begin to guess how he would ever find his family. He tried not to think of the other possibility, but the idea kept crawling in with him anyway, like a slinky and unwanted black beetle: Right now they might be lying, quite still, beneath a crushed tree. Or they might have been taken away from the forest forever. The unthinkable was possible.

Little round eyes stared into the darkness, but saw nothing. Alert little ears strained to hear any sound in the chill silence, but heard nothing. Though a long time coming, welcome sleep finally embraced the exhausted young treeclimber.

20

CHAPTER IV

A DISTURBED MORNING NAP

Jt was not the sun peeping over the wooded hill that awoke Ephran from fitful sleep, but the raucous cawing of crows in a grove of nearby butternut trees. Of all the creatures in the big woods crows were among the noisiest -- and the nosiest. They were terrible gossips. Mother pretty much ignored them but father lifted an ear when they were about. They were hard to understand, squawking away at one another like they did, but they flew slowly above the forest (some said beyond it) and Ephran had come to understand that they generally knew a great deal of what was going on below them. So now he lay quietly and listened.

He wasn't able to comprehend everything that was being said, and much of what he did understand was of no concern or interest to him. Then, just as he was about to try closing heavy eyelids for another few winks, a bit of conversation caused them to fly open. Did one of the black rascals say something about a group of squirrels -- squirrels traveling through the trees toward the resting place of the sun? Or had he misunderstood?...had one of them just said something concerning squirrels teaching their sons about trees? He listened as hard as he could but they were talking about something else now. Should he or shouldn't he jump out and ask them, "What about squirrels? Did you see some gray squirrels running through the trees today or yesterday?" He was quite sure the crows wouldn't harm him.

He was too late. By the time he made up his mind and climbed out of the old nest the big black birds had flown lazily away, across the glistening hills. Yesterday's clouds were gone and sunlight sparkled off the dusting of new-fallen snow. He watched the crows, cawing loudly to one another as they flapped off toward Fox Brook. Nothing graceful about them, but he envied them their wings, as they passed high above the hills and across shadowed valleys. Then they were gone and a lonely peace settled over the woods.

How he wished he could have talked to them! Was it possible that they had actually seen his family? If his family was running free in the trees, would they leave him behind? They wouldn't have time to look for him. That thought brought tears to his eyes once more. Even with the cold season sighing its last chill breath, shelter would be necessary for quite a while yet. Especially for Odalee. Her belly was heavy with Ephran's unborn second brothers and sisters and she, most of all, needed a warm and comfortable place to rest.

His stomach grumbled again. Not surprising, considering that he'd slept away most of the cold season, eating very little. The layer of fat that made his stomach round and heavy at the end of the warm season was long gone. And the need for food had not been made less since he woke up. He'd had plenty of exercise already, had no idea how far he'd have to travel, how long it would be before he'd see food again, and how difficult things might get in this snowfilled forest -- without mother or father's advice. He'd have to find something more substantial than rock-hard berries.

Ephran's eye lingered on the trees where the crows had perched. He looked again. His heart beat a little faster. Unless he was badly mistaken these small and leafless branches, that he'd not even noticed the night before, were a kind that grew nuts.

Warm air and sunshine had melted all evidence of the cold season from the hilly slope, and the forest floor beneath the trees was golden brown in color. Ephran realized he was looking at some of last warm season's leaves. They were not particularly appetizing, but it was possible they hid something that was.

Ephran had not forgotten yesterday's close call with the owl. The short trip toward the butternut trees was slow and wary. The trees that grew nuts were not as tall as the surrounding ash and elm and he had to jump from a quivery high branch into their slender limbs. Nearly forgetting to take a precautionary look around, he scampered to the ground.

Now this was more like it! The lack of snow and the goodness of sunshine made it feel like the warm season -- secure and friendly. After a little scratching through layers of leaves, Ephran found his breakfast. And what a breakfast it was! Some of the nuts he uncovered were spoiled, but he expected that. Enough of them, those that had fallen at the very end of the warm season, were preserved, and soon a respectable pile of empty shells surrounded him.

Wonderful feeling, his stomach was finally full...really full! It was cozy among the leaves and Ephran wrapped his tail around his legs and lay down. He hadn't slept well in the abandoned nest. He felt more relaxed and unafraid on this radiant sun-drenched hill. After all, he told himself, most hunters are creatures of the darktime.

Far away a hawk wheeled slowly in the sky, too distant to be a threat. A breeze, spiced with a hint of the warm season, hummed a gentle tune as it swirled through the spruce and fir trees. He thought drowsily about which way he should go. Well, he thought, no harm in running the way the crows spoke of, toward where the sun sets. Or shouldn't he pay attention to what crows said? Did he have a better idea? All right then, it was settled, he'd go that way. In a minute. Right now it was very difficult to hold his eyes open. They very much wanted to close. For a moment. Just a moment...

The hour was very late for Maltrick to be going home. Weary and disappointed from a long and fruitless hunt, the red fox shuffled along the familiar path at the edge of the butternut trees. Things had not gone well today -- and yesterday had been worse. If it hadn't been for those miserable deer, jumping over The Hedge and confusing him... He could almost taste the cottontail that got away, and he licked his lips.

Head down, squinting against the glare of sunlight, he very nearly trotted right by Ephran, who lay curled in a tight fuzzy ball just a few leaps from the path.

Maltrick stopped, hunched his shoulders, and leaned toward the little gray treeclimber. He sniffed. He held his ears erect. Was the squirrel frozen? No...there! A wee breath. What do you know? Sound asleep in the sun. A change of luck. He gathered his legs under him.

It must have been the crackle of a crisp leaf that saved Ephran. The sound was not loud, but it did not belong in that quiet place. Ephran's ear knew, before he himself did, that something was amiss. He opened one eye the tiniest bit and saw the fox, muscles bunched, ready to leap. Maltrick was no slouch when it came to speed, but he didn't know that Ephran was awake. If he'd known, he might have planned his attack differently -- like putting himself between the squirrel and the trees. As it was, Ephran, with amazing reflexes, jerked and twisted out of harm's way at the last possible second. And, as fast as he ran, he may still have been caught had not the butternut trees been so close at paw.

The fox, snarling to himself, watched Ephran scurry into the upper branches of a short and sturdy tree. He sat down in the leaves. Ephran held tight to the trunk and looked down.

Maltrick, forcing a wide grin, said, "Please excuse me for disturbing your nap, little fellow. I was concerned that you might be injured, laying so quietly on the cold earth."

Ephran's breath came in spasms. "I...I am...I'm not hurt."

"Yes! Yes! I can see that you're just fine and full of bounce. I'm really quite pleased about that," said Maltrick. The smile never left his face.

Ephran, struggling to breathe normally, said nothing. The fox spoke again. "I feel badly about waking you. I can understand why you found it so comfortable here in the sun."

Maltrick made a great show of rolling about in the dry leaves and grass, emitting satisfied barking sounds, and generally looking pretty silly.

"Please come back and resume your nap," he said, laying on his side and peering up at Ephran, a broken leaf hanging from his nose. "I'd like to spend some time visiting, but I'm afraid I have to leave. Social obligations, you know. Expecting visitors at my den. Actually my mate's rather boring uncle. But I must hightail it home soon, in any case."

The fox stood up, as though he were going to leave, but he didn't move his paws. Neither did Ephran who said, "You jumped at me."

"Well, my goodness, laddie, please don't take it personally."

Maltrick looked up with a wounded expression. "I was only going to say 'hello' and then you bolted and frightened me and so I jumped too. I didn't mean to frighten you in return. I've tried to apologize." Maltrick sighed. "It would be so nice to have a chat with an intelligent young squirrel before I have to face that uncle. I wish you'd come down and be pleasant to a tired old fox. I'm getting a stiff neck from looking up at you. My name is Maltrick. What's yours?"

Ephran had been taught to be polite, as is any young squirrel with proper upbringing. He wasn't quite sure if good manners should be extended to a fox.

"My name is Ephran. And I think I should stay where I am. I'm quite comfortable up here."

Maltrick had used this route on his hunting forays many times and was quite certain that no family of squirrels lived nearby -- not since the old nest in the tall tree had been abandoned. He also knew that a treeclimber would not usually be alone in the woods at this time of season, not at Ephran's age. There was only one conclusion to be reached; the little nuteater was probably lost. The fox had an idea.

"Ephran, I think I can help you find your family," said Maltrick.

Ephran spun around on the tree, and blurted, "My family! Do you know where my family is?"

"Well, I may. Yes indeed, I just may. As a matter of fact, I believe I saw a group of gray treeclimbers earlier," said the fox, smiling broadly once more.

"Oh my! Where did you see them? Which way were they going? Did you hear them say anything...?"

"Hold on, hold on! Please! One question at a time," said Maltrick, "one question at a time. And come down here to talk if you want my help. I am really getting a very stiff neck."

Ephran started down the tree. His heart was skipping along, faster than his paws. His family was well! And evidently not too far away. He'd reached the lowest boughs and, before scurrying down the trunk, he glanced at the grinning red and white face turned up to him. A drop of saliva sparkled at the corner of the fox's mouth. For some reason Ephran was reminded of a nearly forgotten warning.

One night in the nest mother had said, "Those of us who are hunted can never completely close our eyes or ears. The hunter will be upon you when you least expect it. When you are awake do not look into the fascinating eyes of the hawk or hear the sweetness in the words of the fox. They are your enemies. They will use the very senses you need for survival to mislead you."

Oh dear! He didn't want to miss any chance of finding his family but he didn't know if he should trust the fox. What would father do? Father, most certainly, would test the fox. Father would discover if the fox was being truthful. Father would outsmart the fox. It was

Ephran's turn, and an idea, from who knew where, popped into his head.

"Did you see all five of my family?" he asked innocently.

"Yes, indeed. All five," confirmed the fox with a solemn nod.

"That's very strange," said Ephran as he sat back on the base of a thick branch, "since without me there are only four in my family."

"Hmmm," said Maltrick, "perhaps it was another family. Or perhaps your family picked up a straggler in their travels. Someone lost -- like yourself maybe. In any case, come down so we can discuss this. I mean you no harm."

"Did you mean no harm to the rabbit by The Pond."

At first Maltrick said nothing. He looked very thoughtful. Then he mumbled, "Looks like field mouse hunting again today."

"What's that?" asked Ephran. "I can't hear you."

"Nothing," said the fox, smiling up at Ephran one last time. "We'll continue our little talk another day." He stretched, yawned, and trotted off through the trees.

Shivering occasionally, Ephran sat for some time after the fox disappeared into the woods. He'd forgotten how helpless he was and very nearly had the air taken from him because of it. To fall asleep on the earth was a mistake few squirrels could tell of. Certainly, none would brag of it. They would have to be either very brave or very foolish.

How Phetra would scoff at him. How sad mother would be to see how careless he'd been. For a moment he was relieved that they weren't here to have witnessed this terrible lapse of attention. Only for a moment though. No, he'd suffer his brother's ridicule, Mianta's superiority, mother's scolding, and father's disappointment if he could only see them all again. What he'd give to curl up, with his family around him, as darkness covered the forest!

A tear ran down his cheek and dropped on his paw.

CHAPTER V

ADVICE FROM MAYBERRY

he early hours were spent traveling away from the ascending sun; not so much because the crows had mentioned squirrels going that way as because it seemed as good a way as any. Progress was slow, for he stopped often to look and listen. How he wished he could fly...high above the branches! How much easier it would be to see far away and in all directions. How much better would be his chances to see father and mother.

Sometimes his path was blocked by a snow-clogged field or a hillock, where the trees were not close enough for jumping. He would become impatient and uneasy then, dreading another night alone, but he forced himself to plan an alternate route. His general heading remained true and he was spurred on by hope and fear at the same time.

About the time sunbeams reached the lower leaves Ephran stopped in an oak to rest and review his progress. The tree looked as though it would not turn green again, and it leaned heavily against its neighbor. There were a few acorns in its lower branches. He cracked one of them open and chewed slowly, ignoring its stale taste, peering into the woods. He knew it was far-fetched, but he hoped to catch a glimpse of a familiar shape in one of the trees.

The trees were deserted, but in thick currant bushes crowded under a clump of basswood his eye caught a flicker of movement. He dropped the acorn and strained to detect any motion among the brown stems. There...he saw it again! A rabbit! There was a brown rabbit hidden in the brown weeds.

"Another rabbit with a crooked ear?" he wondered. Not likely. This must be the same cottontail he'd seen yesterday.

At first he was surprised that the long-eared buck had covered so much ground so quickly. The Pond, after all, had to be some distance behind them. Then again, rabbits could move right along. Snow didn't seem to bother them and their big broad paws all that much. They didn't have to choose their path from tree to tree as he did. Besides, he'd been one slow-moving squirrel, often unsure of his direction and afraid that if he went too fast he might miss a clue to finding his family. He probably hadn't traveled as far as he thought.

Ephran picked his way through the trees until he found a comfortable branch in one of the basswoods. He murmured a greeting to the rabbit who was munching contentedly on faded, unappetizing greens. Cocking his head to one side to look up at Ephran with a big brown eye, the cottontail nodded. Then he went on chewing. Ephran had a mouthful of questions but the rabbit had a mouthful of grass. So, for the time being, Ephran had to be patient. It was a difficult thing to do. The sun did not delay in its long arc and Ephran knew that his family could be getting further away by the minute. He played with a twig for a while and then began to fidget on the branch.

The rabbit leisurely swallowed and said, "You seem impatient, longtail."

"Kind of...I guess," replied Ephran, startled when the silence was broken. "I'm looking for my family, you see."

"Ah," said the rabbit. "I understand. You're lost."

"Well, um, someone is. I suppose...I suppose I am. It was those of Many Colors. They destroyed our home with a great noise. Our den...it was in a great oak. My family was inside. I can't find them. They, uh, sort of disappeared."

The words tumbled out of his mouth, like water gurgling down Bubbling Brook. He was too embarrassed to tell the rabbit that he'd run away without waiting to see what happened to his loved ones. And he didn't mention why he hadn't been in the nest with them when the oak fell.

"I see," said the rabbit, swallowing again, and clearing his throat. "Took your tree down, you say. Well, The Many Colored Ones do things like that. I don't know why and I don't know anyone who does."

"I'm afraid that I won't find father and mother if I don't hurry. And I don't know for certain which way they went."

The rabbit nodded his head. "At times it does seem that the trees go on and on, doesn't it?" he said, not waiting for an answer. "But there are not as many gray treeclimbers as there are trees. For someone who can travel as quickly and safely as you can, the forest is really not so big." He scratched his long ear. "I often wish I had the advantages you longtails have with those sharp claws of yours. You can see much farther from up there than I can from down here."

Ephran remembered what mother had said about the high branches. He could indeed see a long way through the leafless limbs. And he could move rapidly if he made up his mind which way he wanted to move. It was true; even if he couldn't fly, he had some definite advantages. He was hardly aware of the tiny spark of confidence that the cottontail had ignited.

"Actually," the rabbit continued, "I might have seen your family just after the sun came over the hill. There were some gray squirrels feeding on hickory nuts..."

"Oh...where...where did you see them?" Ephran's tail stood straight up.

"Hmmm, over there, I believe. I didn't pay a great deal of attention, to be honest..."

"How many squirrels did you see? Did you hear them say anything?"

"I'm not sure. More than one. As I said, I didn't really pay much heed to them. Nor they to me."

"Might there have been two older and two younger?"

The cottontail shook his head and shrugged his shoulders. "I'm really very sorry, little longtail. You are asking many questions I cannot answer."

Ephran took a deep breath. "Yes. I just wish I knew if my family is running...and which way they might be running. Thank you anyway, Mr. Rabbit."

"You are welcome for what little I can tell you," said the cottontail with a smile, "and my name is not Mr. Rabbit. I am called Mayberry."

"I'm very pleased to meet you," said Ephran solemnly. "My name is Ephran." Then, in a voice so low that Mayberry had to strain to hear, he added, "Actually, I've seen you before. Yesterday, by the edge of The Pond."

"Hmmm," said Mayberry thoughtfully, "Do you mean when the deer jumped over the brambles?"

"Yes..."

"Did you see the fox as well?" asked the rabbit.

"Yes, I did," admitted Ephran. He looked away from the cottontail's eyes and suddenly seemed to take a keen interest in cleaning some specks of wood from his tail.

"I'm afraid I'm getting old and careless," sighed Mayberry as he sat back on his round bottom and scratched his other ear, the long one. "I didn't realize the cunning old rascal was there until the deer alerted me. In any case, he didn't get me."

"Through no fault of mine," blurted Ephran. "I could have warned you and I didn't. I was...I was...I just couldn't move. Or even make a sound."

"Ah, don't feel so badly. Your attempt to alert me may have caused the fox to attack before I could get away."

"You're just being nice," said Ephran, "and trying to make me feel better about my not doing...doing something."

Mayberry looked up with a puzzled half-smile. "Well, I appreciate the thought. Most animals in this woods are interested only in looking out for themselves." He looked pensive. "Rabbits, too, for that matter. Look how little attention I paid to the gray squirrels I saw. Anyway, I feel that the episode by The Pond ended well. The fox may perceive it differently."

He grinned up at Ephran. "I suspect that you will find another chance to show your courage. Don't give up your feelings -- or your search for your family. It may well have been them that I saw."

"Thank you for your help, Mr. Mayberry," said Ephran. "I am going to keep looking. I hope I see you again."

29

"Oh, I have an inkling that we'll meet another time. I certainly hope so. Goodbye, Ephran. Good luck in your search."

Mayberry went back to munching uninteresting things he found hidden under the snow and Ephran left him beneath the leafless bushes. He looked back once and Mayberry waved. Ephran was very pleased that Mayberry had not ended up as the fox's lunch. There was no way of being sure whether or not it was his family the cottontail had seen but, as Mayberry said, it very well could have been. Wise and loving father and mother, playful Phetra, sweet and snippy Mianta might be somewhere ahead.

Somehow it seemed a good deal easier to see through the bare trees than it had just a little while ago. And there seemed a little push of air from behind, urging him along as he leaped from bough to bough.

Every rise and dip in the land was another obstacle to be overcome. Perhaps over the next hill. Twice he stopped at tree dens that looked as though they might be occupied, but both were empty. Though anticipation drove him on, short legs became weary nevertheless. After traveling for a particularly long stretch he paused to rest in a golden aspen tree, and was fascinated by two vast and unbroken expanses of snow on either side. He'd never seen such a huge grassless and treeless place. He had no idea he was passing between two lakes.

As the sun passed overhead, and he crossed yet another hill, Ephran came to a sudden halt. Directly in his path lay a group of huge shapes, square ones and oblong ones and roundish ones, they rose from the earth like some sort of gigantic and misshapen mushrooms. Though it was another thing he'd not seen before, he remembered mother's description. How could he forget? These must be the dens of some of the solitary Many Colored Ones.

Oddly enough, they were not all different hues. There was a big red one to be sure, like oak leaves just before they fell to the ground. There was one the color of old wood. The one that seemed to be the best kept was white. To make it hard to see against the snow? To hide? To hide from what? From what he'd observed of these bold creatures he was hard pressed to think of anything They might have to hide from.

On the sides of the white den were many squares of darkness that reflected the sun, probably what father thought was a thin layer of water, frozen by the cold. That explanation didn't satisfy Ephran, though he had none better. Smoke curled lazily from a pile of rocks atop the den. It would have been frightening had not mother explained that Many Colored Ones used "fire" to warm themselves. He didn't know exactly what fire was, but father had said it was light and heat -- like that from the sun. Fire was supposed to be more heat than light, and more uncomfortable than the hottest sun. Jafthuh had told his wide-eyed young ones that fire was not really a breathing, moving animal, but was able to "eat" things in its own way and would, given the chance, devour both trees and grass in great gulps. And, as it ate, it gave off great, foul-smelling clouds, called "smoke."

How strange these Many Colored Ones were! To use something so very dangerous to keep out the cold. Might their fancy pelts be more for looks than for comfort?

The red den was much larger than the white one. It had fewer dark squares and it leaned slightly to the side. Tufts of golden straw dangled from a large hole near its top. This would have to be the nest of those animals that belonged to The Many Colored Ones. Cows and such.

The big wooden dens that they built for Themselves and their animals might have been inviting to Them, but not to Ephran. His parents told him to avoid places like this, the home of unpredictable hunters, possibly spawn of Lomarsh. Maybe this was the home of Those who carried the things that ate wood with many shining teeth.

Raising himself from the branch he'd been lying on, Ephran was about to turn and make a wide circle around the dens when he noticed the corncrib.

The young treeclimber had figured out that this was a farm and had an idea about farm animals. But corncribs were a brand new marvel. No one had mentioned them. Later, when he had a chance to think about corncribs, he would correctly surmise that they were storage places, a kind of den built by The Many Colored Ones to store some of the wonderful foods They grew in their large fields of black dirt. This one seemed none too well constructed. There were big spaces between the slices of wood making up its sides; big enough to allow a squirrel to crawl in -- and snatch a few samples.

Ephran, as everyone who knew him realized, loved to eat. Acorns and hickory nuts were great. Butternuts and walnuts were a fine treat. But corn! Well, a stick of bright yellow corn was nearly total happiness! He'd tasted it just once and he still remembered the day that father brought home that thick stick covered with yellow seeds. The whole family had feasted on that one stick and Ephran would never forget the delicate sweetness. And here -- why, here were more sticks than there were rocks in Rocky Creek! The crib was nearly half full.

He sat stock still for some time, eyes never wavering from the treasure. He mustn't go near it. No telling who or what might be around. But it certainly looked peaceful. He could eat his fill now and even store a few kernels in his mouth as he traveled. That would be a great way to be sure that he didn't go hungry tonight. Mind made up, Ephran set out on the most direct route toward the farm.

Luckily, the corn crib was not far from the edge of the woods and there was very little snow around it. Shriveled grass could be seen, here and there, where something had scraped the area clear. He would need but a few leaps on the ground to reach his goal.

31

As he approached the mountain of corn he tried to go slowly, tried to keep watch in all directions for signs of danger, tried to remember mother's warnings about approaching a place where The Many Colored Ones nested. He did a poor job of trying.

Just as he reached his goal a plump black and white female cat appeared around the far corner of the corncrib. She must've been hidden from Ephran's view while he was studying the farm. But he should have seen her once he was on the earth -- the floor of the crib was built well off the ground. If he'd only watched for danger under the corn instead of being so fascinated by it!

For a moment they faced each other, one as surprised at the confrontation as the other. In his short life Ephran had not seen an animal like this. The eyes, however, were only too familiar. The slit-like orbs were those of a hunter -- and he remembered all too well descriptions given by the older squirrels and their stories of how very cruel and dangerous cats were.

Ephran turned and streaked for the only safe haven a squirrel knows. He had no time to pick and choose -- and he ran without thinking for the first tree his eyes happened upon. That turned out to be a most unusual tree, with no bark and a single pair of stubby branches, very near the top, sticking out in opposite directions. A tree was not a good choice perhaps, but how was a young squirrel from the deep woods to know a tree would prove no obstacle to an experienced old farm cat?

Ephran raced up the smooth trunk, one step ahead of the cat. Up and up they went, up and up and round and round, until Ephran reached the very peak -- a flat peak -- and had to stop, with nowhere to go. The cat had slowed down and now sat at the level of the two branches just beneath Ephran, blocking his escape, yellow eyes unmoving.

Ephran looked for a nearby tree and realized, in his excitement, he'd forgotten one of the most important lessons a young treeclimber learns. Both father and mother had told him many times: "Never climb a tree that has no neighbors."

Well, that's exactly what he'd done. And now he was trapped. Trapped in the funniest tree he'd ever seen, unable to climb any further and without a nearby branch to jump to.

"Well, well...little treeclimber. You climb...quite well," wheezed the cat. "...But what are you going to do now? Can you fly?"

Ephran gazed into the sinister unblinking eyes, unable to speak. He was a bit short of air, but the cat was breathless. She was very fat and getting old. Ephran realized he could have easily outdistanced her on the snowpacked earth. It was a little late to think of that now.

"As soon as I get my air back...I'm coming up there...and get you," the cat managed to say.

"We'll both fall!" Ephran cried.

The cat's grin got broader. "They say I always come up on my paws. Do you?"

With that, still breathing hard, she stood up on one of the thick branches, narrowing the distance between them. Ephran looked from the cat to the earth, snow glistening far below. It seemed a very long way down. Then, for the first time, he noticed a thick vine, black as darkness, that seemed to grow from one of the branches below him to another identical branch, on another identical tree, a long way off. There were two such vines, one growing from each branch. And from his tree, the vines continued on -- right up to the den of The Many Colored Ones!

He had no time to contemplate how very strange this whole business was. He was nearly frantic. He would have to jump. He would have to hope that the vine was not too brittle, that it was not too smooth and hard to grasp. A tumble to the hard earth would most certainly stun him for a long while. More likely it would take his breath away forever.

It made no difference if his family escaped The Many Colored Ones. He'd never see them again anyway. Wherever they were, they'd never know what had happened to their son and brother. What a mess he'd made of things! The cat took one step nearer...and Ephran prepared to jump -- a leap he knew he'd probably not survive.

CHAPTER VI

END OF THE WOODS

Luckily, the jump was not far, because the black vine was indeed very hard and very slippery. His body struck full force and the vine dug into his soft belly. He closed his legs as hard and tight as he could and hugged it, as though it was mother's neck. About the time he thought he was just fine his body shifted ever so slightly, slid sideways, and he found himself upside down, facing the big fluffy clouds sailing overhead.

The cat was flabbergasted. What amazing nerve -- the little rascal was going to try to make a getaway on the Many Colored Ones' vine! Instinctively she reached out, too excited to measure her chances in the usual deliberate fashion. One paw brushed Ephran's tail -- but she had leaned too far. Her head and upper body swung away from the pole. A front paw reached for the black wire and missed. Her rear claws tried desperately to hold on to the crossbar but couldn't. With a tiny shriek the cat tumbled from her perch, end over end, a black and white blur, struggling in the air to get her paws down. She landed with a dull 'WHUMP' in a drift of snow.

Ephran saw none of it. He was too busy trying to right himself on the vine and to get a grip on his perch. By the time he managed to get his paws under him, and felt secure enough to look around, the cat was gone. He knew what had happened when he saw her picking herself gingerly from the snow. She staggered away from the drift, weaving one way, then the other, as though not quite sure the earth would stand still beneath her.

She would stop now and again, sneezing and blowing snow from her nose and mouth. Snorting one last time, she gave herself a little shake, as dignified as she could make it under the circumstances. Then she limped off, following a crooked path toward the den of The Many Colored Ones.

Ephran felt no sense of victory. The only thing he could think of was how to get away from this place as quickly as possible. He supposed he could crawl back, along the vine, to the barkless tree that he'd just scurried up, but he didn't care to go back toward the dens of The Many Colored Ones -- not even the one filled with corn -- unless he absolutely had to. Besides, that would mean he'd have to turn around or creep backwards, on this smooth and cold perch. He eyed the long and narrow black line between himself and the next tree. It seemed a long way, but he couldn't stay here forever. Sighing deeply and putting one paw carefully in front of the other he inched his way along, far above the frozen earth.

"WITH A TINY SHRIEK THE CAT TUMBLED FROM HER PERCH.". . . .

It was just about the hardest work he'd ever done. He was afraid to look up, though he desperately wanted to see how far it was to the next strange tree. One tiny step after another. In no time every muscle ached and cried for rest. Just when he was sure he'd never make it, that he'd have to let himself fall and hope he landed in soft snow as the cat did, he was delighted to find himself alongside a low-hanging branch -- a real honest-to-walnuts branch, not a stubby squared-off thing! And it was close enough to jump to.

Gathering his quivering legs under him, he launched himself at the limb and caught it firmly in his front paws. It dipped suddenly, like a surprised animal trying to shake its attacker, but Ephran held on tightly and, paw after paw, worked his way up to the thicker part. He hesitated only long enough to take another deep breath and then set off, away from the buildings. He glanced back at the thick black vine and said, under his breath, "Thank you for being there."

He put that fearsome place behind him, and ran off through the branches. He was still traveling in the right direction. He could tell by the position of the sun, and the breeze against his face. Ahead, through the trees, was a bright and open place. A meadow, perhaps. A place where he might be able to see a long way. Maybe far enough to see father and mother.

When he got to the clearing he stopped in astonishment. From where came the cold wind -- where he was certain he wanted and needed to go and find Jafthuh and Odalee -- was a vast wasteland. The growth of big trees had tapered to an end and, as far as his eyes could look, straight in front and to both sides, was a gently undulating field of snow. No bushes, no tall grass, no trees...not even a stump. The clouds -- the sky itself -- faded away and came up to meet the earth in all directions save the one he had come. There was no sign of movement and no sound, not even the harsh cawing of a crow.

He sat there for what seemed a long time, his paws colder by the minute and his heart growing as empty as his stomach. Mother had told of this place, the place where some of The Many Colored Ones, those who dwelled apart from others of their kind, had a den at the edge of the trees. He hadn't believed it when she said it. He thought (and he told Mianta and Phetra as much) that she was simply trying to frighten them into staying near their den. But it seemed that mother had not been joking. Her words had been true. There was nowhere to go in this direction. This had to be the end of the woods.

Ephran was beyond tears, beyond panic. Turning slowly, he walked along the limb. Then he stopped and gazed out over the open field again. Maybe he'd missed something. Maybe, if he looked very hard, he would see a tree...a faraway branch. He looked so hard the horizon grew blurry. He ran to the very top of the tallest tree he could find. There was nothing to see.

He'd have to retrace his steps past the dens after all. There was no place else to go. And so he ran back, past the barn and the corncrib. He purposely did not look in their direction. He should have.

Not two short treelengths from Ephran's path, exhausted from his own long trek through the cold woods, another young gray squirrel lay flattened against the branch of a tall oak, sound asleep.

Ephran kept moving, jumping from tree to tree, trying to pick a good squirrel path. At first all he could think of was getting as far away from the dens of The Many Colored Ones as he could. He saw a pair of raccoons, barely awake, plodding along a rocky hillside with little snow. He tried to hail them but they ignored him and continued on their way. He ran on, jumping and climbing when he had to, trying not to let the feeling of hopelessness overcome him. He stopped and lay down on the branch of an elm, his breath coming in short puffs.

His stomach had stopped growling, which was strange since he hadn't really eaten anything since his breakfast of butternuts. He felt lightheaded. His legs were so weary he wondered if he could get up and run again. It was getting dark.

He thought how wonderful it would be if he could just find his way home, to snuggle between mother and father once more. Then his thinking cleared and he realized home wasn't there anymore. Where was home? Was there any home anywhere? How could he find something if he didn't even know that it existed?

He would stay right here, that's what he'd do. All this running and chasing was getting him nowhere. There was no place to go, at least no place he recognized. He would lay here and watch the sun go down, as he used to do last warm season. And he would figure out what to do and where to go.

"All by yerself, son?"

Ephran almost fell from the branch. The voice came from a tree next to the one he was in, its branches intertwined with those of his. An old buck fox squirrel with a tattered pelt peered at him with one open eye, his head hanging languidly from a ropey limb.

"I...I didn't see you," said Ephran.

"Know that."

Silence.

"Yes. I'm alone."

"Little bit young to be out on yer own, aren't ya?" The old chap scratched his bottomside with one paw. "But then, guess I was a bit damp under the whiskers m'self when I started out."

Ephran tried to stand, but it was too much work. He settled for lifting his nose. "I'm not 'damp under the whiskers' as you put it."

"No cause to take offense, son. No crime ta be young." The fox squirrel grinned at Ephran, sporting a big hole where a front tooth was missing.

Tears nearly dried, Ephran puffed out his chest and said, "I've already outsmarted a fox and an owl, and escaped from a cat as well."

"Ummmm."

The ancient one squinted at Ephran, with one eye again. Ephran couldn't help wonder if both eyes ever stayed open at the same time.

"Outsmarted 'em, eh? No help needed?"

"Ah, not really...," said Ephran, with some difficulty.

"Betcha yer brave, too."

Ephran swallowed hard and looked away.

"Well, all I kin say is I'm right glad to hear that a fox and an owl are no match fer a gray squirrel's wit and courage," continued the buck. "P'raps things are changin' in the forest. Most climbers I been 'quainted with needed a touch a good luck to escape owls and foxes and other issue from Lomarsh. Especially cats."

"I think you have to make your own luck," blurted Ephran.

"Mebbe, mebbe," said the fox squirrel, "I was never too good at makin' luck."

"Well, you know what I mean," said Ephran, feeling his face getting warmer and warmer.

"Guess I know what ya mean," said the old fellow, shifting his weight on the branch, "just hope ya aren't too smug about it."

"Too smug about what?"

If Odalee hadn't taught him what was polite and what was impolite, Ephran thought he would have run off and let this character talk to himself. That would be rude, however, and so he kept still. The fact that he had no idea which way to go, and where to find food, might have been a factor in his staying put.

"Too smug about makin' yer own luck is what I'm talkin' 'bout. I 'spect some of yer 'luck' was some worthwhile teachin' from yer mammy and pappy. Some was built in. And if it han't been yet, some day it'll be from friends. Far as being brave is concerned, I m'self never seem to know from one time to 'nother if I'm gonna be brave or if I'm gonna run like gusty air, away from the thing that I was so blamed sure I was gonna face up to."

The orange-colored squirrel opened both eyes and looked directly into Ephran's. "Son, don't figure you kin do it all yerself. Even if you don't say it aloud, that's called braggin'. As soon as you got it figured that yer pretty special, yer gonna make a mistake and get caught. Then yer luck'll be all bad. And who'll have made that kind of luck?" The weathered eyelids closed again and the fox squirrel lay quietly.

"Sir...?"

"Yep."

"My name is Ephran. I am all alone."

"Ya said that before. S'pose yer hungry."

"Yes, sir."

"S'pose yer pooped out too."

"Yes, sir."

"Well," the old one sighed as he got to his paws, "you kin call me Rennigan. Just over this rise I got me a little nest. Big enough fer the both of us, I guess. Think she's got a few old nuts layin' in there. C'mon along then."

Just holding a paw out there
Sometimes packs a bigger punch
Than swinging it from the shoulder.

Kanthak, A Place of Warmth

CHAPTER VII

FRIENDS OF DIFFERENT COLORS

Rennigan was not the best nestmate. He slept fitfully and snored something fierce. Ephran did not mind. They didn't spend all that much time in nests anyway. And when they popped into one of many shelters the old fox squirrel seemed to have scattered all around the wood, Ephran was exhausted and could barely eat the few seeds or nuts his host gave him -- then fall into a deep and restful sleep.

Rennigan never asked about Ephran's family, or how he came to be separated from them. Ephran knew it wasn't that he didn't care. It was more like he understood it was a painful subject, so he didn't bring it up. He wasn't much into giving or taking unnecessary information anyway.

Ephran once got up the courage to ask him, "Ummmm, sir, just how old are you?"

"Well," Rennigan answered, pretending he was thinking very hard, "considerin' all I seen and all I done, I suspek I'm a tad younger'n than I look. Heh, heh."

Most days, if the weather was not too cold, Rennigan would keep his young friend hopping. They moved around a good deal, at first leaving Ephran often totally lost and confused as to where they were. Little by little, though, he found himself realizing not only where they were, but how they got there and how to get back to where they came from. And when it was unpleasant outside they would lay curled in a den of leaves and Rennigan would talk. He would tell what he knew of the movement of air, the change of seasons, the arc of the sun -- and it all took on new meaning.

The many ideas father and mother had planted, like little seeds, Rennigan encouraged and pushed along, and they blossomed in Ephran's mind like the sun coming up over the trees, often stunning him with their clarity and brilliance. At times like those, when he remembered something they had said, Ephran would feel a hollow place inside.

The cold season finally ended all across the big woods. The air grew warmer and daylight longer. Green buds seemed to emerge overnight on yesterday's bare twigs. The forest, so long quiet under its white blanket, resounded with birdsong; the cooing of doves, twittering of sparrows, and warbling of robins. Courageous winterberry peaked tiny leaves from beneath withered vegetation. Drifts of snow shriveled into puddles of water which meandered along depressions in the earth until tumbling into the waiting stream bed. The brook rushed happily and noisily along, babbling and bubbling through its uneven course.

One bright day Ephran and Rennigan were sunning themselves

following a nice lunch of fresh green buds. Ephran was ready for a nap but it seemed Rennigan wanted to talk.

"Air moves from where the sun sets," said Rennigan, "should be warm 'n dry fer a bit now."

"Yes," said Ephran with a yawn, "I expect it will."

"Good time t' travel -- wouldn't have ta worry 'bout the sky growin' angry."

"I suppose it would," said Ephran, picking up a fresh seed and playing, nibbling bits of it off with his sharp front teeth. "Do you have someplace in mind we should go?"

"Not 'we'," said Rennigan, standing up on the branch. "You. I think yer ready."

"Ready?"

"Yep," Rennigan said softly. "Time's come, son."

"But...why couldn't I just..."

"Gotta give 'er a try, son. Gotta use those things ya been given. Gotta stretch yer own legs. Can't always stretch 'em the same direction as mine."

Ephran got to his paws and looked into the fox squirrel's eyes. "I don't know what to say," he said quietly. "I don't know how to thank you. Will I see you again?"

"Oh, you'll see me 'gain. Promise ya that. I might see you more'n you see me, though." Rennigan winked.

It was no use putting it off. They both knew that the longer he waited the harder it would be. So they said goodbye, trying to act indifferent, acting as though they had just met and spent a few moments passing the time of day.

"Mr. Rennigan, you're not the best nestkeeper and you're a noisy sleeper, but I don't know what would have become of me without you."

With a snorting laugh Rennigan said, "Hope ya end up with somethin' better, ya little twerp. Go see if ya kin find some o'that luck y're such an expert 'bout."

Ephran left him the way he found him, both eyes closed, sprawled on a twisted branch. He marked this place. Not, he supposed, that marking any one place would help him locate Rennigan again.

He'd learned well. He knew which way to go and, when he crossed Meadow Brook and circled the grassy open area, still brown and flattened by cold air and mounds of snow, he came to Great Hill. Tall, proud, and unchanging, it seemed to greet him as one of its own. He knew he'd made the right decision. He was home!

The old family den would be just off to his left, toward Bubbling Brook. He wouldn't have far to go to visit the oak if it still stood. It didn't, of course. He tried to ignore the trembling of his legs when he thought of it, but in his mind he could still see it crash to the earth. He

44

set out through the treetops and around the base of Great Hill, toward The Pond.

He searched for a long while. An elm that had a wonderful view and a nice deep woodpecker hole had no leaves, and should have been green by now. He had to reject it. A noble ash had neither holes or branches large enough to support a nest. An oak with huge branches had to be discarded because one could not get to or from it without using the earth. He'd disobeyed the rule about never climbing a tree without neighbors. He'd certainly not be dull-witted enough to make his den in one.

Finally he found a young and robust ash tree that overlooked The Pond. There were no holes, but there was an excellent place for a nest where the trunk split into three thick and heavy boughs. He would have preferred a den inside a sturdy trunk but a nest in these branches would do until he could find something more suitable. His new home was just a little way from where he'd first seen Mayberry, and from the bramble bushes over which the whitetailed deer had jumped. The Hedge was bedecked with a cloak of tiny pink flowers.

Ephran started that very day to build his nest. He knew he should keep at it, but nest construction wasn't much fun. Eating and exploring was more to his liking. The calm early morning was less than half over when he abandoned work and began to gleefully search the damp forest floor for hidden nuts. Some squirrel -- not him, of course -- but, who knew, maybe father or mother, had been here last warm season and buried walnuts and acorns under a shallow layer of earth and leaves.

His pursuit of nuts had led him away from the trees and close to the edge of The Pond. The black oak and cottonwood were well behind him by the time he had filled his stomach and realized it was time to go back to work. He breathed a tiny sigh, turned -- and was instantly frozen in his tracks. Directly above his head was the most frightening sound he could imagine -- more frightening even than the most ferocious and earthshaking peal of thunder. It was a soft sound, a rustling sound, the sound of air rushing through feathers. He could hope it was a dove, but the murmur of a dove's wings was more delicate -- he knew that song. A shiver passed through him and the fur all along his back stood straight up. It had to be a hawk!

Too far and too late to run back to the trees. If he kept very still and didn't even turn his head to peek he could hope that the skyhunter would overlook gray fur against gray earth.

Wings passed over and two shadows disappeared over brown and bent bullrushes at the edge of the water. There was a subdued splash, then silence. Ephran allowed his shaky legs to lower him to the ground.

He lay there quietly, listening and looking as hard as he could. He wished he could see through the switchgrass and the bowed cattails.

Would hawks land in water, he wondered? If they didn't, then these birds had not been hawks. What kind of birds then, huge birds, had flown right over -- and ignored him?

His eye rested on a small willow tree standing in the rushes at the very edge of The Pond. If he could get to it, that little tree would afford him a clear view of the open water. Ever so carefully, trying to make as little noise as possible, Ephran worked his way toward the willow. Before he climbed he stopped once more to listen, but the only sound that came to his ears was the occasional shrill chirp of a blackbird.

The willow was rubbery and its trunk no bigger around than he was. As he climbed, the slender stalk and its branches waved and danced beneath his legs. The further up he scrambled, the thinner and less solid became his support. It took a lot of care and concentration, but the tree, bowed out over the water, finally stopped swaying.

Ephran lifted his head to find himself nearly eye to eye with two astoundingly large birds. They floated on the water just below him, silent and motionless. He could do nothing but stare. One of them, no doubt the drake, had a chestnut brown breast and a golden beak. A white ring, like a perfect collar, separated the breast from the most striking feature of all, an absolutely brilliant green head. This green was not like the leaves of the elm or the grass of the meadow. This green was so pure and bright that it actually shimmered in the sunlight!

The other bird, obviously the hen, was a drab sight when compared to her companion. Her eyes, however, were deep and kind and gave her a comeliness that brightly colored feathers never could. Ephran knew he was in no danger from her.

The brightly colored bird frowned at Ephran. "Be careful or you will join us in the water," he said, as Ephran began once more to wobble about in the little tree.

"Wh...Wh...Who are you?" Ephran blurted.

The hen smiled and asked, "Have you never seen ducks before?"

"I...I don't think so."

It was true. He could not remember ever seeing birds quite like this, so large and so handsome, up so close. During his one visit here last warm season the only birds he recalled seeing were a lot of blackbirds, a couple of robins, and a lone bluejay. He would not have forgotten birds like this, birds so wondrous he hadn't even thought to be frightened of them.

"Well," said the hen, "we are called mallards. I am Marshflower and this is my mate, Cloudchaser. We are thinking of nesting here. Unless, of course, you know of some reason we should not."

"Oh...of course not! Wait! I mean yes, of course! I mean, you certainly should build your nest here. Why, that would be wonderful. I'm building one too, you know..."

He realized he hadn't introduced himself and so he said, with his most charming smile, "I'm called Ephran." And then, flustered, he added, "I'm not building my nest in the water, of course. My nest is in a tree. Over there."

He tried to point to the pile of sticks in the crotch of the young ash and the tiny motion just about did him in. The willow began to sway wildly beneath him and he grabbed the trunk. Though Ephran didn't think his nearly falling into the cold water particularly amusing, the colorful bird laughed loudly.

When he'd regained his balance and composure, Marshflower looked at him intently and asked, "Young treeclimber; do you know of any fox dens hereabout?"

"I haven't seen any," Ephran replied.

He didn't mention the fox he'd seen, not all that long ago, on the shores of this very Pond. Later on, he wondered if he should have. He had good reason to believe that particular fox lived some distance away, near Fox Brook, but The Pond might very well be in its hunting territory.

"Do hawks ever float high above your Pond?" she asked.

"I've seem them only in the far clouds," he said.

Once more she questioned him. "Ephran, do owls come here when the sky darkens?"

"Why bother with this," broke in the drake, "when you know as well as I..."

"Shush!" said the hen to her mate, never taking her eyes off Ephran. "I'm waiting for an answer from one who knows this place better than we."

"I've not heard them," Ephran said, a bit flustered.

He wondered why the drake had interrupted, and felt both flattered and a little confused at why, indeed, the hen was interested in his observations. He was hardly an expert on the territory and he really couldn't know for certain if owls roamed on this side of Great Hill. After all, he'd only been here a short while himself and he dare not think of the danger that might lie on the far side of that massive slope. Besides, he knew his chosen spot was not all that far from Lomarsh, spawning place of hunters and other bad things. He was being selfish. He didn't want these feathered ones to be discouraged or frightened away. He needed company. He wanted their friendship.

"Very well," said the hen, "Thank you for the information and the words of welcome. Perhaps we shall get to know each other better if we can find a suitable place on your Pond."

The male looked at Ephran a moment longer. Ephran wasn't sure if those dark eyes promised friendship or otherwise.

The ducks turned and swam slowly out into open water, tiny ripples on the surface spreading as they moved away. They paddled along, stopping every so often to inspect an especially dense clump of bullrushes or wapato. They spent a long time examining an abandoned muskrat den of weathered cattails and burreed.

Ephran maneuvered himself back down the willow and jumped across the wet earth at the base of the tree. He bounded happily back toward his nest, pleased that he'd met what he hoped would become new neighbors. One could never have too many friends, he told himself, and it would be wonderful to get to know the ducks.

Preoccupied with thoughts of mallards, and with how he was ready now to finish the nest, Ephran started up the base of his tree. Without warning of any kind he found himself face to face again, this time with a little male red squirrel. So surprised was he that he forgot to hold unto the bark of the tree and he tumbled backward among the roots. Dirt in his nose, he flipped unto his paws. His throat tightened and he hissed beneath his breath.

"Go! Get away from my tree!" the red treeclimber squeaked at Ephran. Teeth bared, tail twitching from side to side, it was trying desperately to look fierce.

Ephran found himself taking a step backward among the thick roots before he stopped himself. "Go away yourself, you of shrill noise," he said. "This is my tree, not yours."

"No! My tree!"

"I've already started to build my nest. See there." Ephran pointed to the paltry collection of sticks and leaves just above them.

"No! No! No! This was my tree last warm season and it is my tree this warm season." The red squirrel didn't even glance at Ephran's nest.

"There are many trees in the woods," said Ephran. "I doubt this was ever yours. There's no hole for a red treeclimber. There's no scattered trash like your kind likes to leave around."

"Move on! Move on!" said the red squirrel, uninterested in anything that Ephran might have to say.

"Tell you what, small one; I'll help you find your tree, but you'd better get your paws off mine. Right now. Or else you're going to have more trouble than you bargained for."

The snarl on the red squirrel's diminutive white face wilted. Father had told Ephran that red squirrels had a loud voice and that they'd use it to try and get their way. And, though they could be fierce fighters if need be, most often their "screech was worse than their scratch".

"Hmmm. I suppose you could be right," said the red squirrel with a weak smile. "My tree was much like this, but it could have been a touch smaller." He scratched his ear with a front paw. "Actually, it might have even been on the other side of The Pond. Been moving around a good deal. Confusing, you know."

Ephran started up the ash.

"I say...," said the red squirrel, "Welcome home! My name is

48

"GO! GET AWAY FROM MY TREE!"

Klestra. I think perhaps I should go and find my tree."

He scooted by Ephran, stopped suddenly, turned and said, "You know, I'll take you up on that offer of help. If you meant it."

"I should really stay and finish my nest. I'll wish I had if dark clouds and gusty air come..." He could not miss Klestra's hopeful expression. The sky was perfectly clear.

"Oh well, I can finish what has to be done in a short time. Sure, I'll go with you to find your tree. My name is Ephran."

"Hello, Ephran," said Klestra. "Are you sure you're feeling all right? After watching you fall off the trunk of your own tree I'm a bit worried about having you run about in the branches."

Ephran flushed with anger. Then, seeing the sparkle in Klestra's eye and the hint of a smile in the corner of his mouth, he broke into laughter. So did Klestra.

They ran off, around The Pond, away from Great Hill. They jumped from low branch to low branch, over thick and tortuous roots that fed the great limbs overhead, through green patches of lacy fern and moss. Klestra, lean of body and light of foot, ran ahead of Ephran and disappeared suddenly near an old basswood stump. Ephran ran to the base of the fallen tree and all around it but Klestra was nowhere to be seen or heard. He sat down, puzzled, and was about to call Klestra's name.

"Hey there!" came Klestra's voice from above, then a laugh.

Ephran climbed the stump quickly, reaching the top in two leaps, but when he got there Klestra was gone again.

"Down here!" came the cry. Klestra had reappeared below, among the decomposing roots.

"Don't look so puzzled, Ephran. There's a burrow underneath this stump and a tunnel through the rotted wood. You could get inside from below, but not through that hole in the side, you're far too big for that."

Ephran understood. It was a strange place to find shelter, right down on the earth, but it was shelter. The tree, though no longer tall and green, still served a purpose.

"I must remember this trick. Such a place might be needed at certain times. You were clever to find it," said Ephran.

Klestra stood a bit taller. "That's easy. I have many hiding places in this part of the woods."

As they traveled along, sometimes playfully chasing, sometimes just sitting in the sun chatting, it became obvious to Ephran that Klestra must indeed have spent a great deal of time in this area. He knew of too many refuges and a number of caches of pine cones, seeds, and nuts to be a total stranger. When they reached the far side of The Pond they found a tree which may have been Klestra's. There was certainly enough junk around; broken corn sticks, half-eaten seeds, lots of nutshells of all varieties. The tree was small and had an unhealthy look to it. Bark had peeled off in long strips. Its trunk was broken just above the lowest branches, and its core was nearly totally hollow. Though cozy inside, it was a tight fit for Ephran. It might well be infested with insects later in the warm season.

"Comfortable den, isn't it?" asked Klestra, smiling at Ephran, who was wedged tightly in one corner.

"Very nice," said Ephran. But he couldn't keep a straight face and began to laugh. "Actually, to be comfortable in here I'd have to leave my legs outside."

Klestra giggled and said, "You're right. Either I'm going to have to find friends of lesser girth or else I'm going to have to scrape this old den out so that you can bring your legs along with your tail the next time you visit."

They grew quiet. Ephran smiled uneasily at Klestra. What would father and mother say if they could see their son wedged in a red squirrel den?

"Sorry I mistook your tree for mine," said Klestra.

"Easy mistake to make if you have weak eyes. My tree's only four times bigger than this one." They giggled. Then he added, "Sorry about my comment about trash and red squirrels."

"Hey! We're messy and proud of it."

They both laughed again, self-consciously.

After a bit Ephran said, "You called me friend."

"No insult intended," said Klestra.

"Red and gray squirrels aren't supposed to be friends..."

"So I've been told," said Klestra, "No one's ever given me a good reason. After today, I still don't know any. I think there's plenty of room for both of us on the shores of The Pond." He looked up. "I hope I'm welcome on your side."

"Its not my side, Klestra. The Pond belongs to everyone who has a nest in or around it. And, as far as I know, friends spend time together. See you soon."

CHAPTER VIII

FRIENDLY VISITS

Ephran set off for his side of The Pond, delighted and more than a little amazed that he'd made another new friend -- and a red squirrel at that! The time with Klestra had not been wasted, but it was high time he got busy on his nest. If he didn't get it finished, no one else would do it for him. The sun was already approaching the treetops and there'd be precious little time to get much accomplished before dark. However, there was one more piece of unfinished business to attend to.

He scampered up the trunk of a honey locust tree that afforded a view of the water. Long shadows across the faintly shimmering pool gave the impression of movement, but there were no ripples on the smooth surface.

Ephran sighed. The mallards must have decided that The Pond didn't meet their needs after all. They must have flown off to look elsewhere. Maybe they would be back. Maybe they wouldn't be able to find another place as wonderful as this. He slowly descended the tree, looking back every few steps. He picked up a small branch and a few leaves as he scurried along -- it was all he could carry.

When he got to the ash tree he wove the small stick between two larger ones and pulled on it with his teeth. He was satisfied when it didn't budge. Then he packed the new leaves as tightly as he could between the twigs. He made two more trips to a twisted oak which must have fallen at the end of last warm season. Its remaining leaves were soft and pliable. They were not only good building material, but tasty as well. Ephran knew he shouldn't eat what would make his nest warm and soft, and he did his best to avoid the temptation. Most of the leaves made it back to pad the nest, which was becoming sturdier and more comfortable with each and every trip.

Two crows roosted on a nearby maple limb. They had watched, beaks shut, as Ephran labored. Finally one said, "Heyya, climfella! Thassa worslookin nesti aver see."

The other snorted and said, "Fi cudn't bilnest bittern at iedlif undrrock."

"Yehha," laughed the first, "hil findself fal thrufloor middledark."

Ephran ignored them, though he was tempted to say a few words about the kind of crows' nests he'd seen. The birds made a few more hard to understand comments, but Ephran acted as though he didn't know they were there. After a while they flew off. He sat in his tree then, nibbling on an old musty-flavored hickory nut, watching the sun descend to the edge of the earth.

The air grew chill and Ephran shivered when the last rays of the sun glinted on faroff Lomarsh. For a moment he thought about leaving first thing in the morning to find Rennigan. But where in the woods would he begin to look for that old rascal? Mayberry had talked about trees and gray squirrels, and there did seem to be an awful lot of the one and precious few of the other. Then, though he tried not to, he thought of Jafthuh and Odalee once more, and tears welled up in his eyes before he knew what was happening. He coughed and blinked them back. It was simply no use to dwell on what was lost. It was one of the first things every animal of the forest must learn.

Just as he was about to snuggle in his almost-done nest he thought he detected movement on The Pond. From one of Fetzgar's old dens came a splash, a distinct "Quack!" and more splashing. A ripple spread on the dark pink water, clearly visible in the fading light. A smile dried the tears in Ephran's eyes. His mallards had decided to stay after all!

The days passed quickly. Many of them were spent with Klestra. The two squirrels explored the territory near The Pond, on their side of Great Hill. They rummaged for food, played in the woods among wild fern and columbine, and followed Rocky Creek or Bubbling Brook for short distances along their gurgling courses. There was no need to hide food yet. Many warm and lazy days stretched ahead. There would be lots of fresh buds and, though it took a great many of them to fill one up, they were a moist and tender treat while they lasted.

The forest suddenly bustled with activity. Wild flowers bloomed wherever Ephran looked. Marsh marigolds flourished near The Pond while Trillium, Jacks-in-the-Pulpit and dainty violets covered the forest floor with whites, purples, yellows, and greens. Honey bees hummed among the blossoms. Tiny shrews, mice, and garter snakes scurried about in their own world beneath a tangled blanket of old vegetation and new greenery. A clump of dried leaves might be pushed up and over in the span of a halfday as a wrinkled mushroom surged from the warming earth.

It was even more wonderful to be near The Pond than he'd dreamed it would be. At water's edge clumps of bullrushes grew in thick bunches. Robust, tightly packed, silky soft brown seeds formed quickly at their tips. Highflying white clouds and red-twigged dogwood, laden with clusters of white petals, reflected in the still water. Arrowhead and wild iris sprouted between and among the buttonbush. Here and there a swamp rose waved shyly in the fresh and clear air.

The shallow parts of The Pond wriggled with silver minnows and shadowy black tadpoles. They attracted a lone blue heron, who would fly a very long way to partake of the delicacy of small fish and frogs.

Old Fetzgar, the muskrat that mother had introduced to Ephran and Phetra last warm season, would eye the intruding heron every time it glided across the rushes. "Shoo! Shoo!" he would hiss at the long-legged bird, "Go away!"

Invariably ignored by the heron, Fetzgar would make a great show of splashing into the water, as though he were going right over and raise "what for". He never did, of course, and would swim in circles for a while, well away from the bird. Eventually he'd paddle off to one of his many resting places, mumbling to himself about "outsiders."

It seemed Fetzgar had been on The Pond forever. He could remember residents and incidents for many seasons past. Ephran visited with him whenever he got the chance. Since familiarity did not seem to lessen Fetzgar's shyness, Ephran generally did most of the talking. One thing that had always puzzled Ephran was why Fetzgar had built so many dens on such a small body of water. Once he felt comfortable that he knew the muskrat well enough, he vowed he would find out.

His opportunity came one sunny day when the air was nearly calm. He was experimenting, chewing on a type of berry that he did not really know, but that seemed to flourish on a kind of scrubby bush that grew in the moist soil. The berry smelled all right but it tasted bitter. As he spit it out, Fetzgar surfaced in the water nearby and crawled onto the muddy shore. He shook himself lazily.

"Good day, Mr. Fetzgar," said Ephran.

"G'day," said Fetzgar, carefully smoothing his wet fur and licking his feet as though, from constant soaking in the greenish water they had absorbed some fresh and wonderful taste.

"I see you're building a new place," said Ephran. "Looks very nice. Uh...you have quite a lot of dens, don't you?"

"Yep," answered the bucktoothed old muskrat, scratching one front paw with the other, "quite a few."

"No family though," said Ephran.

"Nope. No family."

Ephran took a deep breath. "Do you think there might be too many?"

Fetzgar squinted at Ephran and said, "Too many? Too many what?"

"Too many...um...too many dens."

" No such thing as too many."

"'No such thing'...?" repeated Ephran.

"Hey, youngster," said Fetzgar, "I knew plenty a treeclimbers built more'n one nest, y'know."

"Yes, I know that," said Ephran, "but those dens are generally far apart, in different parts of the woods -- in case they're needed when one is traveling and needs shelter. Your nests are all on one small pond."

"Small pond, big pond -- no diffrunce. Not t'hard t'figure out if ya think about it fer a minute. Fer instance; see that one o'er there?" he

55

asked, pointing to a small clump of sticks and weeds near shore and sheltered beneath overhanging alder branches.

"Yes," said Ephran, shading his eyes with a paw. "I see it."

"Fer hot days. Nice 'n shady. And surely ya can see th'big un o'er there." He pointed to the far shore line.

"Yes..."

"Walls on thet un thick 'n strong -- fer cold nights." Fetzgar turned and pointed again. "And th'un out there 'n the middle, in open water; that's fer sittin' on and fer lookin' around. Or when I wanna sun m'self. Then there's the real long un n'thet side there..."

"I understand," interrupted Ephran. "Yessir, I see now. As you said, 'No such thing as too many'."

Many small birds were building nests near The Pond and Ephran tried to get to know as many as he could. His offer of conversation and friendship astounded them. At first none of the feathered ones seemed to know how to respond. Eventually, though, almost all of them got around to treating Ephran as a perfectly acceptable neighbor. And, at the same time, ended up talking to each other a bit more as well.

Janey wren was a favorite. She was building a tight little nest in the Hedge -- the one the deer had jumped over the time he first saw Mayberry. Mr. and Mrs. Oriole were working on a much looser but surprisingly sturdy nest in the branch of the big cottonwood tree that grew near the place where Bubbling Brook flowed out of The Pond. A pair of red and brown cardinals had settled on the bank of Rocky Creek where it made a sharp turn against the broad shoulder of The Meadow. At least three families of sparrows took up residence in thick buttonbushes and young prickly elm which grew in abundance in the shade of the bigger trees. They were so busy and highstrung that it was difficult to get them to sit still and chat. They did liven up the neighborhood considerably, however, and one became accustomed to their nearly constant twittering and whistling.

A sizeable flock of blackbirds were putting together haphazard nests in the rapidly growing vegetation near shore. Although Ephran tried to strike up a conversation on more than one occasion, they weren't especially friendly and usually flew away before he could say much more than "Hello". He decided that he'd have to settle for a more distant relationship with them.

Early in the warm season there were many damp and foggy times. Ephran did not mind them. The woods was quiet then, and big fluffy gray-black clouds would drift, like mountains of cattail fluff, low over the treetops. The heavy air would carry the slightly musty smell of forest floor. That odor, rich fragrance of rotting leaves and grasses, mixed with dark earth, was one of his favorites. He knew that -- somehow -- sunwarmth and skywater mixed with the fertile blackness of earth to make the trees and bushes grow. And from the trees and bushes came the wonder and sweetness of buds and nuts.

Most of the birds stayed near their bushes or trees during those cloudy days. Ephran often curled up and slept in his nest, thick tail covering all of him but his nose. Sometimes he visited with Klestra. Sheltered beneath a fallen tree, they would talk of the many things they'd seen in the awakening forest.

"I found some plump and tasty buds among a bed of yellow flowers near the brambles," said Klestra one blustery day. "I'd planned to invite you over for a snack."

"Well...," said Ephran, "why didn't you?"

A smile spread across Klestra's little face, making his long whiskers point toward the sky. "Because Smagtu, our black cousin with the white stripe, got there first."

Ephran couldn't help laughing and Klestra laughed with him. Smagtu, the skunk, was pleasant enough to chat with, but at some distance, thank you. He was a poor dinner companion unless you could hold your breath for a very long while. And who could enjoy a meal that way? He kept asking to have lunch with them, however, and they knew they couldn't make excuses forever. Besides, he was a gentle and friendly creature -- just a bit shy. And of course, that unfortunate odor seemed to hang about him.

They chose a pleasant sun-drenched day, placing themselves carefully where the air would travel from them toward the skunk. They hoped it would not change direction, as it often seemed to. Ephran began to crack nuts he'd carried from a small hickory grove just the other side of The Hedge. Klestra, for his contribution, had brought a stubby, bedraggled corncob. A few yellow kernels were still attached to the rough red surface.

Ephran finished opening his first nut and glanced at Smagtu, who had reclined in a clump of thick grass. Growing near the skunk were small bunches of violets and a few wild columbine. Smagtu was casually chewing on a violet.

"Do the flowers taste good?" asked Ephran.

"Not 'specially."

"What do they taste like?" asked Klestra.

Smagtu crinkled his face and looked thoughtful. "Acshully, kinda bitter. Don't taste like smell."

"Why eat them then?" said Klestra. "Plenty of delicious buds around. Or here," he held out the stick of corn, "have a nice bit of corn."

Smagtu looked abashed. "Well, no, but thanks...flower smell nice, see? Maybe, if Smagtu puts nuff flowers inside..." He hesitated and looked up at the squirrels.

"I understand, Smagtu," said Klestra, a solemn look on his face. "Good luck."

Ephran's most enjoyable times were spent atop one of Fetzgar's deserted dens -- the one on which the ducks had built their nest. He'd found a way to get there by way of a fallen willow branch. The branch was sturdy enough to support his weight, but a larger animal attempting to cross on it would quickly sink into the water. The forgetful muskrat didn't seem to mind the mallards using his former residence and, as a matter of fact, had been heard to say that he was the one who'd invited them to stay on The Pond in the first place.

A green curtain -- bullrushes, wapato, and switchgrass -- was growing up around the nest and made it nearly impossible to detect from either open water or woods. If any landhunter spied it, a cold swim would be necessary to reach it and surprising the ducks would be difficult. The most likely reward for a hunter's trouble would be a damp and chilly pelt.

It seemed that Cloudchaser was always gone. "Off exploring," his mate would say. What or where he explored she seemed not to know. And so it was with Marshflower that Ephran spent his time. The brown female mallard was well nigh impossible to see in her brown nest atop the brown muskrat den. She rarely left the nest for long since she'd laid her seven perfect little eggs. Ephran was not aware of the eggs and Marshflower didn't mention them.

Although she never complained, the hours were very long for Marshflower. She couldn't leave her eggs and Cloudchaser was too restless to stay with her the whole long day. She welcomed Ephran's company and his curious and buoyant attitude toward everything and everyone around him. She found herself enjoying his visits and so, to keep him coming back, she told him stories. And what stories they were...stories of travels to a world so far removed from his experience that they were hard for the little squirrel to believe!

She told of great rivers that flowed from the woods, twisting their way to a pond so large that even the strongest bird could not think of flying across it! So large that one could not begin to see the trees on the far shore!

"So the end of the woods is not really the end of the woods at all," Ephran breathed.

The idea was really beyond belief. He knew what father would say. But why should Marshflower lie to him? Just to entertain him? Maybe, but he wanted to believe it and not just because it made for such good stories. After all, if the woods did not end near the farm where the black and white cat stayed, then it was just possible that his family might still be somewhere where limbs and leaves grew...

Marshflower told of places where multitudes of Many Colored Ones nested -- more of Them than all of the acorns in the woods! She said their dens spread out as far as the eye could see, and were connected together by gently curving but unmoving streams of rockhard earth. Was it even possible that so many could be spawned from Lomarsh?

She told of places where the cold season never came -- and where the birds and animals had never seen snow. The trees were always green and many of them were laden with delicious and exotic sounding food. Oh, how he'd love to explore those trees heavy with food!

She told of these marvels and added to his amazement when she described how it all looked from high in the sky. Ephran was enchanted. He would lay by the hour, unblinking, begging her to go on when she stopped for breath. Finally she would smile at him, say she was exhausted, and that she'd have to rest a bit. He would thank her and leave then, but he could scarcely wait to return and listen to more of her wondrous tales.

CHAPTER IX

NOT-SO-FRIENDLY VISITS

ne lovely day, sunbeams peeking shyly through high thin clouds, Ephran left his nest and scrambled across the half submerged branch, anxious to hear another thrilling tale of flights through the bright blue sky. Instead, he found Marshflower asleep, head tucked under her wing. He scratched himself and sniffled a bit, snorting through his nose, hoping she'd open her eyes. She didn't. For a moment he wondered if he should wake her with a greeting. That, he decided, would be a thoughtless thing to do. Maybe she was especially tired. Maybe she was like him, sometimes unable to sleep through the entire darktime. After a night of open eyes, a nap in the middle of the day could be very nice.

He had just made up his mind to tiptoe away and search out Klestra when a muffled, high-pitched squeak came from the woven reeds beneath the mallard nest.

He stopped short, held his breath, and listened, muscles tensed. He glanced at Marshflower. Still sound asleep. He crept closer, eyes wide, ready to chatter a warning...then run as fast as he could. Suddenly, almost under his nose, a tiny yellow head popped up from under Marshflower's wing.

"Marshflower!" Ephran barked, "To wing! Quickly!"

The hen's eyes opened but she did not so much as flutter a feather. She only smiled at his astonished expression as another and still another head appeared in the nest. "Ephran," she yawned, "how nice of you to visit. Did you come to meet my young ones?"

"Where...where did they come from?" stammered Ephran.

"Why, from the eggs I have been sitting on, of course," said the duck.

"Eggs?"

"Yes, of course, eggs.

"What are eggs?"

Marshflower stifled a chuckle. "Are you really trying to tell me that you've not heard of eggs?"

Ephran tried to remember. "No. What are eggs?" he repeated, looking up at her with a stunned expression.

"Hmmm. It seems you haven't heard of eggs." She cocked her head at him. "Well, how shall I start? I suppose I could describe eggs as warm little dens. Dens where tiny birds, yet without feathers, grow until they are large enough and strong enough to come into the outside air. I have been keeping mine warm for some time. I have to say that I am amazed; I thought you knew why I sat here day after day."

"I never thought much about it, I guess," said Ephran, eyes still

"ALMOST UNDER HIS NOSE A TINY YELLOW HEAD
POPPED UP FROM UNDER MARSHFLOWER'S WING"

TERRY LEWISON

glued to the bobbing heads, little beaks opening and closing. "I was just happy to find you here. I love to hear about your travels during the cold season."

"I suppose it is obvious that you like my stories. And it makes me happy that you enjoy them so," smiled Marshflower. "I am afraid that they will be far and few between now that my family has arrived. These little ones will demand a great deal of time."

"I'll help you!" blurted Ephran.

Marshflower laughed aloud with a quacking sort of sound. Then she looked at him seriously.

"That is a very kind and considerate sort of thought, Ephran," she said. "What assignment would you like? Would you teach them to swim? Or to dive to the bottom of The Pond for food? Or later, how to fly and land safely in the water?"

"Oh dear," muttered Ephran, "none of those sounds very easy. I don't care at all to be in the water. And, though I'd love nothing better, I don't think I can fly."

He thought for a moment and then his face brightened. "I could teach them to climb trees...how to jump from one branch to another...and how to crack open an acorn without mashing the inside..."

This time Marshflower cackled so loudly that Ephran nearly backed off Fetzgar's den into the water. She was unable to speak for a while but finally looked tenderly into his upturned face and said, "You are a good friend, Ephran. And you are welcome to help me with my little ones. But they will never be able to do the things a treeclimber can do any more than you can do the things a duck can do."

Ephran looked down at his paws. He understood. He had always thought it was okay being a squirrel but, my oh my, wouldn't it be wonderful if these paws were wings! Then he might fly, high over the woods and through the clouds, beholding for himself the sights Marshflower had described. It must be like the feeling during a long jump between high branches -- only the happy, tickly feeling would go on and on.

Marshflower fell silent. Ephran looked up to see her gazing intently across The Pond. He followed her eyes. They were fixed on Cloudchaser, sailing high above the water toward the muskrat den. He glided so smoothly, wings gracefully cupped, and sat down with hardly a splash. He swam slowly to his nest, eyeing Ephran in a way that left little doubt that he was not pleased with what he saw.

"Hello, my dear," said Marshflower. Ephran thought her voice sounded strained.

"Hello," said the big drake. Then, very quickly, "What is that squirrel doing here again?"

"He is just visiting," she replied. Her voice was strained all right. "I've told you he comes often. He enjoys listening to stories of our travels."

"Enjoys stories, does he? Squirrels have been known to prefer eggs and small ducks to stories," said Cloudchaser, a grim and unpleasant look on his face.

Marshflower protested; "Oh, that is not the case with Ephran! He didn't even know what eggs were. I had to explain..."

"They learn quickly enough what eggs are -- after they taste them."

At that, Ephran, who'd been sitting quietly on his tail, listening to the conversation and wondering what it was all about, realized why Cloudchaser seemed so unfriendly and suspicious. Why, he actually thought that his gleeful trips to the nest were in hopes of stealing an egg or a duckling...to eat it, of all things! The thought was horrible. And incredible.

They looked at each other for a long moment, gray treeclimber and drake mallard. Ephran thought of objecting to what Cloudchaser was thinking, but he was too choked to find his voice. Besides, what could he say? How could Cloudchaser imagine that Ephran had the tastes and instincts of a hunter? The idea that he was deceiving Marshflower, using false friendship as a route to satisfy that taste was, no question, even worse.

Ephran's eyes burned and his vision blurred. He nearly slipped into the water as he crossed to shore on the floating branch. Behind him he could hear Marshflower saying to her mate; "Now see what you've done! You've hurt his feelings."

She said other things, too, that Ephran could not make out. And the drake's reply, if there was one, went unheard. He ran straight for his nest, wanting only to be alone for a while. As he approached a cluster of basswood trees, Klestra jumped from behind them, directly into his path.

"Hi there!" said Klestra, "What's the big hurry? Where's the big butternut giveaway?"

"Oh, Klestra," said Ephran, startled at the red squirrel's sudden appearance. He quickly wiped his paw across his eyes. "I'm going to my nest."

"Too nice a day to spend in a nest. How about a little exploring on the other side of Spruce Hill? There's some scenery over there I think you'd be interested in."

"No thanks, Klestra. I just feel like resting a while."

For the first time Klestra noticed the unspilled tears. Alarmed, he said, "Ephran, have you been hurt?"

"Not on the outside," Ephran whispered. "Old Cloudchaser just accused me of wanting to have his new family for a snack. I can't understand how he'd even think such a thing."

"Ah. I see," said Klestra thoughtfully, backing up to rest his tail against a basswood trunk. "Marshflower's eggs have hatched at last. Well, treeclimbers have been known to raid a bird's nest on occasion, you know. I'm sure Cloudchaser knows that. Water creatures have trouble trusting land creatures."

"I would never harm Marshflower's eggs or those wee birds!" protested Ephran.

"I'm sure that's entirely true, but he doesn't know that," said Klestra. "Give him time. He'll learn you're to be trusted."

"Trusted?" said Ephran slowly, looking confused, like a springy green branch had just popped him in the nose.

"Sure," said Klestra, "trusted not to harm his family."

"He has no reason not to trust. How can he judge when I've given him no cause?"

"I think the word you're looking for is 'reputation', my friend," said Klestra. "Not your personal reputation, but that of all treeclimbers. We spoke of this sort of thing before -- when we talked of feelings between red and gray squirrels."

Ephran sat on his tail, breathed a big sigh, and looked about as dejected as Klestra imagined a squirrel could look.

"Maybe he shouldn't trust me, I don't know. Maybe no one should. But he has no right to judge me by what other squirrels might or might not do."

"Listen," said Klestra, "I can see that you're upset, but I'm sure you'll find a way to convince Cloudchaser that you're a true friend. Anyway, you're in no mood for a trip to Spruce Hill today. I must take you there someday soon, though, because there's considerably more there than trees that happen to stay green all the time. I'll come back another time -- when you feel like talking and running."

"Thank you, Klestra. I promise that, very soon, I'll go with you to see this mysterious Spruce Hill of yours."

CHAPTER X

COURAGE DISCOVERED

At first Ephran could not understand why his parents hadn't told him about eggs. He could only guess that the thought of eating unborn birds, curled in their warm little dens, was as distasteful to them as it was to him, regardless of what Cloudchaser thought. So if eggs weren't to eat, and if they posed no threat to treeclimbers, then, considering all else that he had to learn in such a short time, it wouldn't be especially surprising if eggs didn't get mentioned at all.

As far as not noticing eggs, it finally occurred to him that by the time his eyes first saw light last warm season, and by the time he was able to crawl out of the nest and really pay attention to what was going on around him, most eggs had already opened. So it wasn't that he wasn't observant -- it was simply that there hadn't been any eggs around, waiting to be discovered.

Many days went by and Ephran did not go near The Pond. He tried to tell himself that it made no difference how Cloudchaser felt about treeclimbers -- or how any old duck might feel about anything at all, for that matter. He remembered father's words about it being far safer and more acceptable to have friends that were like yourself. Despite all that, his heart felt heavy. And he found himself glancing toward the duck nest atop Fetzgar's old den many times every day.

He spent most of those days by himself, trying to keep busy, trying not to think of his family -- or whether he still had a family. He experimented with ideas to make his nest more comfortable and practical and he found many places to store food for the cold season. In his short trips between Bubbling Brook and the Meadow he made mental note of the location of wild blueberry and raspberry plants as well as dogwood and elderberry bushes. Most of the birds were busy with their eggs or the naked and delicate little creatures that crawled out of them. Everyone around The Pond was involved in one project or another and were too occupied to play Run-and-Look among the thick bushes and tree stumps. They didn't even have time to chat for more than a moment. The days were long and a bit lonely. Everyone seemed to have someone except him.

Klestra had disappeared, evidently giving Ephran plenty of time to recover his normal good spirits. Twice Ephran made the trip to the far side of The Pond and both times he found the hollow tree empty. He wasn't worried. He knew that Klestra often left his den for days at a time. The red treeclimber was almost as restless as Cloudchaser.

Though he didn't go near the water, the middle of The Pond was quite clearly visible from his tree. The edges were curtained with greenery that had grown thick as the days grew warm. He sometimes saw Cloudchaser swimming or dunking for food in the still water, and once or twice caught a glimpse of Marshflower near the muskrat den. The nest itself was pretty well hidden from the branches of the ash, partially by reeds and cattails, but mostly by the little willow that Ephran had first used to introduce himself to the ducks. The tree was thick with leaves.

He often lay, head propped on the smooth stub of a broken branch, watching the water and the woods and the bright blue sky. He wouldn't admit, even to himself, how much he longed to go down to the duck nest. He'd love to listen to Marshflower weave her wonderful tales or to watch as she taught her little ones how to tip under water and gather tender wild celery or wapato from the bottom of The Pond. He knew she wouldn't chase him away if he went to the nest while Cloudchaser was away. However, it might be difficult for her if the drake returned while he was there -- and he could appear very suddenly on those big strong wings of his. Ephran thought too highly of the hen to be the cause of trouble for her.

One splendid young day, when the sun over the big woods seemed especially happy, Ephran returned to his nest after gorging himself at a gooseberry bush. He'd found the bush just ahead of an old female cowbird and he'd been scolded the whole time he ate for "not respecting his elders". According to her, he was eating "her berries". It was no use inviting her to join him; she was far too upset and afraid of him. All he could do was be certain that there was plenty of fruit left on the bushes when he finished.

He was ready for a nap now, and after that he'd try visiting Klestra again. He was getting lonesome for the noisy redtail and if the rascal was off wandering again...well, at least the trip around The Pond would take some time. Time was something he had more than enough of.

Ephran settled himself on his favorite branch and propped his chin up, as was his custom. There was nothing particularly exciting to watch. The sun shimmered on the tranquil water and the air was filled with the monotonous drone of insects and happy birdsong. It was peaceful. The old stomach was satisfied. Heavy eyelids drooped shut.

What woke him, or how long he'd slept, he couldn't be sure. But when his eyes focused the first thing he saw was Marshflower, swimming proudly across The Pond. Behind her paddled a slightly wobbly line of seven yellow and black ducklings. The mallard family was out for their first family swim! He must have a closer look.

Scrambling from his branch and down the ash, he vaulted over a fallen limb and ran across the forest floor toward the willow tree. He clambered up the slender trunk and found a place with a reasonable view of The Pond. He surveyed the still water, along with its clumps of mud and vegetation, making certain there was no movement behind them.

Only when Ephran was satisfied that Cloudchaser was not on The Pond did he relax.

Marshflower, in her glory, wanted the entire forest to see her beautiful family. Actually, the audience was pretty small. There was Ephran himself, of course, and Fetzgar, who watched idly from his most recently constructed den, two blackbirds perched on slender cattails, and a small striped chipmunk who chattered intermittently from a stump near the water's edge. The ducklings were swimming directly toward Ephran's willow, following their mother, peeping occasionally, trying to keep themselves in some semblance of a straight line.

Against the brilliant blue sky, scattered white clouds floated slowly and majestically above the water, reflected faithfully in every detail. From that reflection a brown speck grew larger and larger as it neared The Pond. It eventually caught Ephran's eye.

"Oh my!" he thought, "Cloudchaser is coming back for this happy occasion."

If the drake caught Ephran near his family, apparently hiding above them in a tree, there'd be big trouble. Then he realized that the bird closing on The Pond so rapidly was not a duck -- the wing set was wrong. So was the shape. Marshflower and her young had attracted an audience they hadn't bargained for. This was much bigger trouble than an early homecoming by Cloudchaser. This was a hawk!

And Ephran knew exactly where its attention was focused.

"Marshflower!" he cried, not wanting to startle her, but having little choice. "Hawk! Behind you!"

The ducks were close to the willow. Ephran was so well concealed among the leaves that Marshflower hadn't the faintest suspicion he was there. She recognized his voice and her proud smile faded. Her wings went up as though to shield her young. She jumped from the water and turned to face the threat, whose descent had carried it well over buttonbushes on the far shore.

The ducklings, up to that moment, had been lined up behind their mother. Her sudden and unexpected movement confused and scattered them. They paddled off in all directions, pumping tiny and useless wings.

"The reeds...the reeds!" she called.

If she could only get them into the dense green cover, and to keep quiet, the skyhunter would have little chance of finding them.

Peeping frantically, bewildered and unable to understand their mother's obvious alarm, five of the seven had stayed together; a fortunate accident. Marshflower fluttered to them and, with wings and beak, managed to push them behind a wide stand of switchgrass.

The two stragglers swam off together, almost to the trunk of Ephran's willow, seeing only one other. If they'd noticed their mother, brothers, and sisters slip out of sight and into the greenery, Ephran couldn't tell. They knew something was terribly wrong but had no idea what had interrupted their swim. Their mother had never left them alone before. They could not guess what disaster raced toward them from the sky.

Ephran closed his eyes and tried to wish them into the thick reeds and swampgrass that grew so near. But he understood why they didn't move to safety. They were paralyzed by fear and indecision. He knew the feeling. He remembered very well the day Maltrick stalked Mayberry.

Now they'd stopped swimming. They sat in the water, peeping their hearts out, calling for their mother, only a few taillengths from where Ephran watched.

Marshflower, hidden in the bullrushes, did not reappear. Ephran understood what she must be suffering. But she would stay put -- and keep what she had. He knew she was not afraid. If there was any chance of success she'd try to save the strays without thought for her own safety. But to leave the five in an attempt to save the two could well be the end for all of them. If young ducks weren't lost to the hawk, then to other hunters who would quickly find frightened and inexperienced ducklings wandering unto land or open water. It seemed cruel and unfair but it was the way of the forest. It could not be changed.

Or could it?

Ephran peered up between the leaves. Breath caught in his chest. Massive brown and white wings filled the sky. Talons like huge sharp thorns were yet closed but curled and ready. As though in anticipation, the hooked beak opened slightly. The hunter from the clouds slowed and adjusted his dive. Cruel yellow eyes transfixed the ducklings with such concentration that the skyhunter failed to notice the willow tree, swaying gently and unnaturally on this windless day.

Clinging to his perch, invisible to the hawk, Ephran remembered the other time he'd watched a hunter preparing to pounce. He didn't move then, and he made no sound. He'd been safe on a high branch. He could do the same thing now. The hunter wasn't after him. It didn't even know he was there. No one would blame him. This was a hawk, for Green Leaves' sake! Would Rennigan tell him he was making his own luck right now, "good" for him, not so "good" for someone else? When he looked down at the smooth water, he was sure, for a bare moment, that he saw a lopeared rabbit smiling back at him.

The willow branch was not very sturdy. He couldn't depend on it for a long jump. There should be enough support to reach his target, however. Jumping from tree limbs was, after all, what he was supposed to do best. He remembered running from the big oak as it fell under the attack of The Many Colored Ones. He'd used a tiny branch then and hadn't fallen. It was all a matter of timing and judgment.

70

Just before he committed himself to the leap he looked for a moment beyond the hawk and saw, in the distance, another brown figure approaching in the sky. The hawk's mate, no doubt. Double trouble. Well, it was too late to worry about that.

His timing was perfect. As he launched himself from a clump of leaves he saw, with satisfaction, the big bird appear under him, just as though the whole stunt had been practiced over and over again. He landed solidly on its back.

He was flying! But not for long. His front claws dug into the base of the hawk's neck while the rear ones found hold where one wing joined the heavy body. There was no need to bite. The sudden weight, like a firm blow, caught the bird by surprise. It had no idea what had landed astride its back and was causing such sharp pain in its wing. The skyhunter, mighty and fearsome creature though it be, was unable to maintain any sort of balance and was too close to the water to lift this unexpected load back into the clouds.

They plunged into the water together, nearly swamping the ducklings who, finally, swam into thick cover at the base of the willow. The hawk was furious. It righted itself immediately, sitting up in the water, spinning its head this way and that, searching for its attacker.

Ephran ended up at the bottom of The Pond. He tried desperately to stay under, even considering holding unto the thick green leaves growing from the mud. He could not. It was bitterly cold and, never having been in water before, he had not thought to take a big breath before he jumped. It occurred to him how nice it would be if Marshflower had been able to teach him to hold the air in his chest, as the ducks did when they tipped, head down, for their food. Having no real choice in the matter, Ephran popped to the surface and blinked. He found himself looking directly into the gleaming eyes of the hawk, towering over him.

The seconds seemed so very long. Impaled by the frigid stare of the hawk, Ephran remembered overhearing his parents talking in the nest one dark night. Mother had been out in the woods, where she had discovered a cache of butternuts. She'd stayed out too late, carrying the food nearer her nest, and she was nearly caught by a big horned owl that chased her back to the den. After she'd regained her breath and dignity she asked Jafthuh if he'd ever witnessed a hunter catching a victim. He had, he said, and the unlucky quarry seemed to pass into some sort of daze almost before the claws or the beak of the hunter touched them.

Ephran could only hope it was true. Though he and the hawk were out of their element, he knew he stood no chance against hooked beak and sharp talons. He only wished it would be over quickly.

The hawk was amazed. An insolent treeclimber had attacked him! One of the hunted had the audacity...! One shake of the head

"As he launched himself from a clump of leaves he saw with satisfaction, the big bird appear under him......"

cleared water from its eyes. A terrible smile lit the frightful face as it looked one last time.

The bird looked too long.

What Ephran had seen approaching from the sky as he leaped was not the hawk's mate after all. It was Cloudchaser. From a great distance the big drake saw the hawk descending toward The Pond. He had followed, flying as fast as he could. Despite his great speed, he was too far away to be of any help if, as he suspected, the skyhunter was indeed out to get his ducklings.

Thanks to some help, he was not too late.

Golden feet down, he aimed his heavy body at the hunter, whose total attention was riveted on Ephran. Cloudchaser made terribly loud noises as he struck the hawk with his full weight. For a second time the hunter went down, head over tail, under the cold water.

When the hawk surfaced this time it looked more confused and frightened than cruel. Twice it had been surprised and stunned in the attempt to grab some easy pickings -- once by a grey squirrel, of all things, who must be able to fly. And now by an extremely large drake mallard, who most certainly could fly, who was very strong, and very angry.

Enough was enough. The hawk jumped clumsily from the water, beating its powerful wings. For good measure, and as a parting warning, Cloudchaser quacked loudly at the retreating skyhunter. It flew rapidly across the far shore, slowly gaining altitude. It did not circle. It did not look back. Soon it was just a speck on the horizon.

During the final excitement Ephran had swum to shore, waded through thick bullrushes and sawgrass, and lay down to catch his breath on a tuft of stubby turf at the edge of the woods. The sun's rays were sweet comfort on his wet fur and he closed his eyes and huddled against the warm earth. His heart still pounded wildly against his ribs, more from fright than exertion. He was surprisingly unhurt and he noticed that one of the hawk's feathers was stuck to his left front claw.

Two crows had arrived unnoticed, just as Ephran's ambush of the hawk had begun. They had silently watched the amazing rescue from the top of a nearby aspen. They looked at one another and then again at the shivering gray squirrel below, sopping wet and short of air, but still very much capable of climbing into the high branches. Then they spread their wings and flew off toward Meadow Brook.

CHAPTER XI

DIFFICULT WORDS, NEW FACES

phran was very tired, at least as tired as he was the day he fell
asleep in the leaves and awoke to meet Maltrick. He knew he
should move on, into the woods and up a tree, but there was no fright
left in him. He lay down and closed his eyes. The next moment he
opened them to the sound of dripping water. The entire mallard family
was gathered around him. Cloudchaser stood with head high. Next to
him was Marshflower. Her eyes were bright and she wore a big smile.
The drake and the hen were flanked by their seven ducklings.

A drop of water ran down Ephran's forehead and unto his cheek.
He brushed it away. He looked up at Marshflower and Cloudchaser,
shading his eyes from the bright sunlight with one paw. Cloudchaser
cleared his throat.

"Ahem...," he said, "I have come to say a few words to you,
Ephran..." He stopped and looked toward his mate, who nodded at him,
her beak firmly set. "Yes...well...what I have to say is that what you, a
treeclimber, did just now is...is, to the best of my knowledge,...um, pretty
much unheard of. Treeclimbers do not attack hunters, unless to save one
of their own. Even then..."

The drake cleared his throat a second time, with a sort of harsh
quacking sound. "However, with my own eyes, even far out over The
Pond, I saw. I saw you risk your very breath to save my young ones.
Marshflower was right; Ephran is the mallard's friend. More than a
friend... Ahem!" He blew water from the holes in his beak and shook
his bright green head from side to side. "You are welcome at my nest,
Ephran, at any time you choose."

Cloudchaser bowed his head.

"Thank you, uh, Mr. Mallard...," said Ephran.

Cloudchaser looked up. "I am called Cloudchaser. That is what
friends call me -- those that I trust and those that trust me. I would be
honored to have you call me by my name."

This time Ephran had trouble speaking. It was his turn to
swallow hard. "Then," he said, "Thank you...Cloudchaser."

A long look passed between them, a look that said more than
words ever could.

Ephran said, "You may not have heard of squirrels helping
ducks, but I've not heard of a duck fighting to save a squirrel either. My
father would not believe such a thing possible. If what I did kept your
little ones paddling around, and will allow them to fly to those
wonderful faraway places someday, I'm happy. But, since I'm sure they
were already safe when you attacked the hawk, I think the favor has
been repaid."

Marshflower said, "It is difficult to express what I feel, Ephran. You have taught all of us a lesson today. And not just about courage, though I have not seen greater. My mate knows of what I speak. He judged you by what he had heard about others of your kind. It was not fair."

She glanced at Cloudchaser, who smiled and nodded at Ephran.

"I think," she said, "that I will go now and dream a bit. I want to spend some time recalling very special places and things I've seen. I want to describe them so that you can see -- if we want to keep you nearby I must keep my stories interesting."

Ephran's grin was radiant.

She waddled over and lay her head gently against his. In turn, each of the ducklings, totally unafraid, wobbled shyly up to Ephran and smoothed his wet fur with tiny beaks. Then, like hummingbirds filled with nectar, and frightened by a whimsical gust of air, they all vanished into the tall reeds.

"Well, I'm not sure if you're a hero or just mildly demented."

Ephran spun his head toward the woods. The voice had come from one of the trees near the water.

"Klestra, you rascal, where are you?" called Ephran.

"Right up here where we could watch the whole show," said Klestra.

"We?"

"That's what I said; 'We'," answered Klestra. "Since you wouldn't come to the other side of Spruce Hill to see my surprise, I brought my surprise to see you."

Klestra, familiar grin smeared from one side of his face to the other, appeared on a hickory tree, as though he'd suddenly sprouted there. He looked at his friend in mock horror.

"Wilted Walnuts! I didn't expect to find you sopping wet and generally unpresentable. You are a most unpredictable squirrel."

"Since when did you care how I look?" asked Ephran.

"I don't," said the red squirrel, "but you might."

With his paw Klestra pointed up, into the tree. Out of the leafy branches above him another treeclimber appeared. "Strange...", was Ephran's first thought, "a gray squirrel, not a red. And a female besides. And..."

He swallowed and blinked. This squirrel...the one he couldn't take his eyes from...she simply had to be the most beautiful squirrel Ephran had ever seen!

CHAPTER XII

KAAHLI

Other than his mother and sister, Ephran was acquainted with very few female squirrels. Oh sure, there had been some playmates who nested a short distance from the old oak where he grew up, but they were young, silly, and shy and were more like cousins...or something. Anyway, at the time he hadn't been interested.

This particular treeclimber, looking down at him from the hickory tree, was absolutely the lovliest he'd ever seen. Her fur was thick and healthy, her eyes deep and sparkling, her ears pert and perfectly shaped, and her smile...oh, Sweet Green Buds, her smile!

Ephran had never been one to worry about his appearance, but he realized Klestra was right; at the moment he was not looking his best. Lustrous gray fur was drenched and matted. Fluffy tail lay on the earth, heavy with water, and thin as a cattail stalk. He must look like an underfed Fetzgar. A water weed hung from his ear. He pulled it off.

"In all of our many talks I never heard you mention that you enjoyed swimming with birds," Klestra said, tail switching from side to side and big grin lighting up his white face. "Wanting to fly with them, yes; swim, no."

Ephran, trying to fluff up his fur with one paw, said, "I...I don't suppose I did. I sure didn't do it for fun."

"What then?" asked Klestra.

"You'd have to try it yourself to find out," answered Ephran. "But one thing is certain; a tree dweller should leave these watery places to the fish and feathered ones. There are no nuts at the bottom of The Pond -- and there's no way to breathe down there."

"Don't give me that!" said Klestra. "You've known about water for a long time. Why did you jump from the tree?"

"Jump? I didn't jump. Who said I jumped? Couldn't you tell that I fell?"

"Fell? Ha! Take me for a fool if you like, but it looked to me like you meant to leap on that hawk's back."

"Looks can be deceiving. Maybe the hawk just happened to be there. Maybe it was trying to catch me as I fell."

"Oh please, Ephran!" Klestra begged, "Don't give me this gibberish. Kaahli saw it all just as I did."

"Kaahli...?"

"Oh, forgive me," said Klestra with a shake of his head. "You get me so upset that I forget my manners. As I said, you must remember the time I asked you to come with me to Spruce Hill? As I recall, you didn't feel up to the trip at the time. In any case, what I really wanted to do was to introduce you to someone I'd met there, someone I probably wouldn't have even talked to if you hadn't fooled me into thinking that gray squirrels were worthwhile conversing with. Well, this is her! Ephran, I'd like you to meet another gray friend: Kaahli."

Kaahli. He spoke it silently and her name filled his mouth with sweetness. Her gentle smile was like sunlight on his face. He suddenly felt light-headed -- a most unusual sensation. Perhaps the battle with the hawk had taken more out of him than he thought.

"Hello, Ephran," she said.

"H'lo," he managed. Bitter Butternuts, how he wished he could stop smiling. He knew how silly it must look, but it just stuck there. He couldn't make the corners of his mouth come back down.

Silence stretched until Klestra said, "Actually, Kaahli, sometimes he talks nearly as much as a red squirrel. And he's not as feeble in the head as you might be led to believe, looking at that absurd grin. All things considered, he's fairly intelligent for one of your kind."

Ephran and Kaahli broke into laughter. Then Kaahli's expression became serious. "Despite your jesting, Ephran, I think you meant to save those ducklings by jumping on the hawk. I have not heard of a squirrel attacking a skyhunter, not even in after-dark stories. Do you fear nothing?"

"Only sharp-tongued red squirrels."

They all giggled again.

"Well," said Klestra, after another long pause, "I'd love to stay and listen to more of this drivel but I think I've had about all the worthwhile conversation I'm going to get around here today. Besides, I'm expecting company at my nest. See you two soon, I hope."

He scampered off, disappearing behind a thicket of sumac bushes before they could even say good-bye. Ephran and Kaahli sat for a bit, he in a puddle of water on the ground, she in the hickory tree.

"Do you have a tree nearby?" Kaahli finally asked.

"Yes, I have a nest a short distance from here."

Except for the whisper of air through birch leaves and frogs croaking now and then from cool green water lilies, the forest was peaceful.

"You should dry off, you know," said Kaahli.

"Yes," he smiled. "Running will help take the water from my fur. Will you join me?"

She nodded.

Ephran laid the souvenir of his tussle with the hawk at the base of a bunch of cattails. The handsome brown and white feather was important to him. He would come back for it.

They dashed off through the branches, jumping from limb to limb, from tree to tree, climbing higher and higher until they reached the droopy upper boughs of a gigantic cottonwood. When he came to a sturdy branch with a thick fork, Ephran stopped and moved to one side, making room for Kaahli among the rustling leaves. They lay there, catching their breath. The Pond twinkled and sparkled in the late morning sunlight, looking very small from this distance.

She was close enough, nearly touching him. Ephran had trouble thinking clearly. He struggled to start a conversation.

"Klestra says your home is near Spruce Hill," he said lamely, "I've never been there."

"Yes," said Kaahli. "Klestra comes that way often, I think. I met him near Rocky Point one day while I was looking for fresh berries. They like to grow near the water, you know. Anyway, I heard a great racket coming from Rocky Creek and I had to investigate. The noise -- please don't ever tell him I called it that -- was Klestra. He was scolding a marten. I still don't know why he was making such a fuss. I hadn't heard another squirrel in that part of the woods and I needed to talk to someone. I remember thinking, 'Good Green Gooseberries, this one certainly has a vocabulary!'"

"Sounds like Klestra," said Ephran. "He doesn't need much of a reason to scold. I'll bet he did his chattering from a healthy distance though. Martens like red squirrels for lunch -- and I don't mean as guests."

"Oh, indeed!" laughed Kaahli. "He kept a good many jumps between himself and the hunter. The marten tried to ignore him."

"The day he asked me to come to Spruce Hill I was suspicious. I thought he might want me to meet a female. I mistakenly decided she must be a red treeclimber, though, someone he was interested in. I imagined I was the only gray squirrel with a red friend."

"I didn't think much of it that first time; that he was red and I was gray..." She looked at Ephran. "Does it make a difference?"

"Of course it doesn't!" grinned Ephran. "To hear Klestra is to love him, I guess. How did he convince you to travel all the way to The Pond with him?"

"Much as he tried to persuade you to come to Spruce Hill, I suppose. He told me that he had something special to show me, something or someone that might be important to my future."

They glanced sideways at one another.

"Are you alone in your nest?" Ephran asked.

She hesitated a moment. "I am now. I was born near Spring Creek."

"Does your family still nest near the water?"

"No," said Kaahli. She looked away from his eyes. "My mother was not well, you see. Of four in the litter, only I and my brother, Laslum, survived. She was unable to nurse us. She became thinner and thinner. Soon she could barely climb our tree. She had no appetite, not even for the tenderest buds or the sweetest nuts..."

Kaahli shifted her weight on the branch and took a deep breath.

"One day Laslum and I went with our father to gather berries. We thought she might enjoy them. When we came back to the nest she was gone. Father could barely speak. He whispered that we must not try to find her. He said she sought a softer nest...in a quiet place. A place she'd be comfortable. He said she wouldn't want to be disturbed. At first I didn't understand. I wanted my mother..." She closed her eyes for a moment. "Father did his best to take care of us," she continued. "Laslum and I kept the nest as neat and comfortable as we could. We found some bushes with sweet seeds. We spent the cold season near Spring Creek but we knew we'd have to move when warm air returned. We needed nuts, and the only tree near our den that grew nuts lost its leaves early. So, one day my father and brother left the nest to seek a place where acorns or hickory nuts might be found."

She ceased speaking again and gazed down at The Pond.

"What happened?" he asked quietly.

"I don't know," she said and her voiced cracked. "They never came back."

She lifted her head and spoke in a strong voice. "I searched for many days, even near a dwelling of Many Colored Ones, but I found no trace of them. I almost became lost myself. I couldn't stay in the old nest -- it was a sad place. I looked until I came upon a reasonable tree and built a new nest near Spruce Hill."

"How long have you stayed by yourself, Kaahli?"

"It's difficult to say. The sun has set many times on my tree. Yet, I'm sure it seems longer than it's been."

Klestra had made a remarkable discovery; this female was indeed special. She'd lost her family as he had, only she'd had no Rennigan to lean on. He wondered how well he would have managed all by himself. He wondered if he would have been as brave and resourceful as she'd been. She didn't say any more, but it was obvious that her greatest pain was not knowing what had become of her father and brother.

From Ephran Kaahli coaxed the story of his adventures at the end of the cold season and how he'd ended up back at The Pond. He told her of his family, of Maltrick and the farm cat, and of Rennigan. He told her of all the friends he'd made here, the bounty in the trees and the bushes, the beauty of the place, and how he loved all of it.

When he'd finished his story, he glanced at the sky, jumped up, and said, "I can't believe that the sun has traveled such a great distance while we talked. I haven't even offered you a bite to eat. You must be very hungry."

"A little," she admitted, smiling up at him.

"Come," he said, "I know where there are still some tender seeds. I've hidden a few acorns nearby as well."

When they'd eaten their fill Ephran asked, "Would you like to see my nest?"

"Yes," she said, "I would like that."

"Nest building is not my favorite thing to do," Ephran admitted, "so don't expect anything very grand. I find it comfortable and solid though, and the view of The Pond is wonderful."

As they ran toward his home, Ephran asked Kaahli to wait a moment while he retrieved the hawk feather from the cattails. He carried it in his mouth, running on the forest floor the short distance to his tree. He led Kaahli up the husky trunk, took the feather in his front paws, and pushed it into the leaves of the nest just above the big branch.

Kaahli smiled as he stepped back to check out his trophy. The feather was slightly bent and bedraggled-looking from its soaking in The Pond, and the trip in Ephran's mouth had not improved its appearance. It was a fine prize nonetheless and she knew that what it meant to Ephran was far more important than how it looked.

"I suppose it will be gone the first time the wind moves through the woods," he said.

"Well, we'll tuck it in good and tight so that it won't be blown away," Kaahli said.

She ran to the farthest and thinnest part of the branch they stood upon. With sharp teeth she carefully removed the leaves from three small and pliable green twigs and then nipped them off. She carried the twigs in her mouth and, using teeth and paws, wove the quill of the feather to the nest with the tiny branches.

As he watched her Ephran noticed an unusual feeling inside his chest. Or was it his stomach acting up again? It was hard to be sure. The feeling was not exactly hunger. Besides, they'd eaten just a short time ago. It was a bright and sort of happy feeling, yet heavy, and like there may be a bit of sadness on the other side, if you thought about it long enough. He'd never had such a strange sensation and for a minute wondered if he was getting sick after all. Then he questioned whether it had something to do with Kaahli but he couldn't bring himself to ask her. It would sound foolish.

She finished her handiwork and proved how tightly the feather was bound by tugging at it with both paws. It did not budge.

"You are a talented weaver of branches," said Ephran.

She smoothed the feather with her paw and said, "My mother didn't have time to teach me much, but she did show me how to weave a tight nest."

"Then I should have you rebuild mine," said Ephran. "My mother tried to teach me too, but my mind always seemed to wander off to other things."

Neither of them spoke for some time. They sat on the limb, a little way apart, looking at Ephran's nest.

Finally Kaahli stretched, smiled at him, and said, "The sun comes near the trees. I must start back to Spruce Hill."

81

"I haven't been to Spruce Hill, but I know you can't travel that far before darkness comes," he protested.

"There's no need to worry," she said. "I know of places to stay during the dark hours. I've traveled that way with Klestra, you know, and he's very good at finding comfortable trees."

He spoke before he had time to think.

"Please don't go."

He could hardly believe that it had been his voice! He was probably more surprised than Kaahli. He didn't regret saying it, though. Right then it occurred to him that he never would.

Kaahli looked at him quizzically.

"I want you to stay here with me," he said. "And, if you feel that you have to go back to your own nest, I'm going to ask if I may go with you."

Once again he was astounded at his own boldness. Who was this gray squirrel talking through his mouth?

"You would leave your pond and all your friends to come with me to Spruce Hill?" she asked, astonishment in her voice.

"Yes," he said, surprising himself again.

"Oh, my dear Ephran, are you sure you want me to stay here with you?"

"I'm very sure."

"You think I need the protection of a brave male treeclimber. Is that it?"

"I'm afraid I'm being selfish," he said. "I suspect you have no need of my protection. You seem to have done very well by yourself. All I'm certain of is that I want to be with you."

Kaahli moved near, where he faced her on the branch. They gazed at each other in silence. Neither saw anything there that would change their minds. She put her face next to his and they stayed that way a long while.

Sunbeams, grown long and cooler now, trickled through gently waving green leaves, casting dancing blotches of brightness on the two unmoving figures high in the ash tree.

CHAPTER XIII

GOODBYE FOR NOW

hough she never caught him at it, Kaahli knew Ephran was laughing at her. Not a nasty laugh of course. More like a loving smile...one that had gotten just a little out-of-paw. Besides, at times she had to giggle herself. But she couldn't help herself. It seemed that their nest always needed a new leaf here or a fresh twig there. Although she said she wasn't going to rebuild it, she'd almost done exactly that. Ephran didn't complain. The nest was far more comfortable now than it had been when he'd curled there alone.

Time passed quickly. The days, warmer and greener as the sun grew stronger, were spent acquainting Kaahli with the woods near The Pond and Great Hill, introducing her to Ephran's many friends, racing through silver maple, red oak and tamarack, visiting with Klestra in the whispering willow or with the mallard family atop their waterlogged den.

Janey, the tiny wren who built her nest in the thickest part of the bramble hedge, became a special friend. The squirrels delighted in her deliriously joyous chirping on those mornings when the first rays of light appeared over Great Hill. Even when heavy clouds hid the great ball of warmth, Janey did her best to welcome the day with a happy song.

Smagtu, the skunk, took a liking to the young squirrel couple and dropped by the tree for occasional visits. Ephran enjoyed his rambling conversations, spiced as they were with earthy observations. Kaahli learned to take advantage of moving air, adjusting her position quickly whenever she saw the black and white animal approaching the ash tree.

When they played or searched for food near The Pond, often as not, Fetzgar would show up to "chat" a bit. He prided himself on what he thought was noiseless movement. "I kin sneak a sleepin' humminbird and spit in his eye afore he knows I'm there," he'd say with a lopsided grin. Since he pictured himself cunning and nimble they always feigned surprise when he popped up out of the shallows -- even though they'd seen him slide off his den into the water -- and could hardly miss the long, rippling wake behind as he paddled toward them.

Mr. and Mrs. Robin built their nest in the tree next to the ash. And so the last moments of the day often found the four of them, two feathered and two furred, together, watching the sun disappear over Lomarsh, its last brilliant light slowly dimmed and pulled along behind.

Their best friends, besides Klestra of course, were the mallards. Kaahli was not quite so fascinated as her mate with the stories of long flights to faraway places, but she was certainly not bored, and she listened attentively.

The ducklings grew as quickly as the reeds around their nest, as though each were afraid it might be left behind in the race to swim and fly like their parents. To the squirrels it seemed they went from tiny, helpless featherballs to scuffling, squawking, goodnatured rowdies, stouter than the squirrels, almost overnight. Ephran watched their first short and wobbly flights across the waters of The Pond with undisguised envy. He listened to every word Cloudchaser told the young ducks about flying; how to get the most wingpower to rise from the water quickly and nearly straight up, how to cup the wings and balance on gusts of air when landing, how to use the currents high in the sky to fly fast and straight to wherever one wanted to go.

At first Cloudchaser and Marshflower -- and particularly the ducklings -- thought his attention to this flying business, of which he could never partake, was very amusing. But he didn't retreat or get flustered when they giggled at his rapt interest in every detail. He wasn't in the least embarrassed to practice, with his front legs, the wing exercises taught the young ducks. And so, because they loved him, they stopped laughing. And though they knew he could never rise from the earth without using a tree, they made certain that he was included in every flying lesson they had.

"After all, who can say...," remarked Cloudchaser to Marshflower one quiet evening when the smell of plum blossoms filled the air, "that a squirrel who will fight a hawk may not be able to find his way into the sky?"

The ducks learned to enjoy fresh buds brought to them by the squirrels -- freshly plucked, green branch and all -- dragged out to the nest on the muskrat den. For their part, the squirrels found that wild celery and duck potato, dug from the bottom of The Pond by the young mallards, was really very tasty.

All in all, life was marvelous. Except that, as the days passed, Ephran became more and more concerned about Kaahli. She became less and less talkative. At times her mind seemed a long way off. Though she smiled gently and lovingly at him when he interrupted her thoughts, there was no question that something was definitely wrong.

Late one sunny day Ephran and Kaahli were curled on the far side of the muskrat den. Cloudchaser was paddling around, down the shoreline, inspecting his domain and harvesting a bit of wild rice at the origin of Bubbling Brook. Marshflower contentedly watched her young playing and diving in the shallow water near the nest.

"How rapidly they grow," sighed Marshflower, "and how fast the warm season moves on."

"Very true," said Ephran, stretching lazily, "before you know it we'll have to start collecting nuts for the cold season."

"Oh, there's plenty of time for that, Ephran," said one of the three young drakes.

"Ha! Listen to my wise young friend speak...," said Ephran, "he who has never experienced a cold season. I tell you the bitter air will sneak up like the fox. Those of us who have to stay here must get busy. You're lucky, none of you will ever really have to endure a cold season."

A second young drake said, "Ephran, if you wish I will carry you on my back to the warm places far away."

Ephran laughed. "How wonderful that would be! One of you would have to bring Kaahli as well. Isn't that so, little one?"

He was looking right at her, but she didn't answer. Her glazed eyes stared across the water at Fetzgar, who sat on his newest home chewing on the usual limp white root. Ephran doubted that she even saw the muskrat. She certainly hadn't heard her own mate's voice speak to her.

"Kaahli...," he said gently.

Her tail twitched, as though he'd wakened her, and she gave him a tiny smile.

One of the young hen mallards, more perceptive than the others and less inhibited, said, "Kaahli, are you sad?"

"My dear," Marshflower said sharply to her daughter, "you seem unable to mind your own business."

"Don't scold her, Marshflower," said Kaahli, turning her soft smile on the embarrassed young duck. "I'm afraid that there is something inside that's not happy. It shouldn't be there, but it is. It's not because I have no friends, and I certainly don't feel alone. I have Ephran -- and all of our wonderful friends. But I am sad because I don't know what has become of my father and brother. I must believe they are somewhere in the big woods. And, wherever they are, they have no idea where I am."

Everyone was silent.

"A friend of mine named Mayberry once told me that the woods is large but not as big as we think. For those who can travel through the treetops or in the sky, it's much smaller than for those who must stay on the earth," said Ephran.

"True words," said Marshflower, "but what do they have to do with Kaahli's father and brother?"

"What I mean is, if we set our minds to it, I believe we can find Kaahli's family," said Ephran, then he paused for a moment. "And maybe my own in the bargain."

"Wonderful idea! Wonderful idea! I will help," quacked the young drake.

"You help?" scoffed one of his brothers. "How do you plan to help? You can barely fly across The Pond."

"I know you'd help if you could," said Ephran, "but you'd be unable to recognize Kaahli's father and brother...even if you could see them through the warm season's thick leaves. Thank you for your offer, but I think Kaahli and I must do this alone."

Cloudchaser swam up just in time to hear the tailend of the conversation. "What is it that you feel you must do, Ephran?" he asked.

"We're going to search for our families," answered Ephran.

"I suspected as much. I felt this coming every time you spoke of them. How long do you think you'll be gone?"

Ephran looked at Kaahli. "I don't know, my friend. I'm going to plan on searching until we find them."

"Thank you, Ephran," said Kaahli, her eyes sparkling with gratitude and excitement.

"I understand. I do wish you good luck...and have a safe journey," said Cloudchaser.

"We all wish you success," said Marshflower. "But please, please be careful."

The young ducks gathered around Ephran and Kaahli. "Hurry back," said a young female. "Mother says it won't be all that long before the water in The Pond becomes hard and slippery. We want to see you again before that happens."

"If we plan to stay here through the cold days, we must be back long before that," said Ephran. "We must store nuts and seeds. And, before snow covers the bushes, Kaahli wants to find a den inside a tree."

"Which way will you go?" asked Cloudchaser.

"We'll follow Rocky Creek to Spruce Hill. If you have need of us, fly along the water and make your quacking sound. If we can hear you, we'll come out of the trees."

"I and my young will be flying that way from time to time -- as practice for our flight to the warm places. We will watch for you," said Cloudchaser.

"Will you see Klestra before you leave?" asked Marshflower.

"Oh, of course!" said Kaahli. "We must say goodbye to Klestra."

"I'd love to talk to Klestra," said Ephran, "and get his advice about this whole business. He's traveled through the trees further upstream than I have. But saying goodbye to him wouldn't be easy, even if we could find the roving rascal. I think he would insist on coming with us. And I'd very much like to have him along. For that matter, I'd love to take everyone along! But, the more of us together, the better the chance of attracting hunters. Besides, we have no idea of what we might face and I have no interest in endangering our friends." He sighed and looked at Kaahli. "No, I'm afraid we'll have to ask you to say goodbye for us. As I said before, I think this time it must be just the two of us."

Through misty eyes Kaahli looked one last time at the Mallard family and said, "I will miss you as I miss my father and brother."

Kaahli and Ephran jumped to the willow and then to the earth.

In their nest they tried to close their eyes, though darkness had not yet crept into the woods. Ephran wondered, just before he fell asleep, how long it would be before he would again curl in these cozy and familiar leaves.

As the sun sank below the tops of the trees, its last rays seemed to hesitate at the fork of the big ash and at a fine looking nest of twigs. They illuminated a single, slightly discolored feather, fluttering proudly in the evening breeze.

CHAPTER XIV

OF ROGUES AND RESCUES

Kaahli was awake long before the sun gilded the dark sky over Bubbling Brook. She'd slept fitfully, and finally a dream woke her up. In the dream she had heard her father and brother. They were calling to her, calling from far away. Their voices echoed -- they were in a hollow place -- maybe a rotted tree, or a hole in the earth. She couldn't see them and she didn't know if they could see her. She dare not make a sound to let them know that she was near. Her fur was damp with fear, her teeth set in frustration. She had no idea how to help them and, when her eyes flew open, she realized she had been crying aloud.

"Ephran, Ephran...," she'd been sobbing.

Ephran was very sound asleep and her tiny cries had not gotten past his ears. There was no need to wake him now, so she lay quietly as her heart slowed. After what seemed a long while she heard the first sounds of the approaching day. Bright streaks of orange light sprayed a cluster of elm along the far edge of The Pond. At the same time Mrs. Robin greeted the rising sun with a series of happy warbles. Silence of darkness broken, Janey wren responded with her own song. A mourning dove joined in. "Hooo, hooo, hooo," it sighed, and was answered by one of its own kind from across the water.

Kaahli nudged Ephran gently. He grunted and curled his thick tail more tightly about his ears.

"Ephran," she coaxed, "Ephran..."

He stirred and thrust his back legs into the leaves of the nest. Front legs moved stiffly up along his ears as he stretched. Slowly his tail came away from his face and he looked up through heavy lids.

"Time to start out!" she said cheerily.

"Ummmm," he answered, not so cheerily.

Ephran did not care to rise with the sun. As far as he was concerned the early hours belonged to the wrens and robins. However, as sleep floated away, he remembered that this was a most special day and his eyes flew open.

"Yes," he said, "you're right...time to get moving."

Kaahli kissed his nose and scampered out of the nest. Ephran yawned and followed her outside. The air was refreshing; cool and damp on his face. Fine white mist rose from the still water of The Pond. Through the haze he could see the sleeping mallard family, too many and too large for their nest, crowded atop the muskrat den, heads beneath their wings. He looked for Kaahli and saw her above him in the next tree, climbing toward the high branches.

"Hey there, little one!" he called.

She stopped and looked back with a puzzled expression.

"Where do you think you're going in such a big hurry?"

"Oh, Ephran. Don't tease. Come, I want to get started."

"We'd better eat first."

"Is your stomach all you can think of?"

"My dear," he said, "I've told you my story. You know that this old stomach figures often in my thoughts. Except, of course, when I'm thinking of you."

"Ephran! Be serious."

He grinned. "Actually, I am quite serious. We must eat before we set out. We know where food is near The Pond, but who knows where or when we might come across something to eat again."

Despite the fact that she was eager for the next branch, Kaahli understood that what he said was important. She scurried back down the treetrunk and together they ran toward a small patch of stubby bushes at the near end of The Hedge. The bushes seemed a constant source of fresh sweet buds, and Ephran had hidden a few acorns nearby.

Ephran generally enjoyed taking his meals slowly and with a lot of interspersed conversation but, this particular day, he bolted down three tender buds, wet with morning dew, along with two crispy acorns. Kaahli didn't even touch the acorns he'd set before her and she had barely nibbled on the huge green bud he'd placed under her nose.

"Kaahli," he said, "please eat something. We're liable to need all our strength."

"I'm sorry," she said, "I'm too excited to eat just now."

Ephran knew how miserable it could be to travel with an empty stomach, especially when you had no idea when or how you were going to fill it again. It could be distracting enough to cause serious mistakes to be made. He could only hope that, once they were underway, she would settle down and regain her appetite. He would watch carefully for promising bushes and nutbearing trees.

"I'm ready," Kaahli said, eyes sparkling. "Which way?"

"We'll follow Rocky Creek along The Meadow. I think we should start our search at Spruce Hill." He hoped he sounded confident -- like he knew exactly what he was doing and that he understood just where they must go.

There had been no time to prepare for this journey, except for the few moments just before he fell asleep. Though he'd never been there, from conversations with Klestra and Cloudchaser he had a general idea where Spruce Hill was. Klestra wandered along Rocky Creek on a regular basis, and Cloudchaser had flown above its curved path some of those many times he was absent from The Pond. There was just one problem: If they didn't find her family before they got to Spruce Hill -- or at least came across a few clues to direct them further -- what then? He knew nothing of what lay beyond. And Kaahli's memory of the area would be dim. She'd traveled that way only once and then when she'd been upset and frightened. She would remember little of it. Ephran wondered if his reassuring words the evening before might have been a mite hasty. He kept his worries to himself. Kaahli was so excited that he couldn't bring himself to dampen her hopes.

They set out, running and leaping through the boughs of trees that grew near Rocky Creek. They stopped for a few moments to watch the red sun lift itself over the far side of The Meadow. Sunbeams cut through the smoky mist that lay gently on long brome grass. The beams illuminated an enormous spider web woven among tall milkweed and burdock. Dewdrops sparkled in the latticework, like bright silvery stars on a cloudless night.

For a while they traveled in silence while the sun climbed higher and higher into the sky. Ephran ran ahead. As they neared a fork in the waterway below, he descended into lower branches. He came to rest on a drooping linden branch.

"Why do we stop?" Kaahli asked. She was flushed and breathless, but he didn't notice.

"Just ahead Rocky Creek and Meadow Brook join. See?" He nodded. "We'll cross here and put the sun to our backs."

No water had come from the sky for some days now and the creek was quiet. After black clouds rolled away, or when the cold season grew weak and snow turned back to water, the peaceful little stream became a frothy and noisy river, white water boiling over the rocks that gave it its name. Clusters of beggarwort and Jimson weed grew thickly along its banks. A wild iris leaned over, as though admiring its own wavering reflection. Birds of many kinds hid in the green leaves, feasting on clouds of insects. Every now and then a graceful monarch or yellow swallowtail butterfly appeared around a bend, floating lazily along the watercourse, stopping to rest on a bunch of cowslip that thrived in the damp soil.

Ephran surveyed the stream below and spotted a sizeable fallen branch that spanned the stream. Although the limb was old and decayed, it looked solid enough to use as a bridge. He climbed slowly down the linden, ever watchful for what did not belong. Except for an occasional blackbird chirp, and the constant buzzing of gnats and deerflies, all was serene.

Kaahli was moving slower and slower, with steps less and less confident. She was near exhaustion. Ephran was so intent on his route across the stream that he didn't realize that she had fallen far behind him. He crossed the water on his crooked bridge, pleased with himself for having found it. As soon as he had crossed he began scanning the woods ahead, looking for the best tree from which to resume their journey. He must not hesitate. He must not disappoint her.

When she reached the stream Kaahli felt as though she should call to him, ask him to wait a moment. But it was too great an effort.

Besides, he would surely stop when he got to the trees. She could make it that far. They would rest and talk then.

She started across the branch. It was damp and slick with rot. A musty smell rose to her nostrils from dark and stagnant water. A large dragonfly lay motionless below, filmy wings spread wide, head missing. Her vision blurred and her right front paw slipped. She reached blindly with the other paw as she slid sideways but the soft wood pulled apart in her grasp and she tumbled into the water.

Rocky Creek was not particularly wide or deep at this point, perhaps ten to fifteen taillengths across and as many pawlengths in depth. Though it was not moving rapidly, there was a most definite and insistent current beneath the placid surface. Kaahli came up almost immediately, revived by the cool water. She wanted to shout out for Ephran but she had sucked some of the dark liquid into her chest and had to gasp for air. It was all right though. She would be able to swim to the bank. It was only a little way. Then she would catch up to Ephran...

Kaahli stopped in the water as though her legs had suddenly been given to someone else and they were not hers to control.

From a clump of grass at the bottom of the bank, a short distance in front of her, a mink appeared in the scummy water. Its body was large, sleek and muscular. It smiled at her, sharp teeth bared. Its eyes shone like stars in a black sky. She felt as though she had been impaled by them.

"A veesitor," it grinned. "Velcome."

Kaahli's entire body went numb. Her paws stopped treading water. She was so terrified it didn't even occur to her to wonder how she stayed afloat.

"You haf no thing to say?" the mink asked. "Thot hokay. Becass I haf nothing else to say to you eether. Now I vill taste your legs, zen your neck, and zen, ven I feenesh..."

The mink ceased speaking as though something or someone very important had told him to close his mouth. He not only quit talking -- Kaahli noticed his eyes growing wider and wider by the moment.

Only then did she realize that she was moving in the water, without so much as wiggling her paws. Was she imagining it? No, there were tiny ripples, spreading out in every direction from her! She was moving all right...moving slowly upward and, at the same time, closer and closer to shore. It occurred to her that she should jump back into the stream. It would not be safe to stand on the bottom of the creek as it moved. But before she could act, she found herself standing above the mink, who cringed away from her. She looked down at her paws and saw the dark and spiny back of an immense snapping turtle. The mink could still not see what caused his intended victim to rise in the water. From where he lay, low in the water, it looked to him as though this amazing treeclimber, who could swim to the surface without moving its

"BUT THE SOFT WOOD PULLED APART IN HER
GRASP AND SHE TUMBLED INTO THE WATER"

legs, was about to actually walk on the surface of the creek!

As the turtle swam near the far bank Kaahli jumped off its back -- just as its stubby legs reached land. She scurried up the embankment without looking back and heard the mink hiss and shout; "Vait...!"

She almost ran headlong into Ephran, who had finally noticed she was missing and had started back to find her.

"Kaahli! Where have you been? What happened?" Then he saw that her fur was soaked. "You've been in the water?..."

It was over. There was no need for him to know. He would only feel guilty because he hadn't stayed with her -- just as he'd felt guilty about not warning Mayberry that snowy day on The Pond.

"Of course," she said, "I went for a swim. I've seen you do it."

"Kaahli," he said earnestly, "Don't joke. Squirrels don't go for swims. Are you all right?"

"I fell off your rotten bridge," she said, "that's all. Well... just about all."

"You aren't hurt?" Ephran asked again, scampering around her, looking for scratches or scrapes.

"I'm fine," she said, "but I have to admit that my stomach is very unhappy. Its my own fault, I know. I think I'll just say that swimming gives one an appetite."

Ephran smiled and said, "As I always -- or nearly always -- say, 'The only way to travel is with a full stomach'. I see some budding bushes just ahead and I bet I can find a butternut as well."

He was true to his word. He told her to rest in the grass while he brought her fresh nuts and a decent butternut from last warm season. It was gratifying to watch her eat everything. At first she returned his happy grin, but her smile faded. A shadow had fallen across his face.

"Ephran," she said, "the sun..."

Indeed, the warmth from the sky no longer shone down on them. He sniffed the air. It smelled heavy and dark. And there was something else there -- something he could not name.

She heard the alarm in his voice when he said, "Kaahli, we must find shelter. Quickly."

CHAPTER XV

ANGRY SKY

Kaahli's first thought was to wonder why Ephran seemed so agitated. Intent on the food he'd set before her, she'd been aware of no rumbling except that coming from her own stomach. Now she heard thunder in the distance and looked up to see massive black clouds with green-tinged edges, rolling like waves over the motionless treetops.

"Come," was all he said.

She dropped a half-eaten bud in the grass and ran after him, along the uneven ground near the wood's edge. "Ephran!" she called, "Shouldn't we go up -- into the trees?"

"No...," he shouted over his shoulder, "no trees. Follow me." He looked back again, to be sure she was with him. "Follow me closely."

He scampered around a clump of sumac and she ran so close behind that his tail brushed her face. What in the big green forest was he thinking anyway? Was not a high branch the safest place for a treeclimber when danger threatened? Did he have a plan? Did he know what he was doing?"

Ephran abruptly stopped and Kaahli skidded to a halt at his side -- just as the air erupted in enormous gusts. Trees that had stood stockstill just a moment before now bent and swayed in a wild dance, branches flailing furiously against one another. Leaves and twigs danced, whirled, and finally sailed away. Kaahli closed her eyes to tiny slits.

A sharp and bright light flared over their heads, followed immediately by a tremendous clap of thunder. Above the steady whistling of the wind there came a "CRRR-WHUMP!" as a thick bough from high in an ash tree crashed to the forest floor.

"I see now," Kaahli said in his ear. "Even the high places are not secure! But where can we go? Where can we hide if the trees are not safe?"

At that moment Ephran spied what he'd been looking for -- and with no time to spare. It was plain that his mate was about to panic and to run off into the woods, just as he once had.

What he'd been searching for was a hole in the earth. If the truth were known, such places frightened him just as much as they did most gray squirrels. His parents had never so much as mentioned the idea of seeking shelter in the dark and damp ground. It simply wasn't done. There was no freedom there, no chance of escape through clean air and on solid branches. Most likely he would not have thought of such a thing all by himself. The bizarre idea came of friendship with a red squirrel.

"Kaahli!" he called, above the roar of the storm.

She had sat down in the grass, twigs blowing past her ears. Her legs refused to move. Confusion and fear were written all over her face. In two leaps he was back at her side. His teeth gripped the fur of her neck and her eyes widened in surprise. He nodded to her and she followed, not caring one bit for where he was going. But she followed anyway -- into a very dark tunnel beneath a ragged elm stump.

The tormented air reversed itself and began to howl from the other direction, away from the hole they'd entered. Leaves and showers of soil flew past, but did not enter the hole.

The smell in the darkness was simply that of earth and slowly decaying tree roots. Ephran breathed easier -- the den had been vacant for some time. The previous occupant, whoever it might have been, had excavated enough dirt from among the roots to make a cozy space. It was lined with grasses and soft milkweed down. There was room for both of them to lay down, facing the entrance. Side by side, protected by thick elm roots and solid earth, they listened to the shriek of air as it passed through branches that groaned and squealed in pain. Debris of all kinds soared past the stump. Tall thistle and fireweed thrashed in one direction and then the other. The day became darker and darker, even though it was far from time for the sun to sink below the trees.

"THUMP!"

Something very solid struck the thick wooden stump directly above them. Their bodies went rigid. Another "THUMP!" And yet another -- this time a softer and more muffled sound. Something was falling on, and all around, their hiding place...something like the large stones in the bottom of Rocky Creek! Was it possible that the wind moved so strongly that it was picking up rocks from the bed of the stream?

The battering continued for a very long time. At least it seemed that way to them; not only because the clamor and darkness were so frightening but because they didn't understand what was happening. Ephran knew full well that time passed very slowly indeed when you were frightened. This was most certainly one of those occasions. They lay very still, Kaahli with her eyes tightly closed, Ephran's gaze directed to the roof above them, hoping the old knarled roots were as tough as they looked. Neither of them would have been able to count their own heartbeat, and both wished, for all the world, that they were curled in their warm nest by The Pond.

Then, almost as suddenly as it started, the furor stopped. The clatter of stones against wood and earth was gone, and gusty air fell still. Droplets of water began to fall. Ephran rose slowly to his feet. He stood for a bit, then crawled toward the hole through which they'd entered. She could see him put his head outside and, almost as though he'd been pulled out by the ears, his body and tail disappeared.

"Ephran!" she gasped.

He didn't answer for a long minute, but then he called back, "Kaahli, come out here!"

She was none too sure about the wisdom of poking around in the woods so soon after something so dangerous had nearly caught them in the open. Father had taught her that one should stay in the nest until it was safe.

"Wait until your heart slows," he'd said, "and then, count as high as you can...and wait some more."

"But how much more, father?" Kaahli asked.

"What will certainly seem a very long while, my dear. You cannot be assured that the enemy is gone. You must be more patient than the hunter. Use your ears to listen for any sound that does not belong to the woods."

It hadn't been quiet long enough for her to feel really safe, but Kaahli heard no threatening sounds now -- only the gentle patter of water on leaves and grass. Besides, Ephran was out there, and it was his voice that told her to come. She poked her head out. All around the ground was strewn with leaves, twigs, and a few larger branches. That part was no surprise. But there was something else.

Laying everywhere were translucent stones -- stones of different sizes, many of them nearly half the size of her head. Most were rounded but some had rough edges. They glittered, wet and dim, in the cloudfiltered light. Ephran bent his head and licked one of them with his tongue.

"What in the name of spruce leaves are you doing, Ephran?" cried Kaahli, thinking he was planning to eat the rock.

"Why...these aren't stones at all," he said, with a lopsided smile on his face.

"What are they then?"

"They're turning to water, right in front of our eyes," said Ephran. "Very cold water. These stones are of the same stuff that covers The Pond during the cold season. They are ice."

"Where did they come from?"

"From the sky," he said, "there's nowhere else. They must have come from the sky, just like snow."

"Really?...," she said, and tried to look up against the falling drops.

She pulled herself out of the tunnel. A bit hesitantly she put her tongue to one of the stones. It was cold, just as he said, and it was wet. She walked slowly along, watching in wonderment as the smaller stones exuded tiny droplets of crystal-clear water as they shrunk.

The bushy end of a big bough, still green with new leaves, lay in her path where it had fallen. Something was partially hidden, something that looked like an especially large gray-colored stone was sheltered under the limb. Kaahli moved closer...

Ephran was carefully examining the stump and the cavern beneath. He'd know what to look for next time a storm descended on them. Wouldn't it be a fine thing if he could find such a shelter near The Pond? Maybe...maybe one could be dug. After all, some animal had made this one. If another animal could do this, so could he. Nothing wrong with his paws. No doubt of one thing; that rascal Klestra was clever. And the next time he saw Rennigan, he would have to tell him of this too.

"Ohhh, dear..."

The half cry, half gasp, startled him. It came from behind the fallen limb and he recognized Kaahli's voice. Unable to see her, his heart nearly stopped in fright. He jumped from the stump and, fighting panic once more, raced to the far side of the branch.

She was standing alone, staring at the earth in front of her. He drew near, saw she wasn't hurt or threatened, and his eyes followed hers to the ground. There, laying near the remnants of a shattered nest made of twigs and small leaves, was a mourning dove. It was twisted in an uncomfortable-looking position, right wing spread on the wet grass, head turned to the left, eyes closed. Gray and white feathers were in disarray. Kaahli walked slowly to the dove and nuzzled it, as though hoping it might awaken. The bird rolled on its side and lay very still.

How did this happen? The sky provided sunshine and water. Its warmth and moisture was food to the grasses, to the bushes, and to the trees. The sky lay down a protective blanket of snow so that bitter air would not sink to the roots of the trees and bushes -- so that they might wake again in the warm season. Even when intimidating noise and bright light came from the sky, it had never seemed to mean harm to the birds or animals who nested here.

For the first time the squirrels realized that air could be taken from them forever, suddenly and violently, and that the taker could be other than hunters or ripeness of age.

Finally, after it was obvious that the bird was not going to move, Ephran said, "The dove breathes no more. There's nothing to do. Let us go now."

"They're such gentle creatures," said Kaahli, still watching the bird as though she hoped it might get to its feet, smooth its feathers, fly to a low branch, and sing the melancholy song she loved so dearly.

"Yes....," said Ephran slowly. Kaahli searched his face as he looked at the bird one last time. "It seems it couldn't make its own luck."

CHAPTER XVI

DENS OF THE MANY COLORED ONES

phran and Kaahli did not relish the idea of wet fur. Besides, though this was a gentle rain, the water was cold. So they crawled under a large new-fallen branch where thick leaves formed a canopy over them. Droplets of water trickled away and into the soggy earth.

They did not even discuss the possibility of returning to the tunnel beneath the stump. Holes in the ground were for moles and woodchucks and the like. It wasn't really a fitting place for squirrels -- except, of course, in an emergency. And even though the air had become quiet, neither of them felt especially enthusiastic about the idea of climbing back into the branches...not while these particular black clouds still scuttled along above the forest.

The soothing sound of rain pattering on grass and leaves lulled a bone-weary Kaahli to sleep so quickly that Ephran had to lean close to be sure she was breathing. He lay down beside her and, even though his lids were as heavy as hers, he did not let them close. He watched for any movement in the woods. He listened for sounds that did not belong. He'd learned that sleeping on the earth was just plain dangerous. If she wasn't exhausted he would not have allowed it.

Kaahli woke up just as the rain stopped. The surprised and frightened look left her face when she saw him and remembered where they were. "Oh, Ephran, I was so tired," she said with a deep sigh. "I'm sorry that I fell asleep and that you had to keep watch for me."

"No need to apologize. You badly needed that sleep," said Ephran. "But now we must move on. Clouds still cover the sun, and darkness will be here soon."

Kaahli stretched and got to her paws. "Yes," she said, "I'm ready to go. Let's find a place to spend the night."

The clouds were a lighter shade of gray than they had been. Nevertheless, Ephran and Kaahli found themselves glancing at the sky as they climbed into the low branches. Around a curve in Rocky Creek a number of trees lay flat on the ground, roots hanging in the air like huge white worms dragged from their deepearth homes. In the tangled grass they found an entire family of robins, along with a raccoon and a chipmunk who hadn't found shelter from the sky stones in time. There was nothing to be done for them.

"How terrible, Ephran!" said Kaahli.

"Yes. If you hadn't taken your little swim and then had to stop and eat, we would have been right about here when the storm struck. I doubt very much that I would have been able to find a shelter here like the one that saved us."

"Sometimes luck comes wrapped in strange fur," she said quietly.

They came across a small bush laden with green berries and protected by the overhanging branches of a twisted basswood tree. The berries were a tad bitter but neither of them commented about it. A lot of what they were thinking ran in the same vein. The Grand Search for Kaahli's family had gotten off to anything but a promising start. What had begun with high hopes had hit some impressive bumps. They'd already had plenty of bad moments, one that Ephran still didn't even suspect. Most squirrels would have headed back to their own familiar dens by this time. What would happen next?

As day's light faded they found a broken tree, riddled with many holes and without leaves. The long trunk leaned, with a sort of tattered grief, toward a healthy neighbor. The inside core was soft and rotted. It was warm and dry though, and just large enough for the two of them. Stomachs full of green berries, legs sore and aching, heads tired of worrying and wondering, the weary travelers fell asleep immediately.

Morning dawned clear and cool. Ephran and Kaahli awoke with renewed enthusiasm. After a moment or two to stretch and loosen cramped muscles, they scampered off to find something to eat.

The thought of consecutive meals of green berries did not appeal. After a good deal of poking around Kaahli found a cache of nuts, many of which were spoiled. Enough of them were edible to satisfy them for a while -- at least until the sun rose high above the trees.

Once again they set out along Rocky Creek, following its undulating course, stopping now and again to admire the beauty around them. Across the stream, from a field of tall grass and scattered blue flowers, a yellowbreasted meadowlark warbled happily. Ephran tried to imitate the bird, but all that came from his mouth was a pathetic half-whistle. Kaahli laughed. Then her happy expression turned quizzical. She studied the creek and frowned at the field. Slowly, just as the light of a new day rounds the edge of the earth, a glimmer of recognition appeared in her eyes.

"I know this place! We're very near Spruce Hill, Ephran. I remember this little grassy field. My nest is just ahead -- around the next bend and back in the woods."

"Well, I suppose I'll have to see this fancy nest," he said with a grim smile. "I've been dreading this. I'll be put to shame by how much better built it is than mine -- or at least how much better than mine was before you rebuilt it. Lead on."

She giggled and ran off, Ephran following. The soft babbling of the stream faded. They had run only a short distance when she stopped and pointed. Ahead, directly in their path, in the high green boughs of a straight and tall ash tree, was a brown nest.

"Oh, Ephran," she said, "that's my nest! The nest I built. It seems so long ago..."

"It looks very comfortable," he observed.

She drew her breath in quickly. "Do you think that my father and brother might have found it? Do you think they might be inside?"

"Please, Kaahli, don't expect too much..."

"But they could have. They could have come looking for me. Don't you see? It is possible."

She chattered happily as they ran through the trees toward her nest. It was indeed a fine and sturdy structure. For a moment Ephran felt that she might get her wish. He almost expected a treeclimber to pop out through the leaves and twigs. However, the nest was empty -- and evidently had been since Kaahli left. The sparkle faded from her smile.

"Try not to be disappointed," said Ephran. "It would be an amazing coincidence if your father and brother had found the nest you built and then settled into it. Remember, they have no idea where you disappeared to. They might very well be searching for you just as we're searching for them. This was only to be our starting point, you know."

Kaahli's lips were pressed tightly together and she gazed off through the trees. When she turned toward him her chin was steady. "That's true, my mate," she said. "This is where we begin. We'll start looking for father and Laslum from right here."

Now came the part Ephran dreaded. "Start looking" indeed! Looking where? He'd hoped that some clues would show up before they got this far, but none had appeared. How would they start? Which direction would they go? They could pass within two treelengths of another squirrel and never know it was there. The whole illusion, built from bits of hope and shreds of chance, was about to collapse. If he didn't tell her that he didn't know how to start -- right now -- she'd figure it out for herself very soon.

While he struggled with how to break the news that her "hero" was lost and fresh out of ideas, Kaahli set out through the trees as though her destination was precisely in mind. His relief was so great that he asked no questions. He was content to follow through the branches as the sun climbed higher and higher behind them.

Soon they found themselves along the fringe of a great meadow. A few oak stood here and there in the grassy field, twisted limbs stretched to the sky. But there were no bushes at all, and the grass was thick and unusually short. At first that puzzled Ephran. Then he saw why the grass was so short: The kind of thorny vine he and father had inspected near the old nest was barely visible, strung from tree to tree, at the edge of the woods. And far off across the meadow he could see a number of cows, some laying in the shade of a broad oak, some grazing on tender green shoots.

As far as he knew cows were not particularly intelligent or interesting creatures, but they were harmless and gentle. The only thing

Ephran did not like about cows was that they meant, sooner or later, Many Colored Ones would appear nearby.

"Ephran!" Kaahli called excitedly.

He thought she'd never seen cows and was going to ask him about them so he said, "They're just cows, Kaahli. Playthings for The Many Colored Ones."

"I know of them," said Kaahli. "Look beyond."

He squinted. In the distance, barely visible around the border of a large grouping of trees, were the dens he knew would be closeby. Dens of The Many Colored Ones.

"What shall we do?" Her voice was unsteady.

"I was taught to avoid these kinds of dens. We'll find a way around them," Ephran said, and he turned back, facing the direction from which they'd come.

"Wait!" said Kaahli. "Didn't you tell me that when you were searching for your family that you came upon a Den of Many Colored Ones?"

"Well...yes, I did," he said as he sat back again. "But I didn't see any of Them. Just a cat..."

"Which frightened you..."

"Yes, it frightened me."

"And then, after you escaped the cat, you ran back the way you came."

"Of course. I had come to the end of the woods."

"What you thought was the end of the woods," she corrected.

"Yes, that's true. Marshflower says there is a great deal to see beyond our woods."

"You didn't search around that place...what you thought was the end of things?"

"Well, no, I didn't. There seemed no point. There was no sign of my family..."

"Ephran, I think we should go closer."

She'd made up her mind. That was clear. Though she was still afraid, there was something else. More than hope. More than guesswork.

"Before we go on, I must ask: Why did you choose this path when we left your nest on Spruce Hill?" Ephran watched her closely.

She hesitated. "I'm not sure," she said, "why I ran in this particular direction. I think I came this way before -- when I looked for father and Laslum the first time. That den of The Many Colored Ones looks familiar." She paused again. "Why do you ask?"

"I guess because I was so amazed when you set off... especially after you seemed so unsure of what to do only a moment earlier. By the way, did you avoid these dens the last time you came this way?"

"Yes," Kaahli answered, "I stayed far away."

Ephran gazed at the buildings for a long minute. Then he said, "I quit and ran away when I was looking for my family. I was afraid of the dens belonging to these strange Ones. I don't know whether it's a mistake or not, but I feel you're right, Kaahli. We have to go closer."

"Thank you, Ephran."

Ever so carefully they picked their way through the limbs, moving ever nearer to the massive wooden structures that loomed forebodingly in their path.

"There are many trees which grow nuts here," observed Kaahli in a soft voice.

"Yes," agreed Ephran, "and there are signs of squirrels."

Shells from various kinds of nuts, along with remnants of corn cobs, lay scattered here and there on the forest floor. Ephran and Kaahli did not take time to inspect the debris and they saw no treeclimbers in the branches. It would not be wise to chatter or call out -- not so near a place like this.

The largest of the dens was fiery red in color, like sumac bushes just before the cold season. The top was a slanted patch of weathered wooden slabs, one overlapping the next. Three sharp sticks perched along a crest that formed the highest ridge, one at each end and one in the middle, all pointing to the sky. A few holes had been cut into the side facing the squirrels, looking as black as mud from the bottom of The Pond. Two large holes, one above the other, could be seen at the far end. Above the upper hole, perched the likeness of a bird, about the size and form of a pheasant. When seen on end the bird nearly disappeared, becoming a line as thin as whipgrass. It seemed to rotate slowly, pointing its beak into the gently moving air. Astounding!

Standing near the lower hole, at ground level, and surrounded by thick branches stuck into the earth, were three immense animals. They looked a bit like large cows, but more graceful, perhaps some sort of unusually sturdy deer.

Neither Ephran or Kaahli had ever been so close. Neither of them had ever had the time to really study a farmsite. It was mind boggling! There were all sorts of new and fascinating things to look at...and think about...and talk over, but the nearness of Many Colored Ones set curiosity wrestling with fear inside their chests. Perhaps there would be another time.

What was really important now, and they best not forget it, was gray squirrels. If there were any treeclimbers about -- to be seen, or heard, or even smelled, they must be found. Even if they were not Kaahli's family, they might have clues. Conversation with them might be of value.

A short distance from the large den was a much smaller one. It was yellow, like the blossoms of the water lilies on The Pond. It had many black squares, on all sides, and Ephran felt sure that this must be the nest of The Many Colored Ones Themselves.

Then his attention was diverted from the den, for around its corner came two of the curious animals that walked on their back legs. Ephran and Kaahli, hidden in the leaves, sat perfectly still. They were struck with wonder at this sight, mission temporarily forgotten.

These were small for their kind. Either stunted adults or, more likely, young Ones. One had a pelt the color of bright cloudless sky. It hung loosely around the hindquarters. Bird-like legs poked out from the bottom, very white and skinny legs. Furless and featherless. Its paws, at least the ones It walked on, were totally black and unnaturally smooth and shiny. The front paws, swinging at the creature's sides, were small, slender and seemingly useless. Each had five long toes.

The Other, a bit larger and heftier, had red forequarters. Rear feet and hindquarters were brown. Their name would lead one to expect Them to vary in hue but the difference in these two animals was more than just color. While One's pelt was ill-fitting and flapped about its legs, this One's hugged the legs -- all the way down to the rear paws.

The small Ones ran toward a grove of trees, standing between the yellow den and where the squirrels hid in the leaves. The trees were too small to hold any nest except those of tiny birds. And they were not the kind that bore nuts. However, most animals of the forest knew of this tree. They grew a large and wonderfully sweet fruit, sometimes red in color, sometimes yellow. They were a wonderful delicacy for a short time at the end of the warm season. Unfortunately, the old ones said that this treat always grew near the dens of The Many Colored Ones.

In the shade of the little trees lay what appeared to be a long miniature den built of wood. There was no doubt that it was the center of the small Ones' attention. Shaped somewhat like their big dens, this one had no black squares in the sides. What could it be? Why did the small Ones seem so interested in it? It was far too small for Them to crawl into.

Both creatures, red and blue, loose-pelted and tight, crouched near the thing and, from where Ephran was, appeared to be loosening its top. The entire time Ephran and Kaahli had watched, The small Ones had kept up a steady chatter, apparently communicating with one another. The sounds coming from their mouths had varied in pitch and volume, but now became soft and crooning. Above the sounds of their voices Kaahli thought she heard another sound. She leaned forward.

"Ephran," she gasped, "my dream!"

He heard it too. It was squirrels.

Squirrels calling for help.

Calling from a hollow place.

CHAPTER XVII

ESCAPE

It was almost a certainty that the calls were coming from beneath the trees. But, with those smaller Ones right there...

Before Ephran and Kaahli could even begin to ponder their options, a third Many Colored One appeared, just as the other two had, from behind the yellow den. This One was much larger than the two under the trees, but its pelt was similar in appearance to the One with the white twiglike legs. It chattered with harsh, insistent cries and twirled a big silver stick with a rounded end. Though the sounds were not intelligible, the scene was not totally unfamiliar...this larger creature had to be a mother -- a mother calling her young back to their nest.

The small Ones made a half-hearted protest, but rose from crouching positions and ran after their mother. All three disappeared behind the yellow den. Shrill voices faded and there was a muffled thump of wood slamming against wood. Then, except for the shrill call of a bluejay, the grove was quiet.

Ephran glanced at Kaahli. Her attention was riveted on the small wooden structure beneath the trees, barely visible through the leaves.

"Kaahli," he whispered, "you stay here. I'll move closer and try to find where the sound came from."

"I want to go along," she whispered back.

"Aren't you frightened?" he asked.

"Yes. Very much."

She smiled and he smiled back. He jumped to a yellow birch. She followed. The trees became few and far between. Soon they had to leave the safety of the branches. Fortunately, it was a short run to the fruit trees. Still, it was terrifying to have their paws on the earth while the smell of Many Colored Ones hung thick around them. They crept closer and closer, stopping and listening every few steps, trying to keep tree trunks between themselves and the big yellow den.

There were no sounds now. Had they been mistaken about what they'd heard -- or what they thought they'd heard? Had there really been cries coming from this spot? Or had their ears fooled them? Could the sound have come from some strange toy of the Many Colored Ones?

Kaahli was still mesmerized by the tiny den-like structure beneath the trees, which Ephran could now see sat on four wooden legs.

"My mate," he hissed, "stay on this side, away from the yellow place. I'll take one quick look. If there is something dangerous in there I will chatter. Run back to the trees then. I'll be right behind you."

The earth was uneven and, either because of that, or because one of the legs was shorter than the others, the den stood slightly askew.

Ephran ran up the trunk of the nearest fruit tree, far enough so that he could look down onto it. He stopped there, mouth open.

"What is it, Ephran?" Kaahli whispered loudly.

He swallowed. "Come here," he said. "Quickly!"

For an instant she wavered, her mind rebelling against this madness, this intrusion into a dangerous world that she should have no part of. But she gritted her teeth and put the paralyzing fear aside. Scampering to Ephran's side, she looked down -- and nearly swooned. Looking back up, from inside the nest of wood, were two gray squirrels. Thinner than she remembered but...

"Father! Laslum!" she cried.

"Kaahli, is that really you?"

"Oh father...!"

"Shhh," said Ephran. "Time for talk later. We must free them."

"'Free us'?" said the younger gray, with a giddy laugh. "Do you hear that, father? He's going to free us. Tell us, how are you going to do that? Are you going to beat the wood apart with your bushy tail? Are you going to melt it with your bright eyes?"

"Quiet, Laslum!" ordered father. "We have help at last. Now is a time to think and act, not talk nonsense."

Laslum shrunk into a corner, gazing up at his sister and the strange squirrel, his whole body shaking.

"I can see you clearly. Are you too weak to climb out?" asked Kaahli.

"Ah," said father, "my dear daughter, you can see us just as we can see you, but between our eyes is the strongest web of the spider I have known. It is not thick, and it does not stick to our paws, but both Laslum and I have nearly broken our teeth trying to gnaw through it."

Ephran glanced nervously toward the yellow den. Might Those inside have heard or seen the treeclimbers? There was no sound or movement from that direction. Not yet.

"Have you tried chewing through the bottom -- or the sides?" he asked as he looked back down at them.

"Yes," said the older squirrel, "we have tried. But the inside is lined with the same hard webbing you see over the top."

"Oh, Ephran!"

Kaahli looked at her mate with such sadness that he could not speak. He knew what she felt. To come all this way, to be next to those she loved so dearly and sought so intently, only to be denied within touching distance -- by some sort of spider web! It was unthinkable. He must look closer. He must think of something. She expected it.

Kaahli gasped as he jumped from the tree. It appeared that he would fall right into the same prison that held her father and brother. However, his body landed with a soft thump, as though he'd struck an invisible barrier. He tried to stand, but one leg slipped through a hole in the webbing. He regained his balance and seemed to be standing above the captives on thin air. The web was very strong indeed.

"Brave stranger, who are you?" asked Kaahli's father.

"I am the mate of your daughter. I'm called Ephran."

"Ah, her mate! I see. I am Aden. I am grateful that you accompanied Kaahli to find her family."

"He did more than that," said Kaahli. "He suggested the search. He said we would look until we found you."

"If he is as clever as he is brave I think I may give my approval to this union," said Aden.

Ephran wasn't embarrassed by Aden's words because he didn't hear them. He was too busy studying the thin strands supporting his weight, trying to find a way through or around it.

"What is this thing you find yourselves in called?" he asked.

"It is called a cage," replied Aden. "Not the first I've seen. It is a place to hold animals. Sometimes birds. A place from which we cannot escape, a thing only They can open."

Kaahli hissed. "How terrible! Why would They do this? What do They want of you?"

"I have no idea."

"I see what this web really is," interrupted Ephran. "The Many Colored Ones have other uses for this sort of thing. I've seen vines like this, thicker and with thorns, used to keep cows in one place. This vine They've woven together like the spider weaves her web."

"Can it be broken?" Laslum's voice quavered.

"I think not. My father said that his father told him that only water, and sun, and the passage of many seasons will cause it to weaken...," said Ephran slowly as he moved along one edge of the cage, looking for a fault in the weaving, a flaw large enough for a squirrel to pass through.

His heart grew cold. There was no flaw. And the shiny webbing was fastened securely to the wooden frame with tiny sticks made of the same material as the webbing itself. They were all watching him. He had to come up with another idea.

"You must get me out of here," cried Laslum in a distraught voice. "You said you would free us." Terror glistened in his eyes.

Then, as Ephran reached the far corner, the top of the cage tilted beneath him. He quickly scrambled backward a few steps and his roost stabilized. Now he understood that the hard webbing, in addition to lining the entire inside of the cage, had been fitted to a wooden frame that conformed to the top. It was this covering that Ephran and Kaahli had seen the small Many Colored Ones loosening.

In their hurry to answer the call of the large One, They had failed to put the lid firmly back in place. He saw, at the far side, that the frame was definitely displaced toward the end he was standing on. An idea came to him as abruptly as a bumblebee appears at the mouth of a wild rose.

Laslum had begun to weep. Things looked hopeless. The Many Colored Ones would surely be back soon. Aden put his front leg over his son's shoulder and Kaahli whispered over and over; "Don't fret, Laslum. Ephran is here. Don't fret, Laslum. Ephran will think of something..."

"Kaahli," Ephran called quietly, "come over here. I need your help."

She had no idea what he was thinking, but this was not the time for questions. Kaahli jumped onto the cage with Ephran and immediately righted herself on the fine strands.

"Follow me," he said.

He walked carefully to one corner of the lid -- the corner that overhung the edge of the cage. Kaahli watched him from the far side of the heavy cover and, as she moved toward him it began to tilt -- just a tiny bit. A smile came to her lips. However, as she got closer to him, their grins faded. The cover did not budge again. He had hoped that her weight, along with his, would cause it to tip, opening up the far side, but it remained firmly wedged along the edge where it contacted the sides.

They stood together, Aden and Laslum gazing intently up at them, they staring at their paws. Ephran sighed deeply. He was fresh out of ideas again.

Suddenly Kaahli's head came up.

"Jump!" she cried.

"What?"

"Jump! With me!"

"Yes. Of course."

He followed her example and jumped straight up.

Nothing happened.

They jumped again, this time together. Their strong rear legs threw them high in the air and they landed solidly on the overhanging lid. It tilted. Then it slid; ever so little at first. Then it slid a bit more. With an especially well-timed and very high jump it slipped and lurched the full width of a treeclimber's tail.

Aden and Laslum did not need to be told what to do. The caged squirrels stood at the far end of their prison and waited for it to open. When the gap between the lid and the side of the cage was wide enough they scrambled up the mesh and over the side.

Just as Ephran and Kaahli jumped to the ground, the small Many Colored Ones appeared around the corner of their den. They strolled along at first, sucking with thin and fragile lips at something They held in their bare front paws. When They saw the empty cage with the top tilted upward at one end, and four squirrels on the ground, They dropped whatever They'd been eating, and began to shout and wave frantically.

"Run!" cried Ephran. "To the tall trees!"

"Run!" cried Ephran, "to the tall trees!"

Aden and Laslum were weak after many days in the cage. To Kaahli it seemed like another bad dream: Neither of them could move fast enough. The Many Colored Ones were now running -- and gaining. She could hear their heavy paws thud against the earth. She thought she could feel the ground shake. She looked over at Ephran, who ran next to her, urging her brother and father along.

At last they reached the border of the woods. Laslum was winded but he and Aden climbed into the lower branches of a stately maple tree, Ephran and Kaahli right behind.

Ephran turned and looked down at the two smudged and furless faces turned up toward him. Both mouths were open, bellowing wild sounds. Their eyes faced directly forward. They would have trouble seeing what was happening off to their side. Small paws with tiny nails grasped at the tree trunk ineffectually. Funny looking animals, he thought. If They weren't so menacing, they'd be downright entertaining.

The One with brown legs tried to clamber up the tree, legs slipping and sliding on the smooth trunk. Ephran nearly laughed aloud. This Many Colored One was a very slow and poor climber, if It could climb at all. Ephran felt almost sorry for these hapless and disappointed creatures. Almost...

Other eyes watched the futile chase. Other ears heard the frustrated howls. From the roof of the nearby red barn three pigeons looked on, barely able to sit still. They desperately wanted to relate this amazing event to the other residents of the barn, but they didn't want to leave too early. They wanted to be certain that the usual winners did indeed turn out to be losers.

Another pair of eyes, peering through the leaves of a speckled alder bush, took note of the proceedings. It was a fox, far from his usual haunts. Up to this point in his travels he had seen no one he recognized, but this strange scene was carefully recorded and stored in his memory. It was a long way home. He would have time to mull over what he'd seen, including the one familiar face among the treeclimbers.

Ephran and Kaahli's scouting of the woods, when they passed this way earlier, was rewarded. They were able to steer the hungry ex-prisoners toward budding bushes in the shade of a thick oak. The Many Colored Ones did not attempt to follow. It would not have been possible even if They'd tried. The escape route through the leaves was nearly invisible from the ground.

The squirrels stopped to rest and eat in an open place where they could watch the woods and the nearby meadow. It was an extra precaution; these particular Many Colored Ones would be easy to hear long before They'd be seen. As they ate, they talked, and every now and then Kaahli snuggled her nose into Aden or Laslum's neck.

"How did you ever find us?" asked Laslum.

"With luck, I think," she said. "We simply came back to where I

110

built my nest at Spruce Hill and set out from there. We happened to set out in the right direction."

"I don't know that taking the right path was entirely an accident," said Ephran. "I think Kaahli knew, deep down inside, that if her father and brother were still able to run in the trees they would come to find her. Since they did not, they'd either have come to a bad end or...they would have to be trapped by someone who might not take their breath from them. That would certainly not be the fox, or the owl, or the hawk. I think she knew that the only chance to find you was near the den of the unpredictable Many Colored Ones."

"We owe you a great deal, my daughter," said Aden as he picked up his fifth green bud, "and your mate as well."

"Yes," agreed Laslum, "and he has an apology coming. I didn't mean to act so foolish when I first met you -- when you said you'd free us. It was just that father and I had been trying for so long to get out of that...that... place, that I didn't think you'd have a chance. But you did it. And I feel both thankful and ashamed."

"No need to be ashamed, Laslum. I understand. Even if I've never been closed in." Ephran paused. "I've not seen a thing like that -- the den you called a cage. What is it? And how did you come to be in it?"

Laslum looked over to his father and Aden said, "Well, Ephran, I came to know of cages a long while ago. When I was young I lived closer than I care to remember to a place where Many Colored Ones had cages. They kept a dog in a cage, and chickens, and rabbits. Cages are something like the vines that keep cows in one place. Cages are to keep animals in even smaller places."

"But why?" asked Kaahli.

"I cannot answer that," said Aden.

"Then how?" asked Ephran. "If you cannot tell why, tell me how creatures of the branches, of the deep woods, got trapped in a cage."

"My fault," said Laslum.

"It wasn't really anyone's fault," said Aden. "Laslum was tempted by corn. Not the first or last time for that to happen to a squirrel."

Ephran nodded. He'd not disagree with that statement.

"I saw him sniffing at a yellow stick. Before I could so much as shout to warn him, the whole pile of corn, along with the wood it was stacked on, came tumbling down. Laslum was hit in the head, nearly buried. He was stunned and confused and unable to get to his paws. The Many Colored Ones came. I ran off a short distance and watched from a tree while They put him in a cage."

"I was in that tiny place for such a very long time," said Laslum, with a tremulous voice.

"Anyway," continued Aden, "the only time I could get near

Laslum was when darkness came and even that was dangerous because an owl nests nearby. I tried and tried to solve the puzzle of that cage but to no avail."

"Until today," said Kaahli.

"Yes," nodded her father, "until today."

"And what of you, my little one?" asked Aden. "Where did you go when we did not return?"

"Oh, father, I searched so long! But I couldn't find you anywhere. Not a trace. I finally moved away and built a nest near Spruce Hill."

"I didn't mean to abandon you," said Aden with a tight look on his face. "After Laslum had been in the cage a few days I told him that I must find you and bring you to nest nearby with me. I finally decided that The Many Colored Ones must not mean to take his breath away -- at least They seemed in no hurry to do so. I felt that, sooner or later, you and I together would be able to free your brother."

"Oh, father..."

"I was nearly crazy with worry -- about both my young. It didn't help to return to the nest and not find you there."

"I must have been looking for you about that time..."

"I suppose. I, of course, had no idea if you'd left on your own or if you had been taken by a hunter. Since I couldn't find you I came back to Laslum."

"I understand," said Kaahli. "I knew you wouldn't leave me. I was afraid that something terrible must have happened, so I set out to find you. I should have stayed near the nest."

"Well," smiled Aden, with a wink at Ephran, "it seems you found something worthwhile on your travels."

Ephran changed the subject. "Were The Many Colored Ones cruel to you?" he asked Laslum.

"If you mean such as with sticks or rocks, the answer is no," said Laslum, wiping juice from his nose with a paw, "but They did other things, unusual things. As father said, I was stunned when a large piece of wood, along with the corn, fell on me. I got a cut near my ear. When I woke up They were putting water on my head. I scratched and made Them stop." He sighed and searched for another plump bud. "I think the worst thing They did, though, was to keep us from climbing into the branches. They wouldn't let us out of that cage."

Ephran cocked his head. "Did They take you into their dens?"

"No, thank sun and water," shivered Laslum. "We were always left out in the open air...where we could see the trees, and long for them."

After a pause, while they all ate quietly, Ephran said, "Things are pretty clear. There is one more question I must ask, though. I think Kaahli has the same question."

Kaahli glanced at him and nodded. "Yes, father," she said, "We know how Laslum ended up in the cage. But how did you come to be with him?"

Aden looked at Laslum. "I let myself be caught."

Ephran and Kaahli's mouths dropped open in unison.

"I had to do it, you see. My son needed me. When I came back, after being unable to find you, Laslum was not well. He would not eat. I let Them capture me. They were very cooperative."

Ephran shook his head and said, "Now I understand why my mate is brave and thoughtful."

"Son," the older squirrel said to Ephran, "you and I are going to get along just fine unless one of us falls from a high branch while admiring the way the other jumps. Now -- how about a bit of sleep? Tomorrow we must search for a new home."

The night was gentle and they found leafy branches on which to spend the dark hours. Ephran and Kaahli could hear Aden talking to Laslum in a nearby tree. Ephran didn't close his eyes right away. Listening to the soft sounds of the dark and slumbering forest and to her regular breathing gave him a happy feeling he'd not had for a long while. Since they'd first been together he'd not known her to sleep so peacefully. He said a silent goodnight to his parents -- and to Mianta and Phetra, wherever they might be. Then he laid his head between his paws.

CHAPTER XVIII

WARNING FROM HIGH HILL

Ephran awoke before the others. He watched as the stars grew dim and the sun peeped over the far brim of the world. Shafts of golden light swept silently through the trees.

Kaahli slept in a hollowed out place between two big limbs. Aden and Laslum, curled on thick branches in a nearby tree, were barely visible. Ephran hoped they had all slept well. Although they could remain here -- there was plenty of food -- Aden and Laslum wanted to find a new den. Besides, this part of the woods was not a place of pleasant memories.

"Good morning, Ephran," Kaahli smiled up at him, eyes half closed.

"A good morning it is, Kaahli. I hope you are rested. I've never seen you sleep more soundly."

"You two awake over there?" Aden shouted.

"Yes we are, sir," Ephran shouted back.

"Time to find food then. Laslum is hungry."

Finding morning food was an easy task. Though too early in the warm season for fresh nuts, there were plenty of preserved ones. And beneath the bigger trees grew a multitude of bushes laden with buds and seeds. They found a cool and comfortable spot to have their meal, where the trees bordered an open meadow and where the pure newday air, rolling over grass sparkling with dew, filled their noses.

Kaahli bounced around Aden and Laslum; talking, teasing, laughing, and bringing them food. "How do you feel, father?" she asked, as she settled down into a clump of grass and began to clean her fur.

"Surprisingly well, considering all things," said Aden. He turned toward his son. "What about you, Laslum? You spent the most time in that cage."

"I feel pretty weak yet," replied Laslum slowly. "I can tell you all that I won't ever take running in the trees for granted again."

They all nodded.

"Sir, had you any plans in which direction you wanted to search for a new den?" Ephran asked Aden.

"Not really. I suppose you are anxious to get home, aren't you?"

"Actually, I'm in no hurry. We still have time before the cold season settles in and I don't think we are far from what I once thought was the end of the woods...a place I hoped I would find my family. Now that we've reunited Kaahli with her family, perhaps I should try once more to find mine."

"You lost your family?" Aden looked at Kaahli.

"Oh, Great Gray Goodness!" exclaimed Kaahli, a look of

absolute horror on her face. "How selfish can one treeclimber be? Here I gloat over finding my loved ones...and forget that the one who brought me to them, who has stood by me and protected me, who has loved and fed me -- has the same hurt in his heart that he has just helped remove from mine. Ephran, can you forgive me?" She rushed to him and threw her front paws around his neck.

"I had no idea...," mumbled Laslum.

"No need to feel badly," said Ephran, as he patted Kaahli on her back, "It's just that right here we should be close to where I quit searching last cold season. At least we're a lot closer than we were when we left The Pond."

"How would you know which way to go -- if you haven't gone from this place to that before? I mean, it sounds impossible," said Laslum, taking a somewhat impolitely large bite from an acorn.

"Well," said Ephran, "before we found you, Kaahli and I traveled a long distance toward where the sun sets. From Great Hill, according to eyewitnesses, my family apparently set out in a direction between where the sun goes behind the woods and from where cold air comes."

"So...?" Aden squinted in Ephran's direction. "You haven't gone that way by this route, have you?"

"No, I haven't, sir. But, since we've come so far in one direction, I would think we shouldn't have far to go in the other."

"I see," said Aden thoughtfully.

"You do?" said Laslum, wrinkling his nose at his father.

Aden scratched his chin and said to Ephran; "You know, son, that makes sense. Never thought of it in quite that fashion. I've not known a treeclimber who would dare predict a path without having been on it before...and use the routes of the sun and the direction of the wind besides. Quite astounding."

"Not really," murmured Ephran.

"Laslum and I will accompany you on this great experiment," said Aden with finality. "If Laslum feels up to it, that is."

"Sounds like a butternut kind of idea to me," agreed Laslum.

"But you want to find a home," protested Ephran. "The path I take may not lead where you wish to go."

"No hurry on that score," said Aden. "As you just said, it's still a long time until the cold season anyway."

"Let's be on our way then!" cried Kaahli. With a graceful leap to a nearby ash, she led them off through the branches.

The little stream below dove over a steep bank and splashed into a larger waterway that ran perpendicular to it. The merry bubbling ceased as the water united with the deeper and slower moving stream and flowed away toward where the sun would rise.

Ephran cocked his head to one side. "This is Rocky Creek," he

116

said. "See? Down there a bit is where Kaahli and I left the water to seek Spruce Hill."

"You're right, Ephran," said Kaahli, "I recognize that yellow bush near the stand of saplings!"

Aden turned upstream. "Well, then...according to your reckoning, Ephran, we'll have to travel the other way, from where the water flows."

Ephran eyed the gently curving watercourse as it meandered off into the dense trees. "That's right, sir. It certainly didn't take you long to understand how to make travel plans."

Laslum hopped from one paw to the other. "If everyone is ready to move on," he said, "my legs are so anxious to be underway that I believe they are thinking of leaving without me."

Travel was easy through the closely placed trees along the banks of Spring Creek. The squirrels chattered back and forth as they followed Aden through stout boughs. They had not gone far when Aden come to a stop so sudden that he swayed on a small branch he had been prepared to jump from.

"Wait!" he called, "...no further."

"What is it, father?" asked Laslum.

"Thorns. Just ahead."

Kaahli and Ephran climbed into the higher branches. What they saw in their path was not actually trees at all, but very large bushes with small green leaves. Stems and limbs were such a dark brown that they appeared black. And so tightly entwined that they formed a nearly impenetrable barrier.

Ephran was close enough to see the thorns. Three times as long as his own claws, they grew from every branch and in all directions. He knew that, as many as he could see, many more were hidden by the leaves. The thorn grove covered a large area. Although big friendly trees, oak and ash, were visible over the tops of the dense cluster, the distance was too great to be spanned by even their massive branches. To his right he could not see the end of the tangled growth and to his left it grew down to the water's edge.

"We cannot go this way," he heard Kaahli whisper to herself.

Behind the thorns loomed a giant mound of earth that might have dwarfed Great Hill, if not in width, certainly in height. Hardwoods towered so far above that he had to tilt his head far back to see their tops. The bluff sloped steeply to the waterway and to the thorns that stood menacingly in the path of the treeclimbers. Between its base and the impassable growth Ephran noticed something he'd not seen at first; a narrow corridor of young elm trees, nearly hidden among flickering patches of cool shade.

"Shall we go back?" asked Laslum. "I don't think I can climb that steep hill."

117

Kaahli glanced at her mate. "The stream is wide here. And the branches on either side do not meet. We may have to go back a long way if we want to cross."

"Yes," agreed Aden, "and then we would have to get back on this side again, later on, if we are to follow Ephran's route. We might have problems if the water gets wider or the trees further apart. What do you think, Ephran?"

"I think we might follow those young elm along the base of the hill. See them there." He pointed the trees out to the others. "We have to come to the end of the thorns sooner or later."

"But what if the elm stop before the thorns?" asked Laslum.

"They might," agreed Ephran.

"But they might not," said Aden with an air of assurance. "We will never know if we don't try." He winked at Ephran. "The worst that can happen is that we'll have to backtrack. Let's get started. The sun nears the treetops."

Their journey, up to this time, had been accompanied by the occasional jabbering of chipmunks on the ground, the songs of thrushes and bluebirds in bushes, and the chirping of crickets from dark and wet places. These sounds, familiar and ordinary as they were, reassured the squirrels that the forest around them was undisturbed. Talking and laughing as they moved along, relieved that the problem with the thorns seemed at least temporarily settled, they failed to notice that the woods around them had become quiet -- much too quiet. The birds and small animals of the forest had taken cover. The silent alarm had been given. It was being ignored.

Then, from somewhere on High Hill came a burst of sharp staccato chattering. In an instant they all became acutely aware of the hushed woods all around them.

"We are being warned!" said Aden, tension showing in the set of his mouth.

"Of what?" asked Kaahli.

"I don't know yet."

Ears strained and eyes searched. They heard it at the same time, breaking the unnatural calm: Heavy paws on old leaves, a large body moving through the underbrush, occasional snapping of dry twigs. Somewhere in front of them, along the narrow path through the trees they'd been following was...something, something big, something out of place, something frightening.

"Father...!" Laslum's eyes grew wide and his body shivered.

"Hush!" hissed Aden. "Steady, my son. I am certain that whatever comes this way doesn't know we are here."

The older squirrel looked at each of them in turn and said, "Quickly now, Laslum; jump to the thick alder next to you. Ephran; come down from that skinny branch unto the wide trunk. Kaahli, stay where you are. Each of you; keep to the side of the tree opposite the noise you hear. Make sure solid wood is between you and whatever approaches. Keep your tail still. With any luck at all none of us will be seen."

Without another word they obeyed him, moving swiftly and quietly to put a thick branch or treetrunk between themselves and the thing that was moving closer and closer along the base of the hill. It moved slowly. Painfully so. It stopped frequently, as though it might be listening. Listening and watching. The woods remained dreadfully quiet. Perhaps the trees themselves waited to see if harm was meant. The air was unmoving, here near the earth beneath High Hill, and would not carry its odor to them. Nor, of course, would their smell be carried to it.

From where he hid, body pressed against bark, Ephran could see Kaahli and Laslum, hugging their own trees. The look on his mate's pretty face was one of concentration -- almost amusement. The expression her brother wore, on the other paw, was definitely not one of amusement. He looked as though he might bolt at any moment.

Ephran caught Laslum's eye, round and dismayed. Trying not to show his own inner fear, he smiled widely at him as though all of this was nothing but an exciting game. Laslum tried, with little success, to smile back. But Ephran was sure the tension in Laslum's muscles relaxed ever so little. He'd be all right, Ephran thought, if this danger would just move quickly past. Aden was hidden from view by a pine tree, but Ephran was not worried about the shrewd old gray.

It was very near now, whatever it was, almost at the base of Ephran's tree. It stopped moving and Ephran listened carefully. It was so close that he could hear it breathing.

Was it a deer? Unlikely, unless crippled, for it made far too much noise coming through the woods. And the sounds had been too regular for an animal who might be, say, dragging a leg. Maybe a bear? Ephran had heard stories of those massive animals, but they must be rare; no one he knew had ever seen one. A cow perhaps? No. What would one of those poor, simple creatures be doing in the middle of the forest?

The thing started moving again...very slowly. The squirrels circled their trees, at the same pace, like the torpid dance of half-awake mud turtles. Finally it moved far enough away so that Ephran felt he could safely steal a peek around the treetrunk.

"As I thought," the others heard him say.

Aden, Kaahli, and Laslum appeared on their trees just as the intruder turned and disappeared behind the dense stand of thorn bushes.

"What is it you thought, my dear?" asked Kaahli, eyes bright with excitement.

"Many Colored One," he replied, still looking in the direction It had vanished. "Another Many Colored One."

"Was It carrying a stick?" asked Aden.

"I couldn't tell. By the time I looked It was hidden by the bushes."

"Ohhh! It won't come back, will It?" Laslum's teeth chattered.

"No, no, Laslum. Don't worry," crooned Kaahli. She moved to the branch her brother had curled on and huddled next to him, a front leg around his quivering shoulders.

"What do you suppose It was doing in the woods?" asked Ephran, as much to himself as to anyone.

Aden answered, "Who knows? You said They are unpredictable, and you were right. Sometimes They come hunting, but their hunting time is just before the cold season, not so soon after."

Laslum lifted his head and pushed Kaahli's paw aside. "Hunting? Hunting for what?"

"I've heard tell They aren't fussy," said Aden with a grim look. "Maybe deer. Or rabbit. Grouse, perhaps..."

"Or a squirrel," Ephran finished.

"Yes," said Aden uncomfortably, "or a squirrel."

Kaahli sensed the subject badly needed changing. "Who warned us of Its coming?"

"Good question," said Aden. "In the excitement I forgot about that. Who, indeed, would risk their own hiding place -- to tell us we were in need of one?"

They all looked up the steep slope, in the direction from which the chattering had come. The trees were too thick and dense to see through, but something was definitely moving toward them through the upper limbs, causing the leaves to wave and tremble on a day of nearly still air. Laslum and Kaahli stayed where they were, sister whispering quietly to brother, while Aden and Ephran went to meet their visitor.

As they approached a twisted oak tree, an old male fox squirrel appeared in its lower boughs. The thin pelt of yellowing fur was familiar. The squirrel squinted at them with one eye.

"Rennigan!" Ephran cried.

"Yep. That's who it be."

"Rennigan...," Ephran nearly choked on the lump in his throat, "it was you who warned us. I might have guessed. Is this where you nest now?"

"Sometimes, young 'un, sometimes."

Aden observed Ephran, who was laughing along with the bedraggled-looking squirrel, and said, "Obviously you know this noble treeclimber."

Before Ephran could answer, Rennigan faced Aden, tilted his head and said, "Nothin' noble about this twigjumper. Name's Rennigan, as ya heard. Met this here whippersnapper early this warm season. Said he was headed fer Great Hill. Me and Ephran spent a bit a time together." He smiled proudly at Ephran. "Well, he musta made it to wherever he ended up."

"Yes, I made it, Rennigan," said Ephran, "I learned to stretch my own legs. Thanks to advice from friends." Nodding to the squirrels behind them he added, "Back there are my mate, Kaahli, and her brother Laslum. This is Kaahli's father, Aden."

"Howdy."

"Hello, Rennigan," said Aden. "I must thank you for warning us of The Many Colored One. I'm amazed that you could see both It and us through the thick leaves."

"Well," said Rennigan, "I heard The Many Colored One comin' from one direction and saw you in th'other. I was up purty high. Much easier to see down 'n 'round trees rather'n straight through 'em, ya know. Anyway, none of you folks was paying any heed to warnings all 'round you."

"I see," said Aden. "Well, it was certainly very nice of you to call to us, as I said, but I doubt it was necessary. Unlikely It would have harmed anyone in any case. It's not their time to hunt, you know."

Rennigan's twinkling eyes held Aden's, his uneven grin displaying a chipped tooth, and said, "Mebbe it's not their time t'hunt. Not so sure this One knew yer rules though. It may not 'a used it, but t'was carryin' a thunderstick. Didn't figure you'd want me to take the chance that It'd play fair."

"Oh...," said Aden.

"Rennigan," said Ephran, "do you realize that you just did something that you told me you weren't very good at?"

"How's thet, son?"

"You said you weren't very good at making luck. I'm of the opinion that you just made me and my companions some luck...some pretty good luck, actually."

"Mebbe I did at that, Ephran, mebbe I did," he chuckled.

CHAPTER XIX

SQUIRREL IN A STUMP

Rennigan traveled a short distance with them, through the elms at the base of the hill. "So yer hopin' that you didn't look close enough the last time, is that th'story?" he asked Ephran. "Yer hopin' ya overlooked a clue to findin' yer family?"

"Something like that, I guess. I know that what I thought then was wrong. I had not reached the end of the woods. Maybe it's wishful thinking -- that father and mother and Mianta and Phetra escaped and are somewhere in the forest. I was hoping that maybe you'd heard or seen something that would help."

"Wish I could say I had," said Rennigan, "but don't spend much time visitin'."

Kaahli said, "You have seen gray squirrels in this part of the woods, haven't you, Mr. Rennigan?"

"Yep. Gray squirrels every here 'n there in the woods. Always was, always will be. I hope." He smiled at her. "Don't help much though. Never really took the time ta git to know any of 'em. 'Cept this here Ephran fella."

As they neared the end of the thorn bushes he said to Ephran, "Been hearin' that you done a few things some treeclimbers might brag about."

"Maybe," Ephran grinned back, "and maybe I've done a few things that I'd just as soon no one heard about too."

"Sounds normal, anaway. Well, this's where I leave ya. The rest a this business is yers." Rennigan winked and said, "Carry on then. Don't give up hope. Hope may be the best of all things ta keep close at paw."

"Rennigan," said Ephran, putting his paw on the old squirrel's shoulder, "thank you for keeping both eyes open today."

"Welcum, son. And you keep pickin' up friends, m'brighteyed longtail. The way yer goin' ya won't have ta make a whole lot of yer own luck."

"I just hope I can muster enough of it to find my family," said Ephran.

They all thanked Rennigan again, said their farewells, and watched the fox squirrel lope off through the trees, following the stream the way they'd come.

"Fascinating character," observed Aden.

"He is that," agreed Ephran.

They watched until he disappeared, leaping from branch to branch, through a swale where the earth sloped away from the thorn trees. Stunted alder poked up here and there from thick tangles of

123

pigweed, cocklebur and poison oak. Small finches, sparrows, and even an occasional wren could be seen, both in the brush and among the thorns. The trees, forbidding to the squirrels, offered a protected nesting place that shrubs with smooth branches could not.

They were about to set out again when Kaahli pointed and said, "Look there!"

Her paw directed their eyes to fat hindquarters and a stringy tail, vanishing into the grass in a thicket of prickly ash trees. No mistaking that kind of bottom; it belonged to a muskrat. If they were patient, the animal would lead them to water. That's where muskrats always ended up. Though squirrels were not really interested in water for drinking, some of the tenderest and sweetest buds grew near streams and ponds. And, as Ephran often said, it was always nice to know where food was.

Kaahli looked at her father and Ephran. "Shall we...?"

"Why not?" agreed Ephran. "He seems to be heading in the general direction we want to go...and my stomach says it's about time to eat again."

Silently they followed, limb to limb, keeping the animal in sight as it scurried through the weeds. Ephran would have liked to chat with the muskrat. Perhaps it would know Fetzgar...or even be related. Muskrats were shy types though, and to try striking up a conversation might only serve to confuse and frighten it.

The muskrat waddled along the ground, stopping here and there to smell at a tree root or poke his nose into a bunch of blue or yellow flowers. Oblivious to the squirrels overhead, humming softly to himself, Mr. Muskrat seemed to be wandering aimlessly, exploring whatever caught his fancy. He knew exactly where he was going though, and the treeclimbers didn't have to wait long before they found themselves on the grassy shore of a lake. The muskrat, still humming, blew a series of musical bubbles as he slid below the surface.

The lake was not a big one as lakes go, but it was at least five times as large as The Pond and, to the squirrels, was a sizeable body of water indeed. Trees grew down to the water's edge and to bunches of bullrushes scattered in the shallows. It was enough like The Pond to make Ephran a bit homesick. As he looked wistfully at sparkling little waves, splashing against the reeds, movement down the shoreline caught his eye.

He saw many brown clumps in the shallow water, most of them the remnants of last season's cattail roots. Some of those clumps, however, seemed to be moving. He squinted against the bright water.

"Kaahli," he said excitedly, "Ducks!"

"Ducks? Where?"

"Down there. In a bay." He pointed with his paw.

"Could they be our mallards?" she wondered.

124

"Your mallards?" From where he rested in a willow tree, Aden had overheard her question.

"Oh, father," Kaahli laughed. "I don't really mean our mallards. A family of mallards lives in The Pond near our home, you see. They're very good friends."

His eyes grew wider. "You are good friends...with ducks?"

"It's a long story, father. Ephran became friends with them. He saved these ducklings from a hawk and...well, the parents were grateful..."

Aden looked at Ephran, mouth open. At first he could only shake his head slowly, from side to side. Finally he muttered, "Saved ducks from a hawk, you say? Are my ears on straight?"

"I'm going to try to attract their attention," Kaahli said, and she chattered as loudly and rapidly as she could.

The ducks grew still. A few uncertain quacks were exchanged. Then three of the big birds jumped straight up out of the water, beating powerful wings. They flew low over the cattails and directly toward the squirrels.

"Cloudchaser!" Ephran shouted.

The ducks made a wide circle over the deeper water and swooped down into the grassy shoal in front of the squirrels. Ephran and Kaahli, smiling with delight, failed to notice the faces of Aden and Laslum. They were totally flabbergasted.

"Ephran! Kaahli! Is it you?" asked a young drake.

"What other treeclimbers would hail ducks?" Cloudchaser replied, laughing and quacking loudly.

"Yes. It's us! And it's so wonderful to see you!" cried Kaahli. "What are you doing so far from home?"

"More than one reason, dear Kaahli," answered Cloudchaser, flapping his wings. "My young need to test their wings you know, and the flight to Little Lake is about the right distance. I told you we fly this way. We have family here too, as you see. It is good to visit them once in a while. Perhaps the most important reason we flew here is in hopes that we might find you along the way."

"Hello, Cloudchaser!" said Ephran, as he ran to the branch Kaahli was on. "Did I hear you say you were looking for us?"

The drake said, "Hello to you, brave hawkfighter! Yes, we have been watching for you. I wanted to give warning before you returned to The Pond."

"Warn us?" Kaahli said with alarm. "Warn us of what?"

Just then the mallards realized that Aden and Laslum were seated on the branch of a nearby tree, incredulous at this conversation between their kin, her mate, and a group of ducks -- of all things! Cloudchaser fell silent. Ephran realized that the drake's feelings about squirrels, other than those he knew personally, were not -- and probably never would be -- sentiments of warmth and trust.

"Cloudchaser and young mallards: The treeclimbers you see here call themselves Aden and Laslum. They are Kaahli's father and brother. We've helped them escape from Many Colored Ones."

Aden said, "Yes...ummm...of course..."

Laslum mumbled something unintelligible.

"Ah, so that's it!" exclaimed Cloudchaser. "How wonderful! You were successful in your search then. Sometime I must hear the story of this escape. And we are happy to meet the father and brother of Kaahli."

"Why, most surely...and thank you," said Aden. "Likewise, I'm certain."

"You spoke of a warning," said Kaahli.

"Yes, I did, said Cloudchaser. "But I don't care to frighten anyone without good cause. Perhaps I am being too cautious, but Marshflower and I agreed that you should be informed if I found you: The Pond has been visited in your absence -- by Many Colored Ones."

Ephran and Kaahli both gasped. Laslum shivered and closed his eyes.

"Another warning about Them. They have crossed Great Hill then," mumbled Ephran. His smile had evaporated.

"As I say," said Cloudchaser, "I am not at all sure that this portends a problem. They have gone and not returned. Perhaps They never will. I have no desire to alarm you needlessly."

"Did They carry thundersticks?" interrupted Aden.

"I saw no thundersticks," answered Cloudchaser.

"What do you suppose They wanted?" asked Kaahli.

"Who knows? Who can tell what They are after. Sometimes They come just to look. To walk among the trees. But sometimes to make mischief," said the drake.

"Thank you for telling us, Cloudchaser," said Kaahli, "even though your news is not especially welcome. I don't know when we'll return to The Pond. We're going to try and find Ephran's family now."

"Ah. Then your searching is not yet ended."

"It appears not. But when we do come back we will be very careful. Please -- you and Marshflower and the young ones must also be watchful," said Kaahli.

"We will," said the drake. "And we hope that you have a safe journey and are once again successful in finding what is lost."

"Come back to The Pond before we have to fly away," a young hen said to Kaahli.

"We hope to be back before you fly off to those places that my mate loves to hear about," said Kaahli with a smile. "Fly with the moving air now."

"Keep to the high branches," answered Cloudchaser.

Ephran waved at the ducks but his thoughts were a long way down Rocky Creek. The mallards lifted themselves from the water, circled out over the lake, then swung over the tops of the trees, quacking farewell to the squirrels below.

"Unusual...most unusual." It was about all Aden could say.

With an effort that would have been clearly visible had anyone been watching him, Ephran took a deep breath and said, "The ducks are unusual and special friends." He watched as the mallards became tiny specks in the darkening sky and murmured to himself, "I must believe they will not be caught unaware."

As they'd approached the lake Laslum had spotted tall bushes bearing branches full of buds and green berries. They ate and talked until it was nearly dark. Ephran was quiet, Kaahli thought, but Aden and Laslum had a bundle of questions about the ducks and the way Ephran and Kaahli's relationship with them had developed. Kaahli told them the entire story, including the rescue of the ducklings, and they were amazed all over again. As she talked, Ephran wondered if they'd understand the deep friendship with Klestra. He'd wait for another time to tell them of that.

They found comfortable leafy branches in a dense stand of elm trees. The night, warm and soft, lulled the weary travelers to sleep. The moon, like a silver leaf on a starfilled lake, floated over the peaceful forest until the sun appeared at the edge of Little Lake. They awoke to the quacking and splashing of Cloudchaser's relatives.

The bushes that provided their last meal held many more, and they ate their fill before setting out. The calm and restful darkness had renewed Ephran's spirits. It was hard to think of unpleasant possibilities on a day as brilliant as this. Father and Laslum led the way while Ephran and Kaahli lagged behind. They took turns chasing one another around the trunk of an especially thick cottonwood, played "chase-the-frontrunner" on the slender and pliant branches of a young willow, and laughed and rolled about on the forest floor in a soft velvety patch of green moss.

Ephran was still chuckling and tickling his mate when she grew very still. He felt her grow rigid under his paws.

"What is it, Kaahli?"

"Listen!..."

He held his breath.

There was a frightful commotion somewhere ahead, somewhere along the path Aden and Laslum must have taken through the thick treetrunks. A sound -- a voice -- something between a loud scream and a terrible cough!

"What...?" he muttered, straining to hear more clearly.

"Father! Laslum!" Kaahli gasped, and jumped to her paws.

127

She was in the next tree before Ephran could set his claws into a nearby maple. He followed her, bough to bough, through the grass at times, as the intermittent howling became louder and louder. They reached a small clearing at the same moment. The sight that greeted them was a perplexing one, to say the least.

Laslum was perched, high above the ground, on the broken and jagged tip of a leafless elm. He peered down at a large mud-splattered animal with tangled yellow hair, obviously the source of the racket. The creature paid no attention to Laslum, engrossed as it was in a hollow box elder stump near the base of Laslum's tree. The mangy animal would dig vigorously at the base of the stump for a moment. Then, seeming to weary of it, would commence its dreadful howling again.

Aden watched the proceedings from a nearby ironwood, chest heaving with the exertion of having run so far so fast, a concerned look on his face.

"Father," Kaahli called, "what is that...that thing?"

"Dog," Aden replied breathlessly. "Has a...squirrel trapped in there...nearly caught in the open...as we got here...made it into the stump...just in time."

Sure enough, each time the dog stopped digging and barking for a moment Ephran could hear whimpering sounds from the stump. The big animal ignored the squirrels, out of his reach in the trees, though he could hardly miss hearing them speak.

So this was a dog. Jafthuh and Odalee had told their young about such animals, but dogs were rarely seen in the deep woods. It looked a great deal like a fox, only much larger and more muscular. They spent a lot of time around Many Colored Ones. He wondered if they were like cows.

Ephran thought that he should do something to help. Before he could move, however, Laslum disappeared into the opening in the broken elm. He reappeared with a chestnut so large that it barely fit in his mouth. Instead of rushing to Laslum's aid, Ephran thought he might sit still and see what Kaahli's brother had in mind. It seemed an especially good idea since, at the moment, he had no thoughts of his own for aiding the trapped treeclimber.

Without hesitation, and as though it had been carefully planned, Laslum took the waterlogged nut in his front paws. He balanced himself on his rear legs and held the nut far behind his head. Flinging his front legs like stretched green vines, he threw the nut with astounding speed and accuracy. The nut struck the dog squarely on the side of its head, making a dull THUNK! The surprised animal let out a sharp yelp and jumped backward.

"What are ya doin' anyway?" it said, rubbing the base of its ear with a muddy front paw.

"I'm greeting an uninvited visitor," said Laslum.

"Some greetin'," snorted the dog. "And who says I'm not 'vited? You figure this is yer woods? Am I spose ta ask permission t'be here?"

"No, it's not my woods. Nor anyone else's that I know of," replied Laslum. "Certainly not yours."

"Course 'snot mine," said the dog. "I'm just out explorin' m'Master's woods."

"Ah! 'Your Master's woods' you say." said Laslum. "And who might this Master be, this great One who possesses the trees and the bushes and the streams and the flowers?"

The dog looked puzzled. "Why, Master is...is...well, m'Master is m'Master."

Laslum laughed. "That is a most confusing answer."

"Don't think yerself so clever, Mr. Squirrel," answered the dog, wiping his nose with a dusty paw. "Master has a name. Just can't recall it at the moment. Could easy lead Him t'any tree ya think is yours and He'd show ya right quick that He's Master o'these here woods."

"And how would it show me that it is Master of my tree and this woods?" asked Laslum, still smirking.

"Big noise from his thunderstick, that's how. He'd swab that grin off yer face and drop ya senseless from yer branch."

There was a shocked silence. The dog had a Master that used a thunderstick! No question as to what kind of creature it was talking about. Mother had been right again. There was enough evidence to leave no doubt that at least some of The Many Colored Ones were hunters. The only thing that wasn't clear was if this dog was as dangerous as the loathsome creatures it nested with.

Ephran asked, "Have you seen It...I mean Him, do this?"

The dog looked over at Ephran, seeming not one bit surprised at hearing a new voice. It must have known all of them were here the whole time.

"Lots a times," said the dog, and he looked down at the earth.

"To squirrels?"

"Yeah,...and to rabbits 'n birds too."

"Do those who fall recover their senses? Do they fly or run away?"

"Nah. Pretty quiet usually. Mostly done breathin'.."

The dog lay down at the base of the tree with a distressed look on its face, as though exhausted with its digging and barking -- or with this conversation -- or both.

"Why does your Master do this? Does He need the birds and animals for food?"

"Nah. Reckon He's got all th'food He needs. Brings it home in big crinkly brown leaves, squashed inta shiny roundish things, packed inta little squares called boxes..."

It looked up with sad eyes and said, "No...don't believe most 'a The Many Colored Ones really need ya folks to fill their bellies."

Nobody said anything for a while. Then Ephran spoke.

"My name is Ephran. What's yours?"

The dog lifted his head. "Master calls me Fred."

"Well, Fred. Despite what you've done here I suspect you are not the same as your Master. You have neither the look or sound of a hunter."

"Hey! Hold on there fella! Don't sell me short," said Fred, raising one dirty paw. "I like to chase a rabbit er a squirrel once in a while. Give 'em a purty good run too, if I say so myself." He scratched his ear. "Good for my legs, ya know?" He looked over at Kaahli. "Spose yer right though. Wouldn't wanna catch one... Huntin' is kinda messy business."

"May I come out now?" The tiny voice came from the stump.

Curiosity about the dog and its master had caused them to forget entirely about the poor animal still trembling in darkness inside the stump. They looked pointedly at the dog, who still lay very close -- too close -- to where the chase had ended. After a moment the significance of the pointed silence and lack of any action dawned on him, and Fred got to his paws.

"I unnerstand," he mumbled and he ambled a good distance away.

He moved far enough to make it quite obvious that the trapped squirrel could easily escape into the limbs of a nearby silver maple before he could possibly get close enough to cause any harm. Then he lay down again, head on his paws.

A little black nose poked cautiously out of the hole in the rotten stump. Seeing the coast clear, a disheveled, dusty, and somewhat overweight gray squirrel crawled out, eyes still damp and red.

Ephran choked.

"Mianta!" he cried.

CHAPTER XX

FRED

Ephran scampered down the tree without a second thought for the dog. He ran to his sister, who held out her plump forelegs to greet him. He nearly bowled her over with a flurry of hugging and nuzzling.

Mianta could scarcely believe that her very own brother, who the entire family had sadly decided was lost forever, was right here, in her paws. Obviously, one of the voices she heard from the stump had been familiar, but sounds had been muffled in there. She told herself that it couldn't possibly be Ephran. When he finally said his name she nearly fainted with joy.

"Ephran! Where did you come from?" She held him away so she could look at him.

"Not from Lomarsh, if that's what you're thinking," he said.

She laughed, hugged him again, and in the process looked over his shoulder. There she saw, through sudden tears of relief, love, embarrassment, and leftover fright -- three other squirrels. There was an older male...and the young buck, the chestnut slinger, the one she'd been able to see from the hole in the stump. And there was a female too.

Mianta gently nudged Ephran away saying, "I'm such a mess. Let me clean myself up. I wasn't expecting visitors in this part of the woods."

She rubbed her generous flank against the stump to fluff up her fur, brushed off some of the more obvious smudges, and smoothed down the rough spots with her paws.

"I shall be ready to be introduced presently, Ephran," she said, with a dignity marred only by a streak of dirt, just under her nose, that she couldn't quite see. "But first, I must attend to one or two matters."

Ephran smiled and struggled not to laugh aloud -- Mianta had not changed. She strode purposely to the chestnut that Laslum had thrown with such amazing accuracy. She picked it up, carried it to the stump, and stuffed it into the crack she'd crawled out of.

"Food, you know," she said, smiling at the squirrels in the branches. She then turned to Fred, a venomous look in her eye.

"I hope you are very pleased with yourself," she said.

Fred's ears perked up. Was she talking to him? Must be. She was looking right at him. He was too surprised to respond. He lay there, mouth open and tongue hanging.

"Yes, I mean you, you big oaf!"

The squirrels were struck dumb. Mianta was no more than a leap away from the big animal.

"You like to chase smaller folk, do you? Does it make you feel

"I HOPE YOU ARE VERY PLEASED WITH YOURSELF!"

real big and brave to scare the wits out of a creature one-tenth your size? You say you don't care to hunt so you're evidently into terrorizing. Is that a big deal for you?"

The dog's eyes were so large and round that they reminded Ephran of some of the stones on the bottom of Rocky Creek. Ferocious hunter or not, none of the listeners harbored any doubt that, as soon as he recovered from the shock of being tonguelashed by this pudgy treeclimber, he'd make her sorry for her insolence. How long would he allow this to continue? Would she have time to get to a tree before the big white teeth closed around her?

Much to their surprise, Fred dropped his eyes under Mianta's glare.

"Sorry," he said softly.

"I should hope so. Apology accepted."

She then turned to Ephran with a grin and said, "Now I'm ready to be introduced to your friends. Especially the brave one who throws so well."

Mianta greeted Aden formally. She squealed in delight and surprise when she met Kaahli and learned that she was mate to Ephran. But it was obvious that Mianta's main attraction was her "hero". At first Laslum was embarrassed by her attention and compliments but, little by little, he began to respond to the plump and lively female. She was really quite attractive now, since she'd regained her composure and cleaned herself up.

Laslum couldn't explain to them, or even to himself, where or why he'd gotten the idea to attack the dog -- except to say that he knew he had to do something when he saw a squirrel in trouble, a prisoner in a dark place.

And Mianta -- well, Mianta was in her glory. She basked in the praise of the other squirrels, beaming and preening and saying things like, "Oh, no big thing", as they lauded her for her grit when she backed the dog down at such close quarters. They seemed to forget how they found her, snuffling and whimpering inside a hollow tree stump, courage surfacing after Fred's hunting instincts had become suspect. Oh well, thought Ephran, they either have very short memories or very good manners. And, of course, her daring did deserve some credit. After all, even he had been fearful that her scolding of the dog might cause it to revert to its old habits.

Finally, after the excitement subsided, Mianta curled up next to Ephran. "Brother," she said, "what in the Great Green Woods happened to you? We looked and looked. We worried and worried. We waited and waited. We finally gave up."

Ephran said, "I know you have as many questions about what happened since the cold season as I do. We have much to talk about. I have just one question that must be answered now..."

"I know what your question is," Mianta nodded. "And the answer is 'Yes', our father and mother are well. So is Phetra. We are not far from their den right now. I will take all of you there."

Ephran closed his eyes, squeezing back the tears of happiness, and they hugged each other once more.

Fred, who'd been laying quietly on the ground a short distance from the chattering squirrels, chewing on a dry root, said, "Ya folks see all the good I did here? Ya wouldn't a even known each other was 'round if t'weren't fer me. Everybody seems real happy just 'cause I chased the fat...ah, I mean the...ah, healthy l'il treeclimber inta the stump. P'raps I should have some sorta tiny reward, hmm? Any a ya know where a hungry dog mite find a bite to eat?"

"Poor dog," said Kaahli, "I imagine you are getting hungry." To Ephran she said, "Can you think of anything in the woods Fred might be interested in eating?"

"I really have no idea what dogs like to eat," replied Ephran. "Fred, what does your Master feed you?"

"Don't rightly know what 'tis," said Fred. "Takes it outa the same kinda brown leaves he gets his own food in. Brings it to me in a round shiny thing called 'dish'."

"Fred, where is your Many Colored One now?" asked Aden.

"Oh, I expect He's over in his den. One made a trees He laid down. By a big lake. Not far from here." Fred scratched his ear again. "Anaway, don't think it's far from here."

"His den is built of trees without roots?" asked Ephran slowly. Once again he saw, in his mind, the old oak fall to the earth.

"Yep."

"Does your Master grow things near his den?" asked Mianta, a gleam in her eye. "Like corn perhaps?"

"Nope," Fred answered firmly, with a shake of his head. "Don't grow nothin'. Just hangs around there durin' the warm season mostly. Gits far away when the old air gits cold. Brings me out here fer huntin' sometimes."

"Is there dog food at this den of trees?" asked Kaahli.

"You bet," said Fred. "Lots."

Ephran said, "I think that solves the problem then. You best wander back that way. You have to eat and it seems none of us know what a dog eats. Your Many Colored One knows what you're accustomed to."

"S'pose yer right," Fred agreed.

"Well then," said Aden, standing on his two hind legs and patting his white belly, "as long as that's settled, let's be on our way."

"Fred," said Ephran, "before we leave I want to thank you for not harming my sister. I know you could have. Maybe, from now on, you'll think about getting your exercise without including the chasing of small animals."

134

"Try not to," said Fred. "Real sorry I scared Meeanter so bad. Guess I shouldn't chase. Hard to promise too much though..." His dirty face broke into a grin. "So blamed much fun...ya know."

They bid goodbye to the dog, smiling in spite of themselves. They set out behind Mianta, who knew the best and fastest route to the den of Jafthuh and Odalee. They hadn't passed across many branches when something told Ephran he should look back. Sure enough, Fred hadn't moved.

"He's still sitting there!" he shouted to the others, who had continued to jump from tree to tree.

The dog had lain down again near the base of the broken elm, head on paws, watching his new friends scamper away through the trees. Ephran retraced his steps. He ran to the ground and up to Fred's nose. He looked into the sad brown eyes and said: "Fred, don't you want to go to that den by the lake and get something to eat?"

"Yep."

Suspicious, Ephran asked, "Do you know how to get there?"

"Nope."

"He's lost!" he shouted to the others, who were waiting to find out what the problem was. "We're going to have to help him find his way home."

Fred grimaced. "Gosh! Wisht ya wouldn't hafta holler fer the whole woods to hear. Dogs ain't sposed to git lost, ya know."

"Sorry," Ephran said, "Guess I don't know much about dogs."

After a good deal of questioning they learned that Fred had wandered away from his Master's den on the big lake and, apparently delighted to be free in the woods, he'd forgotten to mark his path by leaving scent on the bushes and trees along the way. Except for throwing a panic into a family of chipmunks he happened upon, an odorless faceoff with a skunk, and passing by the smaller lake, he remembered little of his aimless wandering.

Even that little bit helped. It helped because Ephran, from his own travels, knew of a special place where two sizeable bodies of water were close together. He thought he might have a pretty good idea of where Fred's Many Colored One had built its den of trees.

"It shouldn't be far from here," he explained. "We'll just go back to the shore of Little Lake and follow it around toward the side from which the cold air comes. From there I believe we'll be able to see Fred's lake. I've traveled that path before."

They were impressed, all over again, with Ephran's memory, and with his ability to use the sun and the moving air to direct him to a destination. Fred, whose stomach was beginning to growl impatiently, was especially impressed -- and very anxious to be underway.

The path taken earlier was retraced, back toward the clearing where they'd had their morning meal. They did not tarry. The day was nearly spent and the sun was sinking rapidly behind them. By the time they followed the shoreline to its far side -- five squirrels bouncing through the trees, followed by an unkempt yellow dog padding along on the ground -- the frogs in the shallows had begun their sunset song.

Ephran's bearing was true, and soon they could see the blue water of a large lake sparkling in the setting sunlight. He looked down at the dog and said, "The den of your Master must be on the shore of the lake just ahead, Fred. Do you want us to take you there?"

"Oh no!" said Fred. "I know where I am now. I kin make it from here."

"Are you sure you don't want us to take you to your Master's den?" Mianta asked. She wanted to get a closer look at these Many Colored Ones. They were supposedly such interesting animals and she felt a bit cheated that the Ones near father and mother's nest seemed disappointingly dull. That pair rarely came out of their den. And when They did, They just sat, or walked, or worked in the dirt with their white paws. It got downright boring to watch Them.

"No! No! Please!" said Fred. "I want you to go now."

"Fred," said Kaahli in her most soothing voice, "what's the matter? Are you embarrassed because your Master might see that you needed help to find your way home?"

"No," said Fred. "...Well, I'm a touch 'barrassed all right. But that's not the main reason I want you to leave. You gotta unnerstand that my Master would never figure you folks showed me the way. I think 'e reckons that anathing got fur or feathers is a little on the dense side. He an' his friend'd just decide 'twas good luck to have so many squirrels all t'gether in one place at one time."

"'Good luck'?" repeated a puzzled Laslum.

The dog looked up and said, "Sure. Good luck. They'd git their thundersticks and knock ya down from the branches."

Aden said, "Fred, it is the wrong time for The Many Colored Ones to be using the thundersticks. It is early in the warm season. I have not heard of Them using thundersticks until the cold season is nearly upon us."

"I know," said Fred. "They know too. Pretty sure its agin their own rules to hunt now. But my Master and his friend do it anahow."

"They are very dangerous then," breathed the old squirrel.

"Yeah, I guess," said Fred, slowly nodding his shaggy head. "Very dangerous."

CHAPTER XXI

REUNION

Ephran watched Fred's yellow tail retreat through the trees and bushes until he was satisfied that the dog was headed in the right direction.

"I think he'll make it," he said, "unless, of course, he forgets his new resolution when he runs into another squirrel. Or maybe a rabbit..."

"Right now I think he's more interested in something to eat than he is in chasing," said Kaahli.

"Yes," agreed Laslum. "I hope the thought of food wrapped in brown leaves keeps him moving along."

"Astounding thing, you know," mused Aden, "that an animal, even one like that, should take his food, his very air, from a Many Colored One."

"A strange thing," nodded Ephran.

"I can't understand it at all," said Laslum.

Mianta squinted at them and said, "You said the right word. Food. Food is what's important...and his Master provides it. Anyway, with all this 'Fred-business' taking up time, the light has become too feeble to travel by. We must find a sheltered place to spend the dark hours."

They quickly realized the truth of her words. Two robins chirped their serenade to the setting sun from the top of a pussy willow bush at water's edge. The deep thrumming of a grouse could be heard a long way off among the spruce trees. A flock of brown and white sparrows twittered cheerfully as they fluttered past the squirrels in the fading light. A few of the brightest stars had become visible in the clear, blue-black sky.

There were many trees near the lake, and everyone was able to find a comfortable sleeping place among them. Aden settled high in a towering white pine and Mianta and Laslum found a pair of branches in a sturdy hackberry. Ephran and Kaahli snuggled on the boughs of an old elm tree. An owl's lonely hooting reached their ears and, without having to say it aloud, each of them made sure they were well concealed.

Ephran lay awake for a while, at last having the time and peace to savor the prospect of seeing Jafthuh, Odalee and Phetra. Those he thought he might very well never see again were sleeping just a few hills away. A large drop of love and joy formed in his eye. He fell asleep to the sound of Mianta's voice, crooning softly to Laslum under the twinkling, starlit sky.

Morning arrived fresh and cool. As they ate from budding bushes Mianta told them, "Now don't gorge yourselves -- there's still a bit of corn left in the corncrib. We'll be there very soon." She smiled sweetly at Laslum who grinned back through dewsoaked whiskers.

Refreshed after a peaceful sleep and a filling breakfast, the travelers set out, leaping from branch to branch. They laughed and chattered as they ran, spirits high. A group of five whitetailed deer, laying in beds of long grass, lifted their heads and nodded as the treeclimbers passed. A bluebird and a thrush, in the midst of an argument over who had prerogatives regarding a certain gooseberry bush, were so distracted that they both ended up whistling back at the treeclimbers and forgetting to rekindle the disagreement. A family of skunks, out for a morning walk, waved a greeting at the squirrels with long black and white tails.

They hadn't traveled very far when Ephran's steps slowed. Then his legs stopped entirely. He'd just crossed a wooded ridge that overlooked a gently rolling swale of deep and tangled bluegrass, tumbleweed, scattered tamarack and yellow birch. Directly ahead was a familiar landmark.

The corncrib stood slightly askew on its short legs, just as he remembered it. There were fewer sticks of corn inside than on that fateful day late last cold season...and there was the lone tree -- with its thick, long trunk...and the black vine. He'd been so frantic! My goodness, how long ago it all seemed! And lo and behold!...even from this distance he could make out the black and white cat, lying asleep atop flat slabs of wood that led to the entrance of The Many Colored Ones' den.

Kaahli sat silently on the branch next to him, tail around her legs. She did not disturb him, hoping she understood at least a little of what he felt. Meanwhile, Aden and Laslum, led by a happily jabbering Mianta, left the young couple behind as they hurried toward the nest of Jafthuh and Odalee.

Finally Kaahli said to her mate, "This brings back many memories, doesn't it?"

"Yes, it does, Kaahli," he said. "I was trying to decide what I learned here. I made a great many mistakes before I arrived in this place, you know. And I made a big one once I got here. Nearly cost me my breath. And trying to get to the corn wasn't the biggest..." His voice trailed off.

"My mother once told me; 'The leap was not too great if your paws meet the branch'," she said.

"Well," he said, "at last I've found my family. So my paws ended up at home after all. I suspect that it was more luck than anything. Or maybe it wasn't really luck at all. I got a lot of help."

He stood up on the branch where he'd been laying and stretched his legs. He smiled at the quizzical expression on her upturned face, licked her ear, and said, "Let's go. It's hard for me to believe that I'm actually going to see my family. I really thought I would never see them again. I can't wait for them to meet you."

By the time they reached the den, high in the oak tree near the gurgling stream, Mianta had introduced her parents to Kaahli's father and brother. Though Jafthuh and Aden initially eyed each other with feigned disinterest, as was expected, they went out of their way to be polite to one another and to agree on any statement that was made, including the observation that it was a lovely day.

Mother and Mianta were fussing over Laslum, feeding him kernels of bright golden corn. He was swallowing it all; fussing and corn. The two older males had become involved in a lively conversation, laying side by side on a thick gnarled branch just above the entrance to the den. In the small limbs of a nearby maple, four small gray squirrels chased and chattered.

Ephran's mother looked up to see her son approaching through the trees. She carefully took the stick of corn she was holding in her paw and put it on the flat surface of a nearby branch. Her eyes never left him. She looked at nothing else until he was right there in front of her. He hugged her tightly then and, for a long moment, neither could find their voice.

"Ephran, my heart is full," she finally murmured, ever so softly, in his ear.

"No fuller than mine, mother."

"And this, of course, is Kaahli, who Mianta has already told us of," she said, looking over his shoulder.

"Hello, mother," said Kaahli. They embraced as though there had never been a moment in their lives that they had not known and loved one another. Many pairs of eyes brimmed with water of joy.

Jafthuh got to his feet as his son drew near. He hugged him firmly. They looked at one another, said not a word, and hugged again.

"Phetra...?" Ephran glanced around at the nearby trees.

"Mated," said father, "and nested in branches not far away from here, near the lakes. Maybe he will visit soon."

Ephran was coaxed to eat, and while he did so he insisted on hearing what had happened the day the old oak fell to The Many Colored Ones and their things of shiny teeth.

The family, obviously, had escaped the woodcutters after their tree had fallen. The gigantic oak had twisted as it went down and had come to rest with their hole facing upwards instead of into the snow-covered earth.

"It was fortunate it fell that way," said Odalee.

"Yes," agreed Jafthuh, "otherwise we would have been 'up a downed tree', so to speak, and at the mercy of The Many Colored Ones."

The collision with a smaller tree broke the fall and made the shock of striking the ground, if not pleasant, at least bearable. Even so, they'd all been stunned long enough for Ephran to panic and run off toward Meadow Brook before they made their escape. The Ones of Many Colors seemed interested only in the tree and not the least bit in those who called it home. They had made no move to stop the squirrel family and watched silently as they raced away in the treetops.

"We looked all over for you," said Mianta with a stern voice.

"We had no idea where you were," said father.

"The only thing we were sure of was that you weren't where you were supposed to be," said mother.

Ephran cleared his throat. "That's true. I was not in the nest. I made a mistake," he said.

"More than one, I think," said Jafthuh, trying to be gruff and serious. "I'm glad you realize it. I only hope you've learned something."

"I've learned more than one lesson," said Ephran. "But my time alone in the forest nearly came too soon."

Father had remembered taking Ephran to the little clearing where Meadow Brook and Bubbling Brook merged, so the family went that way, hoping their lost son and brother might have wandered away on the familiar path along the watercourse. Besides, it was a path that Jafthuh knew would lead to shelter. They'd traveled rapidly, knowing that if Ephran had gone that way he'd be somewhere ahead, and that they would catch up to him sooner or later.

They could not know that he'd stop to eat elderberries and nearly get caught by an owl. So, by the time Ephran dared peek around the woods to see if Winthrop was still hunting him, his family had crossed Meadow Brook. By the time he spied the abandoned nest of leaves they had passed him by, heading toward the setting sun. After a long and tiring journey they came to this place -- and the sturdy tree Jafthuh remembered from his youth, a tree with a den almost as large as their old one.

"We took turns watching for you," said Mianta.

Mother explained, "We thought you would have to pass this way if you somehow managed to get behind us -- which you did."

"We could only hope you'd come back this way if you were ahead of us," said father.

"I was here," said Ephran. "I even came to what I thought at the time was the end of the woods." To himself he thought, "Until some feathered friends convinced me it could not be."

Father, mother and Mianta looked dismayed.

"You were here? We did not see you," mother finally said.

"Nor I you," said Ephran.

"Phetra, I'll bet," said Mianta, wrinkling her nose. "He never could stay awake when he was supposed to."

"Never mind," said mother. "We were all tired by the time we arrived here. We ran a very long way that day."

The nearness of the den of The Many Colored Ones was hardly an ideal situation. Ephran never dreamed his family would settle near the kind of creature that destroyed their home -- and very nearly themselves in the bargain. But there was the corncrib, of course...and mother decided there were many trees here that would bear nuts. A stream flowed nearby, flanked by bushes bearing abundant buds and seeds. In the time they'd been here, these particular Many Colored Ones had made no threat against the family. They would bear watching nonetheless.

Ephran met the little brothers and sisters who had first opened their eyes about the same time he was building his nest near The Pond. The females; Janna, Ilta, and Tinga, were fascinated by their older brother. They said little, but made sure they didn't miss a word he uttered. The male and the smallest of the lot was named Frafan. He was interested in everything. And he was anything but shy. There were questions for all the visitors but especially for this "new" brother.

After answering a barrage of inquiries about everything from where he built his nest to how they'd found their way to Jafthuh and Odalee's den, Ephran finally turned to his mother and said, "Did I ask this many questions?"

"Very nearly."

"How am I to learn if I don't ask?" objected Frafan.

"How indeed?" smiled Ephran. "Just keep asking, Frafan, and you'll be the smartest squirrel in the woods."

The little females looked at one another and giggled, obviously unconvinced that any amount of question-asking could make their brother the smartest squirrel in this woods. Or any woods, for that matter.

After a wonderful meal of fresh and moist elderberry and gooseberry buds, tender acorns, and crisp corn, the squirrels spent the evening in the thick lower boughs. They most certainly had a great deal to talk about.

His younger sisters loved the story and so Ephran had to tell over and over again about the first day he spent with Kaahli. When Kaahli first told of Ephran's struggle with the hawk everyone thought it was some sort of joke. When she insisted the story was true, and when Ephran did not deny it, they became quiet. Faces filled with awe, they asked hesitant questions. Did he really leap from a branch unto a skyhunter's back? Was he frightened? Was the water cold? What did it feel like to be totally under water? What does the face of a hawk look like close up?

"Ohh, Ephran...," mother breathed.

His family, and Kaahli's, looked at him as though there might be something other than a treeclimber hidden beneath his fur.

They were amazed that Ephran and Kaahli had friends that

included a red squirrel, a family of ducks, even a muskrat. Father shook his head and said, "The next thing I'll hear is that you converse regularly with a skunk."

"That too," smiled Ephran.

Kaahli told of the great storm that had thrown chunks of frozen water from the sky and had taken the breath, once and for all, from some of the forest birds and animals. Odalee remembered seeing very dark greenish-black clouds some time ago, but they had turned away and had not covered their part of the woods. Jafthuh was disbelieving once more when they told about saving themselves by hiding in the earth within the very roots of a rotted tree. Any disparaging remark he might have had about red squirrels was silenced when Ephran told them that the discovery and use of such shelters was just one of the things he'd learned from Klestra.

They were all saddened to hear that Kaahli's mother had taken ill and disappeared from the nest. They were thrilled and proud when told of Aden and Laslum's rescue from the cage and astounded at the description of Mianta's delivery from the stump. Especially the part about the shaggy yellow hunter who really wasn't a hunter at all. Odalee hugged Laslum in thanks for his spirited defense of her daughter, which put a silly smile on his face.

Frafan had so many questions about the dog, and about red squirrels, and muskrats, and cages, that mother finally asked him to be quiet for a while so that someone else could talk.

The stories lasted until it was nearly dark and the young treeclimbers began to yawn. Actually, Janna had already fallen asleep, tucked partway under her mother's front leg. The den of Jafthuh was chock full of squirrels and there was certainly no room for visitors there. However, Mianta was a frequent guest at the den of her parents and her nest was nearby. And so, after they bid one another goodnight, hugged, told one another how glad they were to meet one another, and how good it was to be with one another, Mianta led the guests off in near-darkness.

A brook glistened beneath them in the faint light and soon they approached a stand of elm. Leafless and barkless, the stricken trees stood like naked sentinels, surrounded by tiny prickly saplings and bushes. Some of the trees retained a few stubby limbs. All, save one, were broken off at various distances above the forest floor. Their weathered white flesh shone unnaturally in the dark green and brown woods.

Woodpeckers had been at work here. This stand of dry wood, thought Ephran, must have been a bird's paradise for one entire warm season. Sharp beaks had prepared sleeping places for the squirrels that were so comfortable that one might have thought that the whole process had been an act of friendship -- from winged ones with sturdy snouts -- to treeclimbers with soft noses.

But the driving force for this undertaking had been the same as it was for a lot of the activity in the forest. Ephran was familiar with that motive, and Mianta certainly knew all about it. It was called hunger. The woodpeckers had reaped their reward for making holes in the trees -- hordes of insects no doubt inhabited the rotting wood.

Mianta had her own den, of course, which she'd made comfortable with a bed of soft, sweet-smelling leaves and grasses. Beneath her large den was a smaller one and she'd padded that one nearly as luxuriously as the other. To no one's surprise she asked Laslum if he would like to share her tree and move into the guest nest. He might have been glad it was too dark for anyone to see his face but, bashful or not, he did not refuse the invitation.

Those first few dark hours passed as pleasantly and peacefully as did the following days. Ephran and Kaahli lost track of time as one bright sunny day followed another. The dens were spacious and comfortable and food was plentiful. Hunters were rarely seen and then only at a great distance. Though The Many Colored Ones were unpredictable and obviously dangerous, Aden put all their thoughts into words when he surmised that nesting near one of their dens had a few advantages over nesting in the deep woods. According to he and Jafthuh, who had both been witnesses, the hawk and the fox were not immune to the thundersticks and traps of The Many Colored Ones. Besides, Many Colored Ones often built their dens near running water and that meant plenty of big trees and fresh buds. Best of all perhaps was that They grew things -- things that were good to eat -- things like corn and the big round red fruit that formed on little trees.

Even the cat that had chased Ephran up the lone tree seemed to have mellowed. She could often be seen, laying in the short grass or on the flat sheets of wood leading to The Many Colored Ones' den. At first the squirrels went in pairs to raid the corncrib, so that one of them could stand watch. They soon abandoned the precaution because, even though her quarry was in plain sight, the cat either ignored them or watched with seeming indifference as they pilfered the main course for their next meal.

The warm season turned out to be pretty much what it was supposed to be: Warm. Actually, quite hot -- and very dry. Except for a few intermittent sprinkles of water from a blotchy blue-grey sky, the last storm that anyone could remember was the one which had forced Ephran and Kaahli to hide in the earth beneath the abandoned tree stump. At first the lack of water from the sky did not, in the least, bother them. There was plenty of moisture deep in the forest floor for the roots of the great oaks, hickory, and walnut. The leaves on the bigger trees stayed green, nuts were growing in abundance, and the light and dark times free of flashing light and terrible rumbling in the sky were welcome. It was Jafthuh who first expressed some misgivings.

"The water in the streambed is nearly gone," he observed one evening after they'd eaten. "It lies in small puddles and doesn't move at all."

"And the grass turns brown too early," said Aden.

"There certainly have been no fresh buds for a while," mother fretted, as she pulled brittle kernels of corn from a reddish-yellow stick.

"It concerns me," said Jafthuh. "I don't know what this means for the coming cold season. I don't know if the snow will drift deep or if there will be no snow at all. I wonder if we should lay away some extra corn and nuts and seeds -- if we can find seeds. And should we store them all in the dens and not in the earth...?

"I just don't know," he said finally, and he sniffed the air as though hoping to smell water in the thin clouds that drifted like ribbons of smoke high above.

The younger squirrels listened to their parents and became a bit concerned themselves. They hadn't been in the woods so long as the older ones and they had not seen a drytime. The water had always come from the sky when it was needed...and often when it wasn't. So they tried to worry but found they could not.

Laslum changed the subject to Fred, how big and frightening he'd seemed at first, but how basically gentle he was. And he told of the poor dog's inability to find Blue Lake and his master's den, and how the animal had needed Ephran to show the way. Soon everyone was talking and laughing, and the lack of tears from the sky was forgotten.

CHAPTER XXII

FRAFAN AND BLACKIE

Ephran's second brother and sisters were dazzled by their "new" brother and his mate. Most hours of Ephran and Kaahli's days were claimed by the young ones. Ephran and Kaahli enjoyed the afternoons along the creek and in the high branches with their little charges. Jafthuh and Odalee did not mind sharing their teaching duties. The older squirrels spent the hot days sheltered by clusters of leaves, talking of times past, of the trials and rewards of raising young ones, and of how much easier it used to be to find hickory nuts.

Mianta and Laslum were away from the oak a good deal, exploring the woods and nearby fields, laughing and jabbering constantly. At one point they set out to find Phetra, since everyone agreed that it would be very nice to see him and have Ephran and Kaahli meet his new mate. However, when they got to his nest they found it empty, and a rabbit from a nearby warren told them that the squirrels that nested there hadn't been around for some time.

This news was somewhat disturbing until father reminded those who did know, and informed those who didn't, that Phetra's mate, Roselimb, was a wanderer. "Her paws are very nearly as itchy as Ephran's," said Jafthuh.

"I like her already," smiled Ephran, "but if you think my paws like to travel, you ought to meet an old squirrel friend of ours who lives on the far side of The Pond. He rarely spends two nights in the same nest."

"I just hope Roselimb is able to find her way through the trees as well as you do," fretted Odalee.

"Don't worry, mother," said Mianta, "Phetra and Roselimb will be fine. Phetra might have trouble taking care of himself but Roselimb can watch out for both of them."

"Not nice!" scolded Janna.

"No," agreed Mianta with a giggle, "and not nearly as much fun to say as when Phetra can hear and complain about me to mother."

The afternoon was particularly warm, too warm for much running and playing. After a few attempts, everyone agreed it was just too hot for games. The entire family settled down to nap in the branches, spreading their bodies to catch as much of the capricious air as possible.

Though the heat pressed down on him, Ephran's eyes closed quickly. Then, for no reason he suddenly found himself wide awake. He didn't think he had slept for more than a few moments. He listened for any worrisome sound. There was none. Locusts trilled their high-pitched song in the sweltering woods just as they had been when he fell asleep. He looked around. Kaahli sprawled on a slender limb next to his. Just above were Mianta and Laslum. Confused and a bit groggy, he had just put his head back on his paws when he realized that, among the leafy limbs, not quite enough gray fur was interspersed with green leaves.

Everyone slumbered peacefully, just where they were supposed to be...except Frafan. The branch where his younger brother had rested ("fidgeted" would probably be more nearly the right word, now that he thought of it) was empty. The tiny gray longtail was nowhere in sight.

Ephran's first impulse was to wake Mianta, Laslum and Kaahli, but there was no use alarming the whole group yet. After all, they'd just rested their minds after working up a certain amount of concern about Phetra. Besides, the curious little rascal had to be nearby. He hadn't had time to run far.

Ephran quietly crept along the branch to the trunk, then scampered to the earth. It would be easier to see from ground level. Underbrush beneath the big trees was sparse.

It occurred to him that he should run off into the woods -- that would be where most squirrels would go to explore...or to play...or to visit a friend. But Frafan was not most squirrels. So instead of directing his search to likely places, Ephran turned toward the farm.

At first he saw nothing unusual. A bluejay in a tall bush hopped from one slender branch to another. A lovely black and yellow butterfly glided though the shade. Then he saw a flash of gray in the lower limbs of a stunted basswood.

It was Frafan all right. Little legs were carrying him in the direction the sun would set, directly toward the den of The Many Colored Ones -- and straight for the cat, which lay, apparently asleep, in the shade of a big lilac bush!

Ephran knew that following through the trees would be too slow. He could close the distance much faster if he ran along the earth, especially since lack of skywater had caused the grass and brush on the forest floor to thin and wither. It would be safe enough, if for no other reason than it was too hot and bright for most hunters to be out and about.

Apparently unaware of the cat, Frafan climbed into the upper branches of a cherry tree, all the while moving closer and closer to The Many Colored Ones' den. Ephran was still far behind and he dare not set up a racket too soon. Alerting Frafan to the danger at this point would be sure to waken the cat, laying motionless in the shade, eyes closed.

Though it seemed to take much too long, Ephran finally got close enough to give warning. He jumped to the trunk of a red maple and begin to chatter, trying to make his voice just loud enough -- but not too loud. He didn't want to wake the sleeping family behind him. There was nothing they could do.

As soon as he heard Ephran, Frafan looked back at his brother. There was both guilt and mischief in his bright eyes. The cat raised her head, wide awake.

"Don't look at me! Watch the cat!" barked Ephran.

Confused, Frafan looked first at the tree he was in, then up in the sky above him.

"Not in the clouds! On the earth, Frafan!" barked Ephran. Thunder and lightning! Did he think cats had wings?

Under the lilac bushes Frafan found big yellow eyes peering back at him. He froze. Ephran worked his way slowly up the maple and along a springy limb which leaned toward the cherry tree.

"Keep thinking...," he said softly and slowly to Frafan, eyeing the cat, wondering when she would leap to the base of the cherry tree and race up toward the stricken young squirrel.

"...You can easily jump from your tree into the maple here. Then into the high limbs," he continued, "so relax. Start toward me. Now!"

Memories of his own terror when trapped by this very same cat flooded Ephran's mind. Despite telling Frafan to keep a clear mind, he found it difficult to think. At least Frafan was not in a tree without neighbors. Why didn't the cat attack? What was she waiting for? Frafan still hadn't moved.

"Frafan!" said Ephran. "Come here. Right now!"

"I...I...I didn't see her," stuttered Frafan.

Didn't see her? How in this old knarled woods could anyone miss seeing a big black and white lump laying in the green and brown grass? He knew the answer to his own question. Frafan's mind was on something else -- something that caused him to be careless.

"Right now it doesn't matter whether you saw her or not. Just come over here to me."

Frafan finally moved. He straightened his slender legs, turned quickly, and ran without looking back, right up to his brother. Ephran blew out a long and grateful sigh.

"Well, it took him a while, but he eventually got around to moving his bushy tail, didn't he?"

At that comment from the cat, Ephran, already starting to push Frafan ahead of him into the high branches, almost lost his grip. The hunter lay there, still sprawled in the grass, smiling up at the squirrels. She gave no indication that she intended to move.

"Y..Yes," Ephran stammered, then collected himself. "He's young."

"You aren't exactly the patriarch of the forest yourself," said the cat. "Do you still tend to choose trees which stand all alone?"

"You remember me!"

"Most certainly," replied the cat. "You are called Ephran, I believe. Couldn't help overhearing your family speak of you. My name is Blackie."

Ephran was totally amazed. Not so much at the subject of the conversation (though that was odd enough), but that it was occurring at all. Frafan, curled tightly against his older brother, shivered in the thick heat of lateday.

"Have you quit hunting, Blackie?" asked Ephran.

The cat yawned and stretched lanquidly, then sat up. "Oh yes," she said. "I have indeed. You speak of age as though you know what it means. You don't. I do. I am old. Besides, I've tended to add a bit around the waist. All of which has slowed me down some, though I imagine you suspected that before. What you do not know, and might be interested in, is that I pretty much quit hunting anything save mice the day I met you. I don't even have much luck with the mice anymore." She chuckled. "You were more persuasive than you might have thought at the time, my good Ephran. After the tumble you caused me, I spent three whole days under my master's den, licking my aching body."

Frafan's eyes widened.

"Do you miss the hunt?" asked Ephran.

"Not a great deal. The excitement perhaps. I'm not often hungry. I get plenty to eat," answered Blackie.

"I thought as much," said Ephran. "The Many Colored Ones feed you, don't they?"

The cat's ears perked up. "Ha! My turn to be surprised. How did you know that?"

"I recently met a dog," said Ephran. "He said that his Master fed him and that he didn't need to hunt. I thought that you must be fed also."

"Ah, yes...," said Blackie, laying down again, "I have heard that They feed dogs. Ugh! What a waste!"

"If you've been fed all along, and aren't hungry, then why did you hunt at all?"

Ephran looked down at his little brother, who'd asked the bold question. Blackie tipped her head to the side and grinned up at the squirrels.

"A reasonable thing to ask, little treeclimber," she said. "Why indeed? I suppose that I hunted because my parents did. And their parents before them. Hunting has been a part of us for a very long time. None of us knows when it started. Or when it might have ended. All I can tell you is that, at one time, it was necessary."

They sat for a bit, until a hint of air stirred the leaves. Ephran said to Frafan, "Come. We must return to the others. They'll be very worried if they wake up and find us both gone."

148

"HAVE YOU QUIT
HUNTING, BLACKIE?"

"They won't worry if they know I'm with you," Frafan smiled up at his brother.

Ephran turned back to the cat. "Do The Many Colored Ones know we take some of their corn?" he asked.

"I think They do," said Blackie.

"Does it anger Them?"

"Not that I can tell. At one time They fed many animals with it; cows and pigs. I have observed your small brother explore the place and, as I'm sure he knows, the big animals' den is empty now. What little you treeclimbers eat is of no consequence to the creatures you call Many Colored Ones."

"Frafan told me that They don't eat this corn," said Ephran. "So tasty too. How very strange..."

"Different tastes for different tongues," Blackie said. "I myself don't see what you find in corn."

"I suppose that's true. Well, we must be going. Goodbye, Blackie."

"Goodbye, Ephran and Frafan. Come and visit again sometime."

"I might do that," said Ephran, "I just might do that."

As the brothers scampered back toward the big oak Ephran asked, "Frafan, where were you going? Did you have someplace in mind or were you just wandering?"

"I wasn't just wandering. If you must know, I was going to the den of The Many Colored Ones. I usually go around the far side. I've never seen the cat over there. I just forgot about her."

Aha! thought Ephran. The rascal had taken this daring trip before. "To the den? Who gave you permission to go near the den of The Many Colored Ones?"

Frafan had set a brisk pace, running ahead of Ephran. He was not particularly interested in a confrontation with his first brother and it was quite obvious that he didn't care to look him in the eye. But now Ephran caught up, and ran past Frafan on a large branch. He stopped and turned, blocking Frafan's path.

"Well...?" said Ephran, sitting practically nose to nose with his brother.

"No one gave me permission."

"Why did you go then -- without telling anyone?"

"Because I knew they would tell me I couldn't go. I didn't wake them up today because I expected to be back before they woke up. Before you woke up too. I don't know that they would understand, but perhaps you will. I must learn, you see."

Ephran understood, more than Frafan suspected. "You must learn, you say. Learn what?"

"Many things. There are so many questions. Some, like the

roar of silver birds high above the clouds and the long white streaks they leave behind...I don't know if those questions will ever be answered. But The Many Colored Ones...I want to understand Them. They're such a mystery and yet, I think, important in many ways to what happens in the woods. The more I learn, the better it will be for us. And I have a chance to study Them and learn. I can even see into their den from the high branches."

"You can see into their den?" Ephran was astounded. This brother was more curious and adventurous that even he'd dreamt of being!

"Yes. Through those large black holes. The ones that look as though they're covered by a layer of frozen water. I can see right through them, down into their den. I've only done it a few times but I could already tell you a great deal about how and what They eat, the things They do inside their walls, how They change their pelts. They're not really 'many-colored-ones' at all, you know."

They'd reached the big oak trees where the family, Ephran was relieved to see, still slept away the lazy afternoon. "Frafan," he whispered, "it's good to be curious. And it's good to learn. But it can lead to big trouble if you try to trick or outsmart father and mother. Take it from one who knows. Now go back and lay where you were. This little business with Blackie will be our secret. Some day, when we're alone and have time, I want to hear more about that den -- and Those who nest inside."

Frafan grinned widely.

When Jafthuh awoke a short time later he stretched, looked about to see that everyone was in his or her place, and then called out, "Wake up, everyone! Time to eat." He turned to Ephran, who he thought looked surprisingly wide awake.

"Nice nap, eh son?" he asked.

"Most worthwhile nap, father," Ephran smiled back.

151

Flying must be wonderful.
The view has to be amazing.
The problem is,
to have any effect
on a problem down below,
one generally has to be
close enough to touch.

Odalee, in her fifth season

CHAPTER XXIII

BLACK SKY, BLACK EARTH

𝕿he days grew perceptibly shorter and the sun angled more and more acutely across hazy skies above the big woods. And still no clouds billowed from below the faraway hills. The earth became hard and the squirrels, having found acorns and hickory nuts plentiful (if slightly stunted), had great difficulty scratching a hole deep enough to store them. Grass in open areas, away from the sustaining shade of big trees, was totally brown and crisp. The nearby stream's happy gurgling, one of the delightful sounds of a healthy forest, had ceased. Its bed was reduced to patches of cracked and drying mud.

One day Ephran and Kaahli were carrying chestnuts back to the den of Jafthuh and Odalee. It was terribly warm, as it had been for many days, and they stopped to rest often. The heat was so stifling that it was hard to imagine that the cold season would ever invade the forest. That it would, overnight, turn the leaves gold and orange and red. That it would tiptoe over the grass, leaving it crisp and white. That it would roar through the trees, spitting fluffy snowflakes. But their instincts told them that, unless their world had changed beyond belief, bitter air would descend on them all too soon.

As they neared the big oak Ephran stopped in the shade of an aspen and dropped his nut to the ground. He sat on his tail, took a deep breath and looked over at his mate, who had followed his example. "Kaahli," he said, "I think it's time we go home."

Her face broke into a smile. "Yes, it is," she agreed, "unless we plan on staying here this cold season."

"That would not be a good idea," said Ephran, "for us or the rest of our families. We've been here long enough. This is not the place we choose."

Kaahli pulled up a dry weed with her paw and said, "If we're to leave it must be soon. We must find our own food to last us..." She sneaked a glance in his direction. "And it would be nice to find a warm den in a good solid tree."

The hint flew over his ears. "I want to see the sparkling Pond again," said Ephran, gazing in the direction of their nest. "I just hope there's still water in it. I'm lonesome for Klestra and the mallard family. We promised the ducks we'd be back before they leave for the warmer places. You know, though I never really thought of it before, I would really like to visit with Smagtu and Fetzgar too."

That evening there was genuine sadness when they announced their plans to leave for The Pond. It had been a wonderful time together. A time of peace, tranquility and happiness. None of them would ever forget it. And yet...

"It's probably for the best, for many reasons. At your age you should have some privacy," Jafthuh said to Ephran and Kaahli. "Besides, this many treeclimbers, all together in one place, will sooner or later attract the fox and hawk -- even so close to a den of Many Colored Ones."

"I also must be leaving," said Aden.

"Ah, we will miss you greatly, Aden," said Jafthuh.

Odalee nodded her agreement.

"Where will you go, father?" asked Kaahli, sadly aware that many trees would once more come between her and her father. This time she wanted to know exactly where he'd be.

"You are welcome to come with us," said Ephran. "I know we could find you a good tree near The Pond."

"No, no...thank you all the same, Ephran. I agree with Jafthuh -- you two should be free of family always in your branches. Anyway, I have decided to go back and find a tree in a place I knew when I was a young buck. It is a place you should all visit sometime, a place where water bubbles up from deep in the earth. A place called The Spring."

"Water from the earth?" Frafan looked up from an unbitten bud in his paws.

"That's right, Frafan," said Aden, "a continuous stream of cold and very clear water."

"How curious," said Ephran. "I would like to see this wondrous water that comes up out of the earth. Maybe we'll be visiting you before you get a chance to visit us."

"Is this place called The Spring close enough so that we can visit back and forth?" asked Odalee.

"Most certainly! It lies not far from where Laslum and I were caged. Its water spills into Rocky Creek. In any case, I would not likely be found too distant from the splendid hospitality I've enjoyed at the den of Jafthuh and Odalee. And what of you, Laslum?" asked Aden as he turned to his son. "Will you be coming with me?"

"I think not, father." Laslum glanced at Mianta, whose expression had turned, maybe for the first time, thought Ephran, downright bashful. "We have spoken of it a great deal," Laslum continued, a proud smile on his face, "and I've decided to accept Mianta's invitation and return to her den."

Mianta may have been embarrassed at first, but the modest glow didn't last long. Amid general laughter she turned on Laslum and gave him a big kiss, right in front of everyone. She then playfully accused him of wanting to stay just because her den was so soft and comfortable.

The announcement that they would become mates was, of course, no surprise to anyone, but it made the entire squirrel family very happy to hear it nonetheless. By the time they finished kissing, and hugging, and congratulating, there wasn't a perfectly dry eye in the whole troup.

The morning of Kaahli and Ephran's departure Aden held his daughter and assured her that he was a big squirrel now, that he could take care of himself, and that he'd be just fine where he was going. He'd be only a few branches distant from the den of Jafthuh and Odalee, and not much further from Laslum and Mianta. Why, he'd hardly be off in some remote and dangerous corner of the woods! These arguments seemed to comfort her.

She peered intently at him. "You will come and visit Ephran and me, won't you?" she asked.

"Of course! Of course I will! You don't think I would miss the opportunity to get to know the ducks, do you? I believe I might even like to meet your red squirrel and muskrat friends. I'm not too old to learn new tricks, you know...though I may have a bit of trouble with the skunk."

"And dear Laslum," said Kaahli, "I am so pleased for you. I know you'll be happy here with Mianta. I only hope we find each other in the same branches soon again."

"You will," Laslum said, "you will. Once more, my thanks to you and Ephran for rescuing father and me. And there's no need, I'm sure, to make you understand why I'm so happy that we decided to come with Ephran to search for his family."

"I suppose we should be grateful to Fred as well," said Mianta.

Ephran leaped to the solid limb of a nearby elm. "Keep to the high branches!" they shouted to each other. "Keep to the high branches!"

And so, with many backward glances, they began their long journey home -- to The Pond and Great Hill. The sun was already behind them and the air would soon be chilled. There was no question that the warm season was ending.

Following the dry creek bed along its gently undulating path toward Blue Lake, Ephran and Kaahli were lost in their own thoughts. They did not speak for some time. Ephran stopped in the top of a small birch tree surrounded by red-twigged dogwood bushes. Just ahead the little stream, when it held water, would come to the end of its meandering journey and empty into the lake. The lakeshore was much further from the trees than it had been when they left Fred here earlier. Sudan and buffalo grass grew thick where water had once been deep and cold.

"Isn't the den of Fred's Master somewhere on this lake?" asked Kaahli.

"Yes, it is," said Ephran. "Let's find a big tree. We may be able to see it from here."

A very tall and straight ash tree stood a little way back in the woods. Ephran and Kaahli raced into its highest limbs. They peered out at the lake which glistened and twinkled in the bright late warm season sunlight.

"There!" said Kaahli, pointing with her paw, "I see it!"

Down the shoreline was a squarish den built of interlaced tree trunks. Two large Many Colored Ones sat outside the den and close to a little puddle of flickering red light, dancing at the edge of the sandy beach, very near clumps of thick brown grass. So this was what fire looked like! Ephran had smelled it once before. He'd asked father what it was, and where it was coming from. But father knew not where. Far away across the trees, was all he could say. The smell itself, unknown though it be, was somehow terribly frightening, and it made his legs quiver. Now that same smell, maybe even more repulsive, was moving on the air, toward Ephran and Kaahli.

Kaahli wrinkled her nose. "Is that fire?" she asked, worry in her voice.

"Yes," he answered, "that must be fire."

"What are They doing with it?"

"I don't know. Not for warmth -- not on a day like today. Frafan might know."

How, she wondered to herself, would little Frafan know why these remarkably peculiar animals would make fire when the air was already so warm?

The Many Colored Ones, reclining by their fire, repeatedly put their front paws to their mouths and tilted their heads back. Only after watching for a time did Ephran and Kaahli realize that They were holding some type of smooth and shiny objects, shaped like the thick end of a broken branch, in their long paws. Then one of Them rose from what must have been a sitting position and tried to walk on its rear legs. It wobbled badly, leaned sideways like a tree in a high wind, lost its balance, and fell heavily in the sand. For some reason, that mishap sent both of the peculiar creatures into gales of high-pitched gurgling sounds.

"That One has not learned to walk on its rear legs," a baffled Kaahli said.

"Very strange," said Ephran. "It appears large enough to be an adult too."

"Do you see Fred anywhere?" asked Kaahli.

"No. I suspect he's either sleeping in the den or, Blue Sky Forbid, off exploring in the woods again."

They sat a while longer, puzzled and a little frightened -- even though they were a considerable distance from what had to be Fred's Master. These particular Ones were acting very strange, at least compared to others of their kind Ephran had seen. A visit with Fred would have been enjoyable, and the dog might have explained what these Many Colored Ones were up to, but Ephran and Kaahli felt uncomfortable. Without having to discuss it, they set out once again

156

through the trees, along the shore of the lake and toward where the sun would rise.

Eventually they found a hollow place in a wide tree trunk. The hole would have been fine for one squirrel, but it was a tight fit for two. It was good enough for a one night stay and, curled close together, they quickly fell asleep.

The sky had barely began to brighten when Ephran awoke. He'd been so deep in slumber that at first he didn't realize where he was -- or what had disturbed him. Half awake, he listened for any unusual sounds in the forest around them. He heard nothing. Then Kaahli coughed, and he realized what was amiss. A thick, acrid smell filled the air. He put his head outside the hole. The stars and moon were not visible. A thick gray haze swept over his head and enveloped the trees, giving them a mysterious appearance in the faint light. It looked very much like early in the warm season when the air was full of tiny water droplets, too tiny to see and too nearly weightless to fall to the earth. One knew water was there because one could feel it, cool and fresh and tickly, on the end of one's nose. This air might bear a resemblance to that air, but it was most definitely not burdened with water.

Kaahli woke to Ephran's gentle nudge. She stifled another cough and said, "Ephran...that awful smell. Like yesterday. Is it what I think it is?"

He looked into her face, just below him in the hollow tree. "I'm afraid so, Kaahli." He fought to control a feeling of dread. "It's the smell of fire again. Only this time I'm afraid it's free in the woods."

"We must run then," said Kaahli, trying to squeeze by him, through the narrow hole.

"Yes, we must," he said, holding her back with one paw, "but wait for just a moment."

"Wait?"

"Yes," he said again, face intent with thought, "wait until I can tell which way to run."

She did not understand. Not at all. How could he decide which way to run? What difference did it make? There was danger. It was very near. They must run. They must run soon...and they must run fast. Before the enemy caught them. That was all there was to it.

Then she remembered the time during the storm, when he told her the branches weren't safe. That had been difficult to understand too. It had been even harder to follow him into a hole in the earth. But, against all reason, all instinct, and her parents' lessons, she'd trusted him. She must trust him again. Watching his eyes, she sat back as her heart slowed.

Ephran observed the rolling smoke for a few minutes and then said, "Let's run now."

He ran up the crooked tree and jumped to a neighboring maple. Kaahli was on his heels. At first they moved swiftly and surely through the branches, running in the same direction that the smoke moved.

Ephran felt good about his plan. But he soon found himself slowing. They didn't seem to be gaining any ground. The fire was keeping up. The flames ran as fast as they did. Perhaps faster. It was getting harder and harder to breathe. Kaahli, behind him in a hickory tree, had stopped running but could not stop coughing. By the time he worked his way back to her, she was struggling for air.

Smoke became thicker by the moment. Kaahli's eyes were red and full of sad and frightened tears. More upsetting than the tears was the look of surrender that Ephran saw there.

"Dear one," he said, making his voice as firm and clear as he could, "the smoke seems less dense on the ground. Let's leave the branches and see if the air isn't sweeter there."

Kaahli was in no condition to argue. The ground was dangerous but she was willing to try anything that might make it easier to breathe and to see.

By the time they reached the forest floor the fire's effect on birds and animals caught in its hot and smoky path had become obvious. A group of five whitetailed deer came crashing through the underbrush, silent and graceful movements discarded. Big brown eyes, usually gentle and placid, were wide and fearful. Their flying hooves passed over Ephran and Kaahli, who were trying to catch their breath near the dry earth. Ephran helped Kaahli move closer to the base of a thick treetrunk so that they wouldn't be crushed by larger terrified animals.

A flock of crows flew over, cawing constantly to one another, words clipped and garbled. Two chipmunks ran by in complete panic. Ephran called to them but they seemed to look right through him, as though he weren't really there.

"Come, Kaahli," he coaxed, when he thought she was breathing easier.

They set out again. He couldn't allow her to just lie there, and let the fire overtake them.

Though she struggled valiantly, her legs grew weak and she kept falling behind. Sometimes he'd run back and urge her on. Other times, when he saw she was still moving, and to save his own strength, he'd wait for her and speak words of encouragement. Soon she didn't answer -- or even look at him.

He did not want to give up, but it was no use. Finally, she simply could run no more. She collapsed on the parched and hardened earth and said, "My love, I am done. I can't go on."

Her face was smudged, her beautiful thick fur bedraggled and filled with dust, her eyes red and full of despair.

She tried to smile. "You had the right idea, practicing with

Marshflower's young. I wish now...that we could both fly. Mostly I wish I could have stayed with you. Had your young..."

He thought he should speak, to invent some sort of encouragement, but he could hear the crackle of the fire itself as it attacked and devoured branches and leaves and grasses that had had the water sucked from them during the long drought. The heat on the forest floor was almost unbearable. He knew how Kaahli felt. He too was exhausted. He moved to be close to her. He wondered if it would be painful...if the hurt would last a long time.

"Ephran! Over here!"

The disembodied voice rose from thick gray clouds of smoke. Imagination. Could it be his imagination? Could hopelessness make the mind invent hope? He was desperate to save her, he realized that. But this did not feel like desperation. And this was not a dream. Actually, he might have heard that voice before. Where? He couldn't quite place it.

"Who is it?" he called. And he put his body over hers, trying to shield her from heat and smoke and from strange and unknown voices.

"Hurry! Over here!"

The voice was insistent.

Kaahli's watering eyes looked questioningly into his. All he could do was shrug. She coughed again, harder than before. He helped her to her paws.

Together they crept along the ground -- in the direction from which the voice had come. When he looked quickly behind, Ephran could see the flickering of red-orange flames through the dense black cloud of smoke. The fire was very near.

They found themselves in a clearing, beyond the edge of the trees, in a narrow patch of grass. A gust of air cleared the smoke for a moment; just long enough for both of them to see that they were standing very nearly atop a gaping hole in a hillock adjacent to a dry creek bed. Peering at them from atop the rim of that hole, gray-black clouds swirling around it, was a face. A familiar face. The face of Maltrick, the fox.

Kaahli gasped but did not move. She was beyond running.

"Hurry," said Maltrick. "You best come in quickly."

Ephran looked into the hunter's unsmiling eyes and said, "We'll take our chances out here."

"If you do you will soon be a chunk of smoldering fur," said the fox.

"Better that than a torn and mangled piece of flesh," said Ephran.

"The smell of smoke ruins my appetite," said the fox. "I won't harm you or your mate. And it will do me and mine no good to see you burn."

Kaahli turned to Ephran and said, "Come, Ephran. He means what he says."

She did not wait for his response. Nor did she look back. Without another word she ran the last few steps to the hole. The fox moved aside to let her pass and she vanished into the circle of blackness.

Maltrick and Ephran faced each other for an instant. Their eyes met through the swirling smoke. Then Maltrick turned and followed Kaahli into the hole in the earth. A searing blast of heat nearly crushed Ephran and he too jumped into the hole at the last possible moment.

He rolled over and over, further and further from the heat and smoke. He came to rest at the end of a tunnel in a pile of loose dirt. It was cool and moist. Kaahli was next to him, breathing slowly. The smell was not good in here, but it was far better than the stinging smoke.

As his eyes adjusted to the darkness he could make out Maltrick, laying in a larger chamber just across the tunnel he had rolled down. Next to Maltrick was a smaller fox, obviously his mate, and three young ones. They paid no attention to the squirrels -- at least for the moment. The pups watched their parents while the adults listened to the sounds outside.

Ephran peered about in the dim light, searching for another exit, a possible escape route. He couldn't see one. The tunnel might continue on to his left, but no light came from that direction. Two exits would be a good idea and he knew, if this was an abandoned badger den as he suspected, it probably had possessed that luxury at one time. However, the second tunnel may have collapsed or even been filled in. As he began to breathe and think easier he decided that, if worse came to worse, he'd fight his last fight right here. He would stand his ground. He would protect his mate as best he could.

Kaahli's eyes, like the foxes', were directed up the corridor they'd tumbled down. They were all intent on the fire raging through the forest above them. He was grateful that her attention was directed elsewhere -- that she had not had the time or interest to inspect the den she rested in.

Almost immediately he'd noticed two small piles of white bones. One stack was against the wall in the chamber the foxes inhabited. The other was just to his right. He kept his body between it and Kaahli. With all that had happened he was unsure how she'd react if she saw those remains of some poor creatures of the woods. She might lose all sense and attack the foxes. He was close to that himself. To do such a thing, the rational part of his mind told him, would be a sure way to end it all right then and there.

The angry crackling of the fire, the snapping of dry wood and weed as it was devoured, drifted to their ears. A whiff of smoke came down the tunnel. Just as it had on the other occasion when they'd found themselves in the earth, time seemed to pass very slowly. However,

"Hurry," said "Maltrick, "You best come in quickly."

after a long while, it grew silent above. The roar of flames became occasional spitting and hissing -- then it ceased altogether. A thin shaft of sunlight appeared in the tunnel. Still they waited. Finally Maltrick rose and eased his way up the passageway, toward the entrance.

After a few moments his voice echoed from above, "It is safe. You may come up now."

The vixen and her pups, almost full grown, turned to their very unusual guests, huddled on the far side of the tunnel. No doubt of it, thought Ephran, he and Kaahli were trapped. More surely and more hopelessly than Aden and Laslum had been. There was no way out of here without passing within a paw's length of a fox.

Ephran and Kaahli got to their paws. The foxes did not move. The squirrels trotted up the tunnel. No use to hurry. There were foxes at both ends.

Maltrick stood outside his lair, looking about at a changed world. The thick smoke was gone, but here and there thin streamers of gray-white fumes arose from a smoldering bush or a tuft of blackened grass. Air was moving briskly along the stream bed. It smelled fresh and clean.

Kaahli smiled and ran out unto the charred earth. The fire had cut a swath through the trees on both sides of Fox Brook, following the flow of air, but green leaves could be seen in the direction of The Pond.

Ephran stood for a moment, next to Maltrick. He looked into the gleaming eyes, almost directly above him.

"I am in your debt, Maltrick," he said.

"Farewell, Ephran," said the fox. "When you and your pretty mate have young ones, teach them to outsmart the hunter. I will try to enlighten my own so that they will not be easily fooled. But I admit at the outset that I do not hold high hopes. I fear they may have difficulty outwitting the offspring of those able to open cages of The Many Colored Ones."

Ephran ran a few steps, turned back and said, "I wish I knew if you are as unusual a fox as I think you are. Fortunately or unfortunately, you're the only fox I know."

Maltrick smiled at him, wheeled, and melted into his dark cavern.

CHAPTER XXIV

FAMILIAR BRANCHES

Ephran glanced back, unsure what he expected to see; Maltrick maybe, or one of his family, loping across the black earth in pursuit. No animals were to be seen. Smoke yet flowed from charred grass, winding in and out of clumps of roasted bushes and blackened trunks. Many trees still smoldered, and almost all of them had lost their leaves to the awesome heat. He couldn't believe it: saved by the earth again! Well, he thought, the earth had done its part, but the real saving was done by someone who had learned how to use the earth wisely.

Off toward where the sun would rise were large black clouds, marking the progress of the blaze as it raced away, pushed along by the stiff breeze. Ephran was amazed at how quickly the hungry fire had consumed nearly everything in its path. Green leaves had withered where they grew and a few still fluttered down from scorched branches, crumbling to ash when they touched the earth. But, in some places, and for no apparent reason, the fire had ignored a tuft of grass or a cluster of trees. They stood like green islands, awash in a grey-black lake of desolation.

Ephran's interest in the power of fire was not shared by Kaahli. While he poked along, snooping here and there, she had run ahead, toward the leafy treetops she could see in the distance.

"Kaahli!" he called, when he realized she was far ahead, "Wait for me!"

She stopped and turned, smudges of ash on her lovely face. Her appearance might have made him smile if the terror of the whole experience didn't show so clearly in her eyes. He caught up to her and sat on the warm earth, catching his breath.

"I'm sorry to leave you behind, Ephran," she said. "I felt that I had to run...run as fast as I could. I had to find a green branch..." She hesitated and peered over his shoulder. "Back there, in the den of the hunter, I...I was certain neither of us would ever run again."

"Never mind. I understand. Come now. The air has returned to my chest. Just ahead I think I see that green bough you've been looking for."

Indeed, untouched forest was close at paw. The first leafy tree they reached was a red elm. They scrambled up its sweet limbs, sturdy and full of life. Kaahli sighed, shivered, and lay down on a branch.

"No one would ever believe what we've seen today," she said, shaking her head from side to side.

Ephran said, "Klestra might believe it, but I doubt he'd be able to make ears or tails of it. And our families -- they have enough trouble understanding our friends, say nothing of a fox..."

"Our families!" Kaahli jumped to her feet. "Ephran! Do you think our families escaped the fire?"

She stretched her body upright on the branch, supporting herself against a small twig, gazing intently in the direction of Blue Lake as though she might be able to see, even from this great distance, that Aden and Jafthuh and Laslum and the rest of the squirrel family were safe.

"Ephran, we must go back! We must be certain our families are all right."

"Easy, Kaahli," said Ephran, "No need to worry. Our families are safe -- safe from this fire, at least."

"How do you know that?" she asked, astonishment in her voice. "How can you possibly say something like that when you can see no further than I can?"

"For the same reason I knew which way to run, which was the right idea -- even if we couldn't run fast enough. I'm certain that the fire was somehow set loose by Fred's careless Master and his friend. And their den was between us and the den of Jafthuh..."

"Oh please, Ephran! No lectures about sunset and clouds and moving air right now," she interrupted impatiently. "The fire came after us and it may very well have gone after them."

"No, Kaahli," he said gently, "the fire did not come after us. It didn't care about us one way or the other. It only went where the wind pushed it. It couldn't move in the other direction, toward our families. It could not run against the flow of the air."

It was not the family they'd left near the old farmhouse that worried him. He knew he was right about the wind. But what of Phetra? Didn't father and mother say that Phetra and his new mate nested between the lakes? That was exactly where the fire had started. No purpose would be served by sharing his apprehension with Kaahli. She wouldn't recognize Phetra if she ran headlong into him on a branch but, if she was made aware of Ephran's concern, she'd lose sleep worrying about him anyway. There was really no telling where Phetra might be. Ephran could only hope that he had not returned to his nest in the time since Mianta and Laslum had gone looking for him. He could only hope that he had not been asleep in his den when flames roared through his part of the forest.

While he fretted about his brother, Kaahli had been thinking. It was certainly true that the fire had traveled rapidly with the wind. It had been pushed so fast that it hadn't even had the chance to stray and attack Great Hill. Fire was not as strong as moving air. Their families would be unharmed. Unless Odalee had been watching the sky, they might not even know that flames had laid waste to a large part of the woods.

"Thank you," she finally said to him. "I think I understand."

He nuzzled her neck and said, "Let's rest a while before we travel on. If you aren't exhausted, I most surely am."

Though the sun was far from hiding behind the distant trees, Ephran and Kaahli's eyes were closed almost before their heads were settled on their paws. So they did not notice when the sun grew dim -- or when the air began to move, ever so gently, through the branches. It was not until the rumbling overhead became loud enough to wake them that they looked up.

Blue sky was covered by billowing clouds. Flashing light flickered between massive banks of darkness. Ephran's heart fluttered until he realized that there was no odor of smoke. He sniffed the air. It was thick with the smell of water.

"Ephran!" Kaahli said. "The stones..."

He knew what she meant, and he thought of the mourning dove, denied of its song once and for all by the stones from the sky.

"I think not," he said. "The angry smell is not there. And the air has become still. Are you afraid?"

"Not really. Are you?"

"Not much sense to be afraid now. We just came through a fire bigger and more ferocious than any squirrel would believe possible. And we followed that with a little side tour of a fox den."

She laughed and hugged him close as the first large drops splattered into the leaves. Like any treeclimbers, Ephran and Kaahli didn't especially care for wet fur. But this was a rare occasion. They ran to the earth, deeper and deeper into the woods, chattering and giggling, rolling in the wet grass. Water fell faster and faster, thicker and thicker. They did not mind that their fur became soaked and matted. The earth drank deeply. Ephran could feel its relief.

The sun broke out beneath clouds on the horizon just as they reached the butternut trees and the old squirrel nest where Ephran had spent his first night alone. Across the entire sky, stretching from Lomarsh, across Rocky Creek and The Spring, and all the way to Blue Lake, appeared a majestic multicolored arc of shimmering light. Though it wasn't a new sight for either of them, the wonder and majesty of it never dimmed. This particular arc might be the brightest and clearest they'd ever seen. When he was younger Ephran had asked every older squirrel he happened to meet what might cause such an astonishingly beautiful thing to happen right after water came from the sky. Some tried explanations. Some, like Rennigan, shrugged. None came up with an answer that satisfied him.

They ate fresh butternuts as the sun settled behind the trees. Afterward they lay together on a thick branch as the light dimmed. A distant pair of crows called to each other and a mourning dove cooed its twilight song.

Kaahli wanted to spend the night in the old nest her mate had told her about -- even though it was not in the best condition. The need for repairs didn't matter and, despite their short nap, weariness overwhelmed them and they fell asleep to the wonderful and nearly forgotten smell of wet earth. Even if he'd been aware of it, Ephran probably would not have cared that his tail was hanging through a hole in the bottom of the nest. It swung back and forth in the cool air, like an oak leaf at the end of the warm season, undecided whether to stay where it was or float to the forest floor.

They awoke at the same moment, and to the same sound that had roused Ephran that first day after he'd lost his family. Crows. Crows laughing. Crows harsh and scratchy laughing.

"Eeyah! Hoo many treeclumbers figure packed in'ere?" asked one voice.

"Dunno," squawked another, "but one fallin'ut bottum."

There came another screech, and loud cawing.

"Think tak anip outa fuzzy t'ing."

"Yeh. Like bik catapillar. Nice'njuicy maybe, huh?."

In the nest Kaahli turned to Ephran and whispered, "What are they talking about?"

"I don't know," replied Ephran and, just as the words left his mouth, realized how cold his backside felt. "Oh, my! They're talking about my tail!"

He jumped up and out -- unto a nearby branch, expecting at any moment a big yellow beak to close around his beautiful tail... and pull him through the hole.

Five crows perched in nearby branches. They took one look at the expression on Ephran's face and started laughing all over again. Kaahli's head popped out of the nest to find her mate, four legs wrapped around a slender limb, waving slowly to and fro. She tried not to, but couldn't help herself, and she burst into laughter.

"Very amusing, I'm sure," said Ephran, with an injured look on his face.

"Oh, my dear," Kaahli managed to gurgle, "you look...you look...like Frafan, trying to climb to the top of a skinny milkweed to see what's inside its pod."

Ephran peered at her and then at the crows. He grinned widely and started laughing himself. The crows fell silent. They watched the giggling treeclimbers for a few moments, then flew off.

Breakfast was butternuts -- again. The lack of variety in their diet didn't bother them. Fresh nuts were always a treat. Besides, this was not the time to think of food very long or very seriously. After all, Meadow Brook was just a short way ahead...and Meadow Brook bordered Great Hill...and Great Hill loomed high over The Pond. They were nearly home.

They passed the clearing with the berry bushes while the sun was still climbing. They ran around the base of Resting Hill and reached Meadow Brook when the sun was high above. They stopped to eat and rest. Meadow Brook was not totally dry but it held little more than a trickle. The water from the sky had helped, but it would take a great deal of it to fill the stream.

"Let's follow Meadow Brook to Rocky Creek," said Ephran. "Then, if we follow Rocky Creek to The Pond, we'll pass right by Klestra's den."

"Do you think we'll find him at home?" asked Kaahli.

"Not likely, I suppose," said Ephran.

They started along the weed-choked channel and, as they approached the union of Meadow Brook and Rocky Creek, they heard a happy gurgling sound. They ran to a small ironwood near the bank and from its top branches they could see clear water tumbling along the rocks.

"There is so much water here, Ephran!" said Kaahli. "It's not like the other streams."

"The rain helped," said Ephran, "but I suspect that Rocky Creek has held water this entire warm season."

Then she remembered. "The Spring," she whispered.

"Yes. Aden told us of water from the earth, from the peaceful place he plans to live. This water comes from The Spring -- and it flows into our Pond."

"Oh, Ephran! That's exactly what it is...Our Pond! Let's find our nest."

They jumped from high limb to high limb, chattering and laughing, recognizing landmarks, greeting every bird and chipmunk they saw. Then The Pond appeared, shining and winking, beckoning through thick green leaves. And they laughed the harder and their cheeks became wet with tears of joy.

"Noisy, noisy! You both might as well have red fur."

There was no mistaking the shrill voice. Klestra appeared on a cottonwood stump, wearing a grin as wide as his face.

It had been a very long time. Kaahli hugged the little red treeclimber so long and so hard that he finally begged her to stop saying; "Please, dear Kaahli! I won't survive your homecoming if I don't get a chance to breathe!"

Ephran and Klestra looked at each other. Klestra said, "Welcome home, my friend."

"It's good to be back," said Ephran.

"I congratulate you on your successful search for Kaahli's father and brother. But I shouldn't be civil to you, you know. What kind of friendship is it where someone ups and runs off...without so much as a simple 'goodbye'?"

"It was something we had to do, the two of us," said Ephran. "You must understand that I knew you would want to come with us if you heard of our plans. And, if you'd been along, you would have led the way and done all the work. Then where would I stand in Kaahli's eyes?"

Klestra laughed and said, "You're right! You're right! I would have done all the thinking and all the rescuing. I would have embarrassed both of you. You are pardoned on the basis of using good sense. Besides, I wasn't at home when you left. I didn't even know you were gone until the sun rose and set three times."

"Klestra, how did you know we found my family?" asked Kaahli.

"The ducks, naturally. They told all of us here at The Pond that they met and talked to you at a place called Little Lake."

"Did you know that we found Ephran's family as well?"

"Good gracious, no! How wonderful. More to talk about," said Klestra.

"I should have remembered that the ducks would bring you word," said Ephran. "How are our friends, the mallards?"

The smile faded from Klestra's face and he bit his lip.

"Klestra...?" Ephran tilted his head, trying to read his friend's face.

"What is it, Klestra?" asked Kaahli, alarm in her voice, "What's the matter?"

He looked away from their searching eyes and said, "Not all news is happy news, I fear. Your homecoming will not be without sadness."

CHAPTER XXV

SOLEMN HOMECOMING

Kaahli and Ephran were stunned. Sadness?

"Klestra," began Ephran, "what exactly do you mean...?"

"Wait. In a bit," interrupted Klestra. "I said too much for now. I'll tell you the whole story very shortly. At the moment we must get over to your side of The Pond. There are a lot of folks waiting near your nest."

Klestra's diversion was successful. For the moment at least, what was going on across the water, at home, was easier to think of than any sad tidings he might have. After all, he could not know that, since the sun came up, Ephran and Kaahli thought they were at the end of breathing twice. He could not know that his friends had little desire to consider unhappy possibilities right now. He could not know that the credit he gave himself for distracting them was largely undeserved.

"Who is waiting near our nest?" asked Kaahli.

"Oh -- Janey wren. Smagtu and Fetzgar. Probably the chipmunk family, among others," said Klestra mysteriously.

"How...?"

Before the question was asked, Klestra answered. "How did we know you were on your way home? This time the forest's most talkative messengers."

"Crows!" said Ephran.

"Sure. The old black blabberbeaks themselves. Come now, there is much to speak of. Let's join the others."

With that he turned toward The Pond and emitted a long, shrill chatter. The announcement flew across the sparkling water to those on the far side, those who'd been waiting for just such a signal. Thanks to the crows, Klestra knew his friends had approached the Pond by following Rocky Creek and he had been watching for them since shortly after sunrise. He jumped from the stump, ran off across the forest floor to a small poplar, and up unto its trunk.

He looked back and said, "Well, come on you two! Let's get a move on. Light from the sky will be gone before you know it."

Klestra led the way. They passed The Hedge, thick leaves sustained by deep roots. Then Great Hill loomed ahead, bathed in sunlight. The nest of brown leaves was just as they'd left it. At the base of their tree were a multitude of birds and animals, many sizes and shapes, some in the bushes and some on the ground.

Smagtu and Fetzgar were easy to make out. Two chipmunk families were there with all their young. The entire wren and oriole families perched in nearby dogwood branches below a large contingent of mourning doves. Old Mrs. Cowbird sat in a stunted bush. A group of robins, three or four cardinals, and even a few blackbirds were scattered in the higher branches. Ephran was surprised to see two large black crows land quietly a short distance away. He hoped that they weren't there just looking for an opportunity to make sport of the animals and smaller birds.

Most interesting, perhaps, were two figures on a limb near Ephran and Kaahli's nest, and another pair on the ground beneath the dogwood. Those in the tree appeared to be gray squirrels. Those on the ground had very long ears and one...one had a crooked ear!

Smagtu was the first to see Klestra coming through the trees with Ephran and Kaahli and he tried to direct all the animals and birds to shout together. He wasn't very successful, and the "WELCOME HOME" chorus was a bit off-key and ragged. It didn't really matter though.

At the time, Ephran didn't think about how very unusual this gathering was. The idea was as eccentric as the red treeclimber who'd arranged it. What a thought! A welcoming party for gray treeclimbers. And he'd invited all sorts of birds and animals -- creatures that generally ignored each other when at peace, creatures that could be rather vicious rivals when things weren't going so well. Like when berries got a bit scarce. Or when someone seemed to be spending too much time in someone else's territory. The best part was -- they all came!

The rabbit in the bushes was, of course, Mayberry, and with him was his lovely, longeared mate, Truestar. Needless to say, Ephran and the lopeared rabbit were extremely pleased to see one another again. Kaahli was delighted to meet Mayberry, the rabbit Ephran spoke of so frequently, and Ephran was equally charmed by Truestar. They greeted all the birds and talked for a moment to the chipmunks, who spoke so fast that it was hard to be sure if they were saying "Nice to see you" or "Lice on knees too". Janey sang her "Song of Welcome" for them. It sounded very much like her "Good Morning" song. Everyone cheered anyway, as though it was an original composition, and she became so rattled that she hid her tiny head beneath her wing.

Fetzgar and Smagtu, bashful bachelors that they were, tried to stay in the background, but Kaahli coaxed them over to where she could talk to them. Everyone moved aside pretty briskly when Smagtu waddled into the group but, much to their credit, no one held their nose or made any cutting remarks like, "What's that terrible smell in the woods today?".

After everyone had greeted the guests of honor, Klestra chattered loudly. When he had their attention he announced, "And now the big surprise for our hawkfighter!"

Just as Klestra pointed in their direction, Ephran remembered the shadowy figures he'd seen on the branch near his nest. "Hello, brother," said one of the shadows, as it moved out of the shade of an overhanging limb.

"Phetra!"

They clung to each other and Ephran closed his eyes tightly, to push back the water of happiness.

"I thought you were gone forever," Phetra managed.

"I had the same fear for you," said Ephran.

"We've been fine. The family escaped The Many Colored Ones who took down our tree. Father and mother now live near Mianta in a place..."

"I know," said Ephran, "we spent most of the warm season with them."

Phetra backed away from Ephran as though someone had pulled his tail. "What?" he said.

"We found Mianta, and then father and mother's den," said Ephran. "It's a long story, but I'll tell you all of it. And you must tell me how you found your way back here. I know that traveling is not your favorite thing to do. I'm just relieved that you weren't trapped by the fire."

"Fire? In our part of the forest?"

"I'm afraid so. It started between the lakes and ran toward where the sun rises. It ate many trees," said Ephran.

Phetra's face fell. "Our den was just this side of Blue Lake. I suppose our tree will be gone."

"Cheer up!" said a voice behind them, "there are a lot of trees in the woods. Just be thankful we weren't asleep in our nest. We'll find a new den if we have to."

"Ephran," said Phetra, a smile returning to his face, "I would like you to meet my mate, Roselimb. As you can hear for yourself, she is not easily disheartened. And, since you wondered how I found my way back to Great Hill, she's the reason. She seems unable to stay in one place for very long."

"I'm pleased to meet my brother's mate. And I admire a treeclimber who can shake off bad luck with such good humor," said Ephran.

"I am honored to know Ephran," she said, "very probably the most famous gray squirrel in the woods."

"That is highly unlikely, but thank you for your words," he said, and he directed their attention to Kaahli. He introduced her to his brother and Roselimb. She greeted them with a hug and said, "At last! I was afraid I might never meet you two. My goodness, I've never seen so many travelers in one squirrel family!"

"So you've spent the warm season here," said Ephran.

"Yes," said Phetra. "At first we stayed on, thinking you and

171

your mate would return any day. We enjoyed ourselves and the time just slipped away. Until the day..."

"Maybe you should look for a good tree nearby," Klestra interrupted nervously. "Plenty of food for another squirrel family. Isn't there, Ephran?"

"No. I don't think so," said Phetra. "After what happened here I think we're ready to move on. My mate has itchy feet anyway. We were preparing to leave when we heard Ephran and Kaahli were on the way here."

Ephran's brow furrowed. "'After what happened here'? What does that mean? What's all the mystery around here anyway?"

"Come 'n git it!" shouted Fetzgar.

Fetzgar, Klestra, Mrs. Chipmunk, and Roselimb were in charge of refreshments and they had assembled a fine assortment of delicacies. Klestra had visited his secret place and, with Roselimb's help, this time found some reasonably fresh golden corn, still on the stick. Fetzgar had brought a wonderful array of soft white roots from beneath the water, at least three kinds, along with some large green tubers. The chipmunks had collected a great many seeds, both large and small, and more green buds than anyone would have thought possible this late in a dry warm season.

The sun seemed to sink quickly as the friends ate and talked and laughed. Janey, the mourning doves, and the robins had rehearsed a number of songs. They sang them beautifully.

When the last tune had been sung and the cheers and congratulations had quieted, Ephran stood on the fallen bough where he'd been laying and said, "My good friends...my brother and his mate: I can hardly express our happiness to see all of you. And my heart is glad to be back at the nest I built. The same one my mate rebuilt."

There was loud laughter and Fetzgar used the noise to cover a belch.

Ephran continued, "Kaahli and I thank you for welcoming us as you have. We are greatly honored..." He hesitated, looked around at the gathered friends and said, "However, not everyone I would expect here is here. And not everything that should be said here is being said. I suspect something is very wrong. Where are the mallards?"

There was no answer. Ephran and Kaahli waited, looking into one face after another. Everyone stopped eating. Eyes were either cast down, as though inspecting their own feet, or else raised to the darkening sky, perhaps to count stars. Phetra started to speak, but Klestra interrupted.

"It's all right, Phetra. I told your brother while we were still on the far side of The Pond that I would be the one to tell him of the ducks. The time, I fear, is come."

Klestra turned to Ephran and Kaahli, swallowed once, and

asked, "Cloudchaser and some of his young met you at a place called Little Lake, did they not?"

"Yes, they did," said Ephran, putting a front leg over Kaahli's shoulder, and holding her close.

"They told you that Many Colored Ones had visited The Pond?"

Ephran and Kaahli both nodded, worry beginning to cloud their faces. Ephran's stomach did not feel right, and this time it was not because he was hungry.

"Cloudchaser was unsure that They meant harm to any of us," continued Klestra. "There were two of Them and They came without thundersticks. But it worried him that They took a long branch from the ground and tried to poke it into your nest. So he wanted you to be warned before you returned. He thought They might be interested in whether or not squirrels lived here. Obviously Phetra and Roselimb were nearby but they stayed out of sight in a tree near The Hedge..."

"What else did They do aside from trying to reach our nest?" asked Ephran.

"Very little. They came back two other times and mostly just sat beneath your tree, stretching their long rear legs in the grass, looking out at the water, and babbling to each other with those funny sounds They make. They didn't try to be quiet either time They came. We all had ample warning to hide. And the mallards had time to fly away, long before They got close. They didn't stay long. They left when the sun did."

Klestra stopped talking and took a deep breath.

"When They came the third time They moved noiselessly. As near as any of us can guess, They must have crept on all fours along Bubbling Brook. When They stood on their hind legs, right at the edge of the cattails, everyone was totally surprised. And this time They both carried the terrible sticks.

"Cloudchaser and Marshflower were in the water near their nest while two of their young ones played nearby. The rest of the family was off, testing their wings on a flight to Little Lake. Marshflower saw the hunters first. She quacked a warning and took wing toward Great Hill, telling the young to follow her. The brother and sister got up quickly as well. But they became confused. They flew in the wrong direction..."

Kaahli choked, as though a nutshell had caught in her throat. Ephran gasped, disbelief and horror on his face. Grimly, Klestra went on. "Thundersticks make a very loud noise, as you probably know. So loud that it knocked the young drake from the air. He fell at the edge of the bullrushes. Cloudchaser was quacking loudly, shouting instructions at his daughter, telling her to fly low over the water and away from The Many Colored Ones. When he saw she was safe -- and only then -- he got out of the water himself. He flew rapidly. He was nearly over the edge of The Pond when They pointed their sticks at him. The sticks made noise and smoke many times. At first Cloudchaser seemed unhurt. Then one wing buckled and he began to fall.

"I watched all this from my tree, you see. I saw Cloudchaser right himself with great effort as he flew over me. I shouted to him. 'Fly on, greenheaded one! Fly to safety!'

"He looked down at me. He was close enough that I could see pain in his eyes. He smiled anyway. He struggled to go higher in the sky, but he must have tired, for he set his wings then and glided through the air a long way. I lost sight of him over Lomarsh."

Kaahli wept openly and Roselimb drew close and tried to comfort her. Ephran, one leg around Kaahli, looked as though he himself might have been struck by the noise of a thunderstick. There was silence except for Kaahli's sobbing. No one could think of a word to say.

"When did this happen?" Ephran asked quietly.

"The sun has set five or six times since they fell," answered Klestra.

"Did the young drake escape?"

"The Many Colored Ones picked up the young one in their paws," said Phetra. "His breath was gone."

After a moment Ephran asked, "Did anyone try to find Cloudchaser?"

"Marshflower and two of her young came back later, after the hunters were gone," said Klestra. "They flew over Lomarsh but saw no sign of Cloudchaser."

"I've not been to Lomarsh," said Ephran with a cracking voice, "but I've heard it's very dense. A bird would not be able to see down into the weeds. Did any, other than birds, go to search?"

An involuntary snort, a sort of communal gasp, rose from the assembled forest creatures.

"Go to Lomarsh on the ground?" asked a shocked Truestar. "It is far too dangerous. It is one place where foxes share territory. Hawks fly over it almost constantly and it is said that there is an owl in every tree. Large snakes hide in tangled grass -- and there are no high branches for treeclimbers. The earth is soft and wet, and provides no shelter for us groundrunners..."

"Lomarsh. Everyone is afraid of Lomarsh -- afraid of its hawks and foxes. Even when there are places much closer which conceal far more dangerous enemies. I will go at the next sunrise," said Ephran flatly.

"I will go and find my friend."

CHAPTER XXVI

UNEXPECTED HELP

After a long while of silent tears, Ephran fell asleep. He dreamt that the cold season had come and gone, and that the water on The Pond again sparkled in warm sunlight. He dreamt that Cloudchaser and Marshflower and their young, now radiant with feathers of bright green, rust, and blue, returned to joyous greetings of all the birds and animals that nested near and on the water. He dreamt that he and Kaahli had young of their own, and that they were healthy and clever and full of breath and joy. And he dreamt that it was all a dream, and he woke up with the fur on his head and paws damp and chilled.

He crawled out of their nest and lay on a thick branch in his tree; the tree he'd chosen when he first returned here, the tree he pointed out to the mallards the first day he met them, the tree he'd watched from as the little ducklings grew into young adults.

The air was cold and unmoving. The woods was bathed in a gentle glow from an almost perfectly round moon. It was bright enough to see Fetzgar's den -- the one that held the deserted duck nest. High above the treetops were stars, twinkling in uncounted profusion. Some were large and shaded red or orange. Some were very tiny and clustered, like a sparkling silver cloud.

Kaahli joined him and they lay close together for some time, sharing their warmth and the branch, gazing into the dimly lit woods and at the stars reflected in the still water. Their friends had all found shelter and none could be seen.

Finally Ephran said, "I didn't mean to wake you, Kaahli."

"You didn't wake me. I haven't slept soundly."

"Why is that? Are you also upset that no one looks for Cloudchaser?" asked Ephran.

"I'm upset about Cloudchaser; that much is true. What has happened here is tragic. But what has happened has happened. There is no help for it. It's you I'm upset about."

"Me?"

"Yes, Ephran, my love -- You. My dear, impulsive treeclimber who would risk everything in Lomarsh."

"What would you have me do, Kaahli? Abandon a friend?"

"It's been a long while since Cloudchaser fell. Do you really think you could find him in that thick tangle of reeds and high grass and muddy water?"

"You sound as though you've been there," said Ephran, "yet I know you haven't. What you know of Lomarsh is what I know -- what all of us know. And we don't even really 'know' that. It's only what others have told us. Believe me, what evils our friends think dwell in Lomarsh is greatly exaggerated. And badly misplaced."

"What we hear may or may not be exaggerated," she said. "The point is that an attempt to rescue Cloudchaser would be a dangerous thing. Once we found father and Laslum we knew they would be able to run through the branches before we endangered ourselves. This time we not only don't know exactly where Cloudchaser is; we're not even sure that he'll ever fly again."

"Again I ask you: Would you have me put worry about possible, maybe imagined, hazards ahead of concern for Cloudchaser?" asked Ephran.

"I would have you weigh carefully what there is to gain and what there is to lose -- for both you and Cloudchaser." She looked into his eyes and he saw the tears collecting in hers. "Ephran," she whispered, "I don't want to be without you."

While they talked the sky behind Great Hill began to brighten, ever so little. Sunrise was less noticeable than usual because of the moon's splendor, but now the more penetrating and realistic golden light of day started to mix with, and slowly replace, the dim and dreamy silver of the night. Kaahli observed, out of the corner of her eye, a rabbit she recognized as Truestar hopping slowly and jerkily between the trees, looking for an early snack beneath the bushes. Then another silent shadow caught her attention almost as soon as it detached itself from that of a big ash tree.

"Ephran!" she screamed.

A glance at her face told him where to look. He whirled on the branch just in time to see an owl swooping through the misty dawn.

There would be no heroic leap to a skyhunter's back this time. Ephran was much too far away to be of any immediate help. But he shouted "Truestar!" into the silent forest anyway, and his voice seemed to echo back to his ears with a hollow sound. Though he knew he couldn't get to Mayberry's mate quickly enough to save her from harm, he could only hope she could keep the owl on the ground for a few moments. Then perhaps he could get there in time to prevent her from being carried away in the sharp and fatal claws.

Though he'd never run with such frantic speed, he hadn't even reached the base of his branch before two heavy black bodies struck the owl.

A puff of feathers, brown and white -- a few black -- floated in the air. This time the loud cawing was not to welcome the sun, which had just arrived over the edge of the earth.

By the time Ephran reached the earth, the owl was on the ground, feathers in disarray, back against a black cherry tree. Wings up, he attempted to fend off two crows, one flapping back and forth over his head and one on the ground, both pecking at him ferociously.

176

Ephran ran up to Truestar who was standing, untouched and spellbound, watching the battle. He said, "Run into the woods, Truestar!"

At the sound of his voice, her eyes cleared and she quickly obeyed. He then turned to the crows and the owl. He'd tell the crows to get out of his way -- to leave the owl to him. He wanted to tear, and scratch, and bite. He wanted to see the hunter's feathers turn red. He wanted the owl to struggle and plead for mercy. And, at that moment, he truly felt he could make it all happen.

However, the fray was obviously over before he could get into it.

"Please! Please!" said the tattered owl, "What in the name of moon and stars is the matter with you fellows anyway?"

One of the crows asked, "Eeyah! What do thi spart wuds?"

"Why, hunting of course!" answered the owl. "You know as well as I that my old territory has been destroyed by fire."

Ephran looked again at this particular owl. "Was your nest near Fox Brook?" he asked.

The owl lowered his wing. He seemed surprised at hearing another voice. It took him a moment to focus on the squirrel in the increasingly bright light.

"As a matter of fact, yes," the big bird answered. Why do you ask?"

"Because I visited your territory at the end of last cold season."

"Hmmm," said Winthrop, squinting at Ephran, "you would not be given to eating frozen berries while perched on fallen trees, would you?"

"I am the one," said Ephran.

"Of course. Of course," nodded the owl. "I would like to know, when you have time, just how you managed that escape. You should have been mine, you know. I had you, no doubt of it."

"Some call it luck," said Ephran.

"Luck, you say?"

The crows stood, like protective parents, at either side of the owl. They crowded the hunter against the stump so tightly that he could not move unless they allowed it, or unless he pushed them aside...and that would be a very difficult thing to do.

One of the crows said, "Lek go 'istime. But nefer combuck 'isplace. 'nough sadness 'ere."

"Cum gen, fine you," said the other crow, "whut star twee finish. Yoo no eyes hun dark -- or light."

Winthrop looked at one crow, then the other. Finally he turned to Ephran and said, "I believe they mean it."

"I'm sure they do," said Ephran. "And I can tell you that if they won't drive you off, there are plenty of other animals and birds around

177

"YOU CAN BE CERTAIN THAT I'M LEAVING,
YOU ARE ALL DOWNRIGHT UNNATURAL!"

here who will." He glanced at the other creatures who had gathered in the trees and around the little clearing after being awakened by the crows' commotion.

"You can be certain that I'm leaving," said Winthrop. "I can scarcely believe this place. You are all downright unnatural. There are other parts of the woods where one can tell the hunters from the hunted."

Gathering what dignity he could, Winthrop carefully brushed past the crows. They moved ever so little, just enough to let him pass. He smoothed his feathers, took three quick one-legged hops on the ground, then spread his wings and rose up between the trees. They watched him fade, like a grey shadow, as he flew along the base of Great Hill and out of sight.

Ephran turned to the crows who gazed back with dark and emotionless eyes. "Thank you," he said.

He didn't know what else to say. He wouldn't have guessed, in the furthest reaches of his imagination, that crows would consider helping any of the woodland creatures. However, whatever their motive, they had indeed helped. They had most assuredly saved Truestar. And, although he didn't think of it until much later, they may have saved his breath as well. Even a brave and strong squirrel, blindly angry at hunters in general, might not have fared particularly well in a skirmish with a large white owl.

The crows didn't respond to his thanks, but he was quite sure that, before they flapped their big wings and lifted off the ground, they both smiled at him. They sailed slowly over The Pond, cawing loudly, waking every creature that might still sleep on this bright Autumn morning.

Ephran ran to where Truestar shivered beneath a wild rose bush. Kaahli was with her. The cottontail shivered as Kaahli spoke softly in her ear. Now, long after the fact, she realized she had nearly been caught by an owl. Fright glittered in her big brown eyes.

Mayberry, obviously distressed, came bounding across the forest floor. "Truestar!" he cried. "The chipmunks just woke me. They talk so fast that I couldn't understand them. What happened?"

"Oh, Mayberry....," she began, but she couldn't continue.

"It's all right now," said Kaahli to Mayberry. "She was attacked by an owl, but it didn't harm her. It's been driven off."

"Oh," sighed Mayberry, as he moved to his mate's side and offered the comfort of his nearness. "They woke me up and Truestar was not at my side and..."

He halted in mid-sentence and looked at Ephran. "...'Driven off'?"

"No, my friend," said Ephran, shaking his head. "It's not what you're thinking. I did not frighten off a very large and hungry white owl. I would like to say I had, but it may have been too large a nut to crack, even if I could get my teeth around it. No -- two crows drove the owl off. It seems I'm destined to owe my deliverance from birds...to birds."

"Crows?" Mayberry's eyes grew wider yet.

"Yes. Crows."

"Why would crows...?" Mayberry's voice trailed off.

"Yes, indeed," said Ephran, "why would crows help a rabbit? I wondered the same thing. Maybe they just don't like owls. But they said there'd been enough sadness here."

The silence was filled with the forest coming awake. Janey wren burst into her song of welcome and the mourning doves answered her. A family of sparrows twittered at each other among the thick leaves of The Hedge. The warbling of a yellowbreasted meadowlark could barely be heard, far away, in a clump of thick sudan grass near The Meadow.

"A wise old fox squirrel once told me that we all need help now and again," Ephran said. "I guess it sometimes comes from where we wouldn't expect it."

"And," Mayberry added, thoughtfully and under his breath, "maybe because even crows can learn by example."

CHAPTER XXVII

MARSHFLOWER RETURNS

T he rabbits and squirrels sat down to eat where The Hedge ended, at the shore of The Pond. They were joined by the chipmunks and, a bit later, by Phetra and Roselimb. Mr. and Mrs. Robin rested in wild honeysuckle bushes, having already had their rather repulsive breakfast of earthworms, pulled from the damp ground at the edge of the water.

Discussion was lively, and each new arrival had to be told of fair Truestar's rescue from the terrible white owl. No one could come up with an explanation of why crows might do such a good deed. Mayberry smiled to himself.

The only one who remained silent was Ephran. During a lull in the conversation Klestra turned to him and said, "My friend, you are very quiet. Do you still plan on going to Lomarsh?"

Ephran, shifting an acorn shell from paw to paw, and staring across The Pond, said, "Yes, Klestra. I'll be leaving very soon."

No one said anything for a moment and then Phetra spoke. "My brother; I must tell you that some of us have talked and we feel that this idea of yours is very unwise..."

"Marshflower!"

The cry came from Mr. Robin, who was the first to see her, swinging widely over the water, then setting her wings and descending toward them. Everyone moved aside to make room for the big brown duck and her six young ones, now almost as large as their mother.

The mallards' neighbors, those who made their home near The Pond and Great Hill, welcomed them with affection. The enthusiasm of the welcome was diminished only because there were seven where there should have been nine. It was not until Marshflower greeted those she had expected to see in this place that she noticed those she had not anticipated.

"Ephran! Kaahli!" she cried. And she opened her wings to them as tears filled her eyes.

"Marshflower," said Kaahli, with a trembling chin, "we are so sorry. We wish...we wish..." Her voice failed her.

The squirrels pressed themselves into the hen's soft breast feathers. Marshflower rested her beak on the back of Kaahli's neck and folded her wings around both of them. The young mallards, along with the other birds and animals, stood silently.

"My dear friends," Marshflower finally said, "we have sorely missed you."

"And we missed you," sobbed Kaahli.

"We were all so happy to hear that you found your family,

Kaahli," said Marshflower. "We had a celebration the day Cloudchaser came home with the news of your success."

"Later we found Ephran's too. We spent many days at his parents' den, with his brothers and sisters," said Kaahli.

"How wonderful that you could be with your loved ones during the warm season!" said Marshflower.

"Wonderful?" Ephran groaned, finally breaking his silence. "How can you say it was wonderful that we were far from The Pond? We weren't here when you needed us. Now two of yours are... are..."

"Oh, Ephran," said Marshflower, "you must not feel that way. There was nothing you could have done."

"Nothing? I might have warned you of The Many Colored Ones' coming. I should have known They'd cross over sooner or later, or sneak around the base of the hill as They did, along Bubbling Brook. I might have heard Them..."

"I don't understand all your words, Ephran, but I suspect that our hearing is every bit as good as yours. Unfortunately, the hunters were very quiet. None of us heard Them coming. Not Cloudchaser, not my young, not Fetzgar, and not me."

"I might have seen Them from a high branch long before They came so near," protested Ephran.

"Perhaps," said Marshflower. "Then again, you might have been asleep in your nest. Or you might have been visiting Klestra on the far side of The Pond. Or you might have been off exploring, or looking for nuts on Great Hill. Mightn't you?"

Ephran lowered his head.

"You have to understand that you cannot blame yourself for what happened. None of us is guilty. It seems hunters are always with us."

Ephran said, "All I know is that my friend may be badly hurt and in need of help. I can't leave him to suffer alone. I want to find him."

"Oh, Ephran...," said Kaahli.

"That would be a mistake, Ephran," said one of the young drakes.

"Why is that? Someone will have to explain to me why it's a mistake to look for the lost." said Ephran.

"We have looked," said a young hen.

"Yes, I know you have -- you have looked from high in the air. But I doubt you can see well enough down into the tangled weeds to tell what is or what is not there. I will be on the ground. My eyes will search from a different angle. I'll be able to find Cloudchaser."

"Perhaps you are right, Ephran. You have certainly proven you can find the lost. Let us say that you were successful. That you find

Cloudchaser. May I ask then; what will you do if you do find him?" asked Marshflower.

Ephran's face registered surprise. "What will I do? Wh...What do you mean, what will I do?"

"Just what I asked. What will you do if you find Cloudchaser?"

"Well, I will...I will...well, it all depends."

"It depends? Depends on what?"

"Well...on his condition. On, uh, what we find around us. What...what we think might be the best course..." He finally silenced his tongue and looked off into the branches.

"There is no reason for it, Ephran," she said. "You have to see that. You have proven to everyone that you would risk the very air in your chest to help. This time it is needless. Even foolish. Before you left to seek Kaahli's family I remember you saying you would not take Klestra because you did not want to endanger him."

Marshflower looked into Ephran's eyes. "Lomarsh is a tangle of vines, burs, thistle, and scrub bushes, all growing in foul-smelling water and mud," she said. "You could pass within a taillength of another animal and, unless you smelled it, or unless it made some sound, you would pass by and never know it was there. But, say by some chance you did find Cloudchaser. What if he was seriously injured? You could not move him through that snarled growth. Where would you take him anyway? Would you protect him from the marauding fox? Even if you were able, to what end?

"If he is not badly hurt, but simply cannot fly, my proud mate can fend for himself. He is clever -- and a very brave and strong duck. If anyone can fall into Lomarsh and come out again, he can. As amazing a treeclimber as you are, if you were there more than likely he would end up with both you and himself to worry about."

For a long while Ephran said nothing. Nor did his friends. He looked from face to face at those gathered around him. He gazed at his brother and then, for an especially long time, at Kaahli. Then, he took in a very deep breath and slowly shook his head.

"You're right," he said, "just as Kaahli was -- when the owl came. I couldn't help Cloudchaser. And I could hurt Kaahli."

"We know this isn't easy for you to say," said Klestra, who had arrived in time to hear most of the conversation.

"Not easy, but wise," said Mayberry. "No one questions Ephran's courage."

"Cloudchaser would be pleased and grateful," said Marshflower. "He picks his friends well." She sighed deeply. "Ephran, Kaahli, we must be leaving. We have a long way to go."

"But it's early yet!" protested Ephran.

"Yes. It is a bit early," agreed Marshflower. "But I can't help fearing for my young now. I know a safe place far away."

183

"Will you be back next warm season?" asked Kaahli.

"To nest on The Pond? I don't know. There are many memories here, good and bad. In any case, we will surely stop to visit; even if we feel we must build a new nest elsewhere."

"We must leave too," said Roselimb. "It's entirely possible that our den was destroyed by fire. We might have to find a new home before the snow flies."

"And we should be getting back to our warren," said Mayberry. "It is much safer there, where we know places to feed and hide from hunters."

"Must everyone leave at once?" cried Kaahli. "It will seem so lonely after we've had so much company."

"I still here," said a sad voice from the back of the group.

"Of course you are, Smagtu," said Kaahli, "and Ephran and I are so grateful that you'll be close b...ah, that you'll be here."

The sun had climbed well over the treetops before all the goodbyes had been said. They promised each other that they would not lose contact with one another, that they would remember that they were friends and, when the warm season returned, that they would all meet here again -- right here at the corner of The Hedge, on the shore of The Pond.

Two by two the animals walked or waddled or hopped or flapped away until only Ephran, Kaahli and Klestra were left, sitting together in the stunted grass near the water. Smagtu lay, rolling about and playing with his tail, back near the trees. A few birds remained in the branches.

Fetzgar had slipped away from the group, feeling the need to inspect the mallard den, and clean up a little bit. He'd had a few meals there and left things a bit on the messy side. Now he returned, soaking wet and obviously excited. He moved as fast as he could -- up the muddy shoreline to where the treeclimbers sat and talked quietly.

"Where'd everybody go?" wheezed the old muskrat, short of breath, "got them ducks' place all ready fer 'em."

"They left, Fetzgar," said Kaahli.

"Dagnab! Jest when I was gittin' use to 'em bein' around, they ups and takes off. Whut 'bout them other birds? 'N them rabbits...'nother treeclimbers?"

"All gone," said Klestra. "Gone to their own nests, or to warmer places. Since when do you care about other birds or animals around your Pond?"

"Foo!" the muskrat said, and slid back into the water.

CHAPTER XXVIII

BACK ACROSS GREAT HILL

Ephran woke to a sharpness in the air that told his nose that the cold season had placed its front paw into the forest. Open water was still visible in the middle, but the edge of The Pond sparkled smooth and brittle among the cattails. Now there was no question; the sun was spending less and less time in the sky above and more and more of it hidden behind the far hills. Brown, yellow, orange and red leaves covered the ground, forming a blanket beneath which tiny creatures of the earth had already begun their long sleep.

Ephran was grateful to Fetzgar for his obvious presence on The Pond, and for Klestra, who seemed to visit more often now. Sometimes he'd find himself wishing he could speak to father or mother for just a few moments. He was lonesome for Phetra and little Frafan...the whole family. Maybe next warm season he and Kaahli would travel that way again.

Smagtu slept in his dark earth tunnel. Mayberry and Truestar were far away with their family. Janey wren, the orioles, and the doves had flown away, across the edge of the earth. The woods was poorer for lack of their songs. A few robins remained, but they sang less and less often.

The brisk air now belonged to massive flocks of blackbirds. Gathering to fly to those warmer fields and forests far away, they would materialize with heart-stopping tumult, a dark whirlwind among the bare trees. After a few moments of nervous squawking from crowded perches, they would fall silent. Then, as suddenly as they appeared, and for no apparent reason, they would swirl away to some other part of the forest.

"Ephran, we simply must find a decent den inside a tree before snow comes." Kaahli took a deep breath and, for a moment at least, ceased picking dusty leaves and sharp dry twigs from the floor of their nest.

Ephran had brushed and fluffed up the hawk feather, attempting to make it look more respectable. The effort was becoming hopeless. Gusty air and hot sun had taken their toll and the feather seemed more bedraggled every time he looked at it.

"I suppose you're right," he said, adjusting the feather to its niche in the nest. "I wouldn't mind the warmth and security of a tree den myself. And there was a time I thought I'd never want to nest far from The Pond, but..."

"We've been comfortable," said Kaahli, too busy to be paying close attention to him, "and we have many friends here. Just in case we stay I'm going to freshen this place up. But there's no reason we shouldn't be able to find something nearby. We've not really taken the time to look carefully for a good tree."

That was true. It seemed there had been something to occupy their attention almost constantly since their return to The Pond. The search for food had begun and they'd found a number of hickory nuts and acorns, along with a few butternuts. If they were to find a cozy den, and move their food supply close to it, they must get down to some serious searching.

"I wonder if there might not be a suitable tree on the other side of Great Hill?" said Kaahli, glancing at Ephran.

Ephran said nothing, but he turned his face to the massive slope. When he didn't respond Kaahli looked up at him and tried to interpret his expression. Was it fear she saw there? She couldn't believe that this special treeclimber of hers was frightened by a hill. Why would he be afraid of that hill, of all hills? It was where he grew up, after all, happy and secure in the den of a loving family.

When he finally spoke it was as though to himself, as though she wasn't even there. "Yes," he said quietly, "The time is come. Time to go back over Great Hill."

"Ephran, would you like me to come with you?" Kaahli asked.

"No!" he said quickly, avoiding her gaze. "You stay. You finish what must be done with the nest..." He calmed his voice. "There's no certainty that I can find a new one."

"When will you go?"

"Now is as good a time as any. Maybe Klestra would go with me. I'll see if I can find him."

She hugged him and he hugged her back, more tightly and longer than usual, she thought. He set out then, without looking at her again.

Lost in thought, he traveled through the branches near The Pond. The sun shone brightly, but with little warmth, and a bank of dark clouds could be seen, approaching from where the sun would set. He stopped in a high bough and gazed toward Lomarsh, barely visible from here. It looked as though it might hold open water, which he couldn't remember being able to detect before. Either a great number of tangled bushes and weeds had shriveled, making things easier to see, or else there was actually more water in that big hole...

"Hey! You up there!" The voice startled Ephran.

"Klestra!" he called back. "I was just on my way to find you."

"Coming to find me, you say. Is that good or bad? May I ask why I'm the object of yet another of your searches?"

"Because I want you to come and look for a new home for Kaahli and me," said Ephran.

"Ah, I see. Sweet Kaahli has decided that she wants a den inside solid wood. Smart treeclimber. It will be safer there."

"Safer?" repeated Ephran. His gaze wandered to the abandoned mallard nest, encased in brittle frozen water.

"By the way," said Klestra, clearing his throat, "isn't that the way this whole relationship started -- the two of us looking for someone's home?"

"I believe you're right," said Ephran, as he joined his friend in the lower limbs of a bare maple tree, "Is that significant?"

"I don't know for sure," said Klestra, "but among red squirrels it's said that, while we breathe, we're only allowed a limited number of trees in which to spend the dark hours. With all the traveling you and I have done I can only assume that we're not exceeding your allowance."

Klestra giggled at what he thought was an amusing fable, but the laughter faded when he realized that Ephran had not so much as smiled. "I hope you're right, Klestra," he said slowly, eyes fixed over Klestra's shoulder on Great Hill. "I hope you're right."

"Ah....where would you suggest we begin looking?" asked Klestra.

"Kaahli thinks the other side of the Hill is a likely place."

"I see. The place of your family's old nest."

"Yes. Where I grew up. Or at least where I was supposed to grow up." With a sigh, Ephran got to his paws and flicked away a loose piece of bark. "Well, I guess we'll never find out what's over there if we stay sitting over here."

They set out, retracing Ephran's earlier path, passing Ephran and Kaahli's nest. Kaahli was not there. Perhaps she was searching on her own, but there was little chance of finding a prime tree on this side of Great Hill. He'd looked here at the beginning of the warm season.

The hill was just as steep as he remembered. He found himself breathing hard and wondered if his chest felt tight simply because of the exertion, or if there might be another reason. He sneaked a glance at Klestra. He'd never asked the red squirrel if, in all his travels, he might have come this way before. Evidently not. Klestra was quiet, which was unusual, and very attentive to what were apparently unknown surroundings. Near the top of the slope they came upon a rotted maple tree, one of its branches laying twisted on the ground.

Ephran pointed and said, "That branch fell last cold season."

Klestra looked surprised; another strange remark. "By the look of it, that's probably true," he said. "But how do you know it for a fact?"

"Because I was here when it broke. The sound of its breaking lured me over the top of the hill," said Ephran. "I left my tree though I'd been told not to."

"You left your den just to see a fallen branch?"

"Not really. Not just that. I was hungry. I was curious. The

187

forest was white with snow. I didn't want to wake my family. The sound of a breaking branch was an excuse."

"I'll bet you didn't want to wake them because you knew your parents would tell you that you couldn't leave," said Klestra.

"Exactly. I wanted no interference with my own little plans, with what I wanted to do."

"Well," said Klestra, "I suppose we're all a bit like that at times."

"You know, Klestra, everyone seems to think me so brave and clever. What happened on this hill proves them wrong. If I would have stayed in my tree that day, as I was supposed to, I would have heard The Many Colored Ones coming. I couldn't have missed Them -- Them with their noisy things of shiny teeth. I could have warned my family. My mother, heavy with young, would not have had to run to the end of the woods. We would not have become separated..." His shoulders sagged. "We were lucky none of us lost our breath. Then, when I was near The Pond that same day, a cottontail rabbit needed my help -- and I didn't give it."

"Ah, my friend," said Klestra, "aren't you being a little harsh? Especially considering that the squirrel who crossed this hill was a very young, curious, and inexperienced treeclimber?"

"I'm afraid that he didn't improve much. Out of selfishness he didn't tell the mallards that there was danger here. And he let himself be talked out of going to search for a friend..."

"Oh, come now, Ephran! You forget disappointed hawks, escape from a cage, friends of all kinds...," Klestra cocked his head. "Are you trying to tell me why you've avoided coming back up this hill? What did you mean when you said there was danger here? Is it more than bad memories?"

"Yes, Klestra. More than memories. Lomarsh is not the place of evil. This is. I've known it for a long time. The Many Colored Ones have claimed this place. I thought They might be satisfied to stay on their own side. But They weren't. Now They want The Pond. It all belongs to Them if They want it. None of us seems to be able to do anything about Them. The trees will be gone -- pulled down by those things with the bright teeth." Ephran shuddered. "I have seen what silver teeth can do."

He hesitated and looked into Klestra's eyes. "You see? Look at me. I'm afraid. Hawks, owls, cages, and spur of the moment decisions aside, I'm really a coward."

"Well, no one is going to believe that nonsense!" said Klestra. "Least of all me. Who in this wide forest doesn't run from The Many Colored Ones? Who are you supposed to be? He who makes no mistakes? Master of all the woods? He who would make The Many Colored Ones creep away in fear and trembling? I doubt it. I think we are all to do the best we can with what we have. All your friends, even your enemies, will agree you have excelled in that. Besides, I don't believe those hunters have claimed the entire woods. I'm not at all sure They want it. You notice They're never around when it's dark. Or when it's very cold...or raining. I think They are too delicate, maybe even frightened, to stay here. They seem to need fire and They require too many pelts. In any case, I'll wager there are none over the top of this hill. Come on, we'll see..."

With that Klestra scurried off, before Ephran could object. Should he call him back? He'd tried to protect his friend from danger before, when they left him at home during the search for Kaahli's family...now he was endangering him for no good reason, just to support his own cowardice...this had gone far enough... But he didn't bother chattering. He knew Klestra would pay no attention. And, quite obviously, one tiny red squirrel could not be allowed to face such danger alone. So Ephran followed, every step a struggle.

Then they were there; looking down the long slope through bare limbs. It was almost as he remembered it. The big oak was gone of course, as were two or three of its neighbors. But many of the smaller trees looked just as they had the last time he'd seen them. And where the big oak had stood many saplings had sprouted. The earth was covered with them; fragile and moist stems, sending slender roots down among the thick and dry ones. They'd found room to grow, now that they were not shaded by their massive parents.

"New trees..." breathed Ephran.

"Yes," agreed Klestra, "Many young trees. Plenty of older ones that might conceal a nice roomy den too. And not a Many Colored One in sight. Shall we start looking?"

"No!" answered Ephran, eyes sparkling.

"No?" repeated Klestra. "Why not? I thought that's what we came for."

"It is!" said Ephran, "...and we will! But I want Kaahli to be here too."

Klestra looked so confused that Ephran couldn't help laughing.

"My friend," he said, suddenly so full of energy that he could barely stand still on the limb, "I can never thank you enough for coming here with me, and for being so understanding and wise. I was fearful, needlessly it appears -- and foolishly as well -- of this place. I don't believe The Many Colored Ones ever returned here after that day They took down these oak." He shook his head slowly, from side to side. "And I thought those who attacked Cloudchaser came from this place. Instead there are new trees. I want my mate to help us pick a spot for a den. Maybe things aren't hopeless after all."

As Klestra scratched his head Ephran ran off, toward The Pond.

He turned back and called, "Come on, you slow-moving red longtail; I'll race you back to the nest!"

CHAPTER XXIX

DREAM COME TRUE

(T)he air began to move again, murmuring through naked branches and stirring fallen leaves. It came from where the sun had risen and, as the friends bounded through the forest, the bright sphere disappeared behind a thickening bank of clouds. They stopped to rest and eat in a hickory tree just over the brow of Great Hill.

"The air is cold, Ephran," said Klestra, wrapping his tail around himself as he nibbled on a hickory nut.

"Yes, and I smell water in the sky. The water may be snow."

"It is very nearly time to curl in the leaves."

Ephran smiled. "It's time for you to find a mate to help keep you warm," he said.

"Don't think I haven't been looking. All those times I was gone from my nest I wasn't just nosing around for corn or pinecones. Not every time anyway. I have some rather nice female friends, actually."

"Would you come nest near Kaahli and me if we find good trees on the other side of the Hill?" asked Ephran.

"Of course I would! I think you need to have me closeby," said Klestra.

Ephran laughed and said, "Kaahli and I have more to discuss than a new nest...we have to decide when we're going to fill it..."

Klestra looked up, wondering why his friend's words had stopped so suddenly. Ephran was peering intently down Great Hill toward The Hedge. "Klestra! Look there -- near the far end of The Hedge!"

The red squirrel followed his friend's gaze, clenched his teeth together, and hissed, "Many Colored One!"

"Yes. Just when I thought that maybe..." He sounded annoyed at first, as though someone might have grabbed an acorn he'd had his eye on. Then irritation turned to panic. "Kaahli!" he gasped.

They ran, faster than usual because it was downhill, Klestra mostly on the ground, jumping over fallen limbs and stumps he wouldn't have thought he could clear, Ephran in the trees, limb to limb, some too small to be safe, heedless of anything except to warn her...to keep the one he loved whole and unharmed.

They came to the bottom. The nest was clearly visible, but Kaahli was not in sight. They moved slower, and very quietly. They watched the forest floor, and the trees in front and to the sides. Ephran was about to chatter, to raise the alarm, when he saw her.

Kaahli hugged the trunk of a plump old elm, her pretty face alert. She had not seen Ephran or Klestra, but she'd obviously seen the hunter. She moved slowly around the trunk, as she'd been taught, keeping the thick tree between her and It.

They could see the longlegged One clearly now. It was mostly red; some brown and some green. A thunderstick lay on its shoulder. It did not turn toward the tree she was on. It must not know she was there.

Ephran was about to heave a sigh of relief when he heard Klestra's urgent whisper: "Ephran! On the ground -- there!"

He'd failed to notice what Klestra's sharp eye had, and he knew at once that Kaahli hadn't seen It either: Another Many Colored One, with another thunderstick, standing perfectly still on its hind legs among the trees at the base of Great Hill! Menacing eyes scanned the tree between Itself and its hunting mate, ever so slowly, ever so carefully. Then Ephran understood what They were doing...and his heart nearly stopped beating in his chest.

They were tricking Kaahli! While she used the noise made by the walking hunter to keep a tree trunk between It and herself, the Other remained silent, watching for anything that moved, any unsuspecting animal trying to escape the One that was making Itself so obvious. Though neither of Them had seen her yet, it was only a matter of time. From where he stood, Ephran could tell that the next few steps of the noisy One would cause her to move directly into the line of vision of the silent One.

It was far too late for warnings. He jumped to a higher branch, legs stretching beneath him, chattering in his loudest and harshest voice. Glancing down as he passed overhead, between the hunters, he saw Kaahli look up at him in astonishment. His noise and the long graceful jumps from branch to branch had the desired effect. All eyes followed him. He ran easily, more easily than he thought he could have, for the far end of The Hedge where it joined The Meadow. Once he got there, he thought, he could circle in either direction.

The first loud report rattled on the twigs just behind him. Why, they were like stones from the sky -- only much smaller! And coming with much greater speed. Aha! It was not the terrible noise that caused hurt and the loss of breath; it was tiny hard pebbles. He wondered if Klestra could appreciate that fact from where he hid. Later they would have to discuss this discovery.

Another roar! Then another. Both hunters pointed thundersticks at him. He stopped chattering and concentrated on smooth jumps. He led Them over as many humps and holes in the woods as he could, through clusters of the thickest trees and thorniest shrubs. He was nearly away. He could hear Them shouting, but their voices were fading.

He bounced off again, his destination a thick cluster of aspen. He'd try to lose Them there. As soon as he got far enough ahead he'd use the same trick; he'd keep a tree trunk between him and Them. They were running together now. Neither was hiding. They'd have no idea

"ANOTHER ROAR, THEN ANOTHER,
BOTH HUNTERS WERE USING THEIR
THUNDERSTICKS"

TERRY LEWISON

where he was. After They got tired of looking and left the forest he'd go back to Kaahli and Klestra.

The next jump, to a thick and bushy oak tree, would be a long one. He bent his hind legs ever so tightly beneath his body. Just as he leaped, a thunderstick spoke again. He felt a sudden twinge, almost like Kaahli's little love nip, behind his shoulder.

He landed solidly on a sturdy branch, slipped for a second, and stopped to catch his breath and inspect his thick fur. He saw nothing amiss, but could not turn his head far enough to see the spot that still tingled. His legs seemed fine. He looked back. The Many Colored Ones were running, as best They could, toward the oak. Good! That meant They had not seen -- or at least They hadn't attacked -- Kaahli or Klestra.

He slowed for a moment to time his jump and realized that one of his front legs felt damp and cold. He looked down. His paw had turned red! He almost giggled. How distressed father would be to see his son turning into a red squirrel before his very eyes!

Another roar sounded from behind. Suddenly he was no longer on the branch. He was tumbling, over and over, ever so slowly it seemed, like the snowflakes which had just begun to fall from the muddy-looking clouds. A thick bough floated upward toward him and he tried to catch it as it went by. Ah, for wings to spread!

"Butternut kind of idea", Aden might have said, but Ephran's timing was off, and his legs refused to obey. His body struck the branch; hard enough to make a sort of flat and pathetic sound. It was as though he was watching and listening to it all through someone else's eyes and ears. There was no pain -- just a numb feeling.

A tangled gooseberry bush broke the final few taillengths of his fall, and Ephran came to rest on a soft pile of golden leaves beneath the quivering branches of the bush. He lay there, on his back, looking up at big white flakes drifting down around him.

He could hear Them. They were searching, but They must be looking in the wrong place. Their voices seemed to be moving further and further away. Soon it was no more than a murmur and he couldn't be sure that all he heard was air -- air moving capriciously among the treetrunks and causing the snowflakes to dance and swing like white butterflies at the beginning of the warm season.

It should be safe now. Time to go back to the nest. He tried to get to his paws. It was difficult. His leg ached terribly and his chest felt as though very nearly beyond hurting. Maybe he should rest for a moment. He lay back. It was really very cozy down here in the leaves. Mustn't fall asleep though. Maltrick nearly caught him the last time he slept in leaves on the earth. Old perplexing Maltrick...

"Come now, Ephran, time to get up!"

The voice was familiar. And very distinct. He rolled over on his side to see who spoke. A huge lump rose in his throat.

"Cloudchaser!"

The big mallard, lowering his head to walk under the overhanging gooseberry branches, waddled up to him.

"Cloudchaser, how...?" he cried again, but tears drowned his words. He choked them back and managed, "You escaped Lomarsh! How are you?"

"Never better," said Cloudchaser, looking down at Ephran with a big smile.

Indeed, he did look as well, or very possibly better, than he ever had. His plumage was as brilliant as it had been at the very beginning of the warm season. His breast was thick and full. His eyes were bright. There was no indication that he'd ever been hurt by a thunderstick.

"I'm so happy to see you, Cloudchaser!" said Ephran, not even trying to hide the water running from his eyes and unto the leaves.

"The sentiment is mutual, I assure you."

"How did you find me?"

"Not especially difficult with all the racket around here. I saw you running through the trees," answered Cloudchaser, "and then I saw you fall. I thought you might need some help."

"Well, I should have learned to accept help, if I've learned nothing else. I seem to need plenty of it," sighed Ephran. He grinned at the mallard. Then his grin faded. He looked deeply into his friend's eyes. "I can't get over how you, who fell wounded in Lomarsh, suddenly shows up to help me when I need it most. Even though I didn't come to help you."

"I'm glad you did not go to Lomarsh. And it does seem that I flew this way at the right time," agreed Cloudchaser, who glanced off in a distracted manner, toward The Pond.

"I'm afraid I can't get up," said Ephran.

"Oh, I suspect you can," said Cloudchaser.

"I've been hurt, you see."

"I would be surprised if one taking a tumble from so high as you did might not have a few bruises to show for it," said Cloudchaser. "I thought you might be trying your own version of flight. Do you think you've been bounced too severely to take that ride high in the sky you've always wanted so badly?"

This was getting harder to believe by the moment! Both his ears and eyes seemed to be deceiving him.

"Really?! Do you mean it?"

"Of course I mean it. What better time? I always loved flying in the snow. Beautiful. Hop on!"

"Can you do this? Can you carry me? How will I stay on?"

"The rider of hawks asks me how to stay on a bird's back? It's easy. Just dig those little claws tightly into my thickest feathers," said Cloudchaser.

"I don't want to hurt you..."

"Don't worry about that. Just climb up on my back."

Cloudchaser lowered himself to the ground as Ephran got to his paws. He clambered up the duck's back, so amazed and delighted at the chance to fly with his friend that he really didn't notice any pain...or weakness. Perhaps there wasn't any. He flattened himself against the soft feathers and held on very tightly.

At first Ephran was frightened -- more frightened than he'd ever been on any branch, no matter how high. There was no nearby tree to jump to either. His stomach fluttered and, for a moment, he felt dizzy. But the view! And the feeling! Goodness of Gooseberries, it was even more wonderful than he'd imagined!

They soared up into the gentle white flakes, through air that felt surprisingly warm. He saw The Many Colored Ones through bare limbs, closer to where he and Cloudchaser had taken off than he thought They would be. They looked funny from up here, like flat brown spiders lost in a maze of twigs. Apparently They had not noticed the very bizarre sight of a large greenheaded duck taking off from beneath a bush with a full grown gray squirrel on its back. He almost laughed aloud when he thought of it.

The wind blew strong in his face as he lifted his head. That must be Fox Brook, far off to his right -- and Lomarsh even further the other way. There was Rocky Point! And, beyond that, Little Lake. Why, he could almost see as far as the den of Jafthuh and Odalee!

He realized he was smiling, smiling the same smile he'd smiled the time he met Kaahli, the one that Klestra had said made him look empty-headed. Oh dear! That reminded him...

"Cloudchaser," he said loudly in the drake's ear, "I must go back now. I must go to Kaahli. Thank you for the wonderful ride."

"Do you tire of the sky so soon?" asked the duck, as they circled The Pond. "I thought you really wanted to get to know what flying was all about."

"Oh no! I'm not tired of it, not at all. I could fly forever and ever. But Kaahli and Klestra are down there, you know. They'll be worried."

"They won't worry for long, my friend. Besides, I would wager that you'd like to give your sweet little mate a nice surprise," said Cloudchaser.

"Surprise her? How?"

"Would she be interested in a comfortable new den? I'm sure I've heard her speak of it."

"Why, yes, she would. But..."

"Good. Because I have found exactly what you need -- the

"THEY SOARED UP INTO THE GENTLE WHITE FLAKES"

perfect den for these times, in the perfect part of the forest. I will take you there and let you see if it might not be just the situation for you and Kaahli. Then I will come back, and bring her to you."

"That would be wonderful, Cloudchaser! Are you certain that it wouldn't be too much trouble? Will Kaahli understand? And what of Klestra?"

"It will all work out. All your questions will be answered. Be patient. Wait and see."

"But...we have to go back. We will go back to The Pond, won't we?"

"Of course we'll go back," said Cloudchaser. "The Pond is home."

Ephran huddled into thick feathers. Warm air washed over him. The big drake seemed confident about his surprise. If he couldn't trust Cloudchaser, then who could he trust? The drake would not tell him something that was not so. Ephran was satisfied. He adjusted his position on Cloudchaser's back, smiled to himself, and let his uneasiness drop away like the shell of an empty nut.

The beauty and wonder of this ride was too good to be true. He really did not want it to ever stop. He felt very comfortable and sleepy and could pretend he was curled next to Kaahli in their warm leafy nest. He searched the trees below, looking for two squirrels, one gray and one red, who he knew must be there somewhere. The swirling snowflakes and the fact that the duck's wings were carrying them higher and higher made it increasingly difficult to make out details.

Ephran could not be absolutely certain but, just before the forest faded from view, and just before he let his heavy eyelids close, he thought he heard someone calling below. It had to be Klestra, shouting words that sounded like; "Keep to the high branches, my friend...keep to the high branches!"

* * * * * *

"Be patient," said Cloudchaser, "wait and see..."

Ephran's adventure continues in
Book II of The Deep Woods Trilogy:
INTO THE HIGH BRANCHES